The Saga of Haram

by
JP Wagner

To Brad, Julie, Crystal, and Sam, you all were the best party a DM could have.

This is a work of fiction. Similarities to real people, places, or events are entirely coincidental.

THE SAGA OF HARAM

First edition. February 24, 2024.

Written by J P Wagner.
Edited by Beth Wagner

Introduction

(As originally featured in my newsletter)

My dad was a Dungeon Master and a Wargamer, I believe he started this back in the 60's and I remember boxes and boxes of his old wargames like Panzier Strike, but there were also fantasy games too like Runequest. But the biggest thing was when he bought Advanced Dungeons & Dragons.

I remember wondering what the difference was between regular Dungeons & Dragons and "Advanced". I don't think it was ever explained to me, but that was my first introduction to D&D.

My mom sewed him a special messenger bag (it was this weird 70's pink, blue and white polyester affair) just to carry his books and of course a dice bag was created for him as well (It was made of simple white broadcloth, and a shoestring was used as a drawstring).

You have to understand, the hobby wasn't as big a deal as it is now. The hobby was still relatively new, so new that the only polyhedral (gaming) dice you could get were white, the numbers weren't painted in, so you had to use Testor hobby paint (the only brand you could get back then) to paint in the numbers. My Dad took some red nail polish to mark off the crits (the lowest or highest you can roll to determine an outcome).

When I was about eight or nine years old, my dad finally decided that I was old enough to play a solo game of D&D. He created a campaign for me and actually used the map that he used with his other players. We played a few sessions, and I can't really remember why they trailed off, I think I got busy with school and Dad was working on articles for the local newspaper so I imagine it was something like that.

Fast forward 40 years...I am looking through my dad's manuscripts trying to decide what to publish next when I came across, *The Saga of Haram*.
I immediately looked at the notes and found a list of place names that were in the story set in a table. The table had the place names, what the names meant (ie, Elizabeth means promise of God) and then D&D map place name.

This was huge! I knew this map because there was only ever one map. I immediately knew that I *had* to publish this manuscript!

For me, this book contains a lot of nostaglia and is in many ways, why I play RPGs to this day.

- Beth Wagner
- February 17, 2024

Map of Eastern Aradair

*A rough partial recreation of the
original map*

JP Wagner

Chapter One

The two boys strode down the narrow winding streets of the Old Quarter of the city. They had grown up together in Ifan Sor, the City of the Moon. The two of them were completely familiar with all the narrow streets and dim alleys of their quarter, and knew the rest of the city well enough to be able to find their way around. They had played in the streets of the city as boys together. The boys had invented monsters to slay and had slain them bravely. They had quarrelled, fought, and made up again. They had stolen sweet buns from the baker together (and been caught and beaten for it a time or two) and had reached an age at which boys want to be doing adventurous things rather than merely playing at them.

The two almost looked like twins, their bodies at fourteen showing some promise of growing taller and broader, their faces wide and smiling, their hair reddish gold in the sun. A closer look showed differences, a slightly narrower and more angular shape to the face of one, a bit more red than gold in the hair of the other.

It was the one with the redder hair who spoke, as they came to a part of the city where baked mud-brick gave way to sandstone as building material. "Are you sure they'll take us, Merrit?"

"Of course I am! Haram, I told you I talked with them last night, and they agreed to consider taking us on both of us. They're not like Saradon's band, not at all, but it'll be a start. It will get us out of this city!"

"They are real Venturers, aren't they? Not just bandits?"

Merrit shrugged. "As near as I can tell. There're three of them, a big warrior, a woman who seems to be a scout, and another man who looks as much as a mage as any man I've seen. They claim to be Venturers, and that satisfies me."

They were now coming up to the front of the squat, grey-tan building with the weathered and peeling sign showing a barking dog atop the skeletal remains of some four-footed animal. That this inn, and not some other, was their destination, encouraged Haram a little. He knew that although the Dog and Bones did not attract the highest class of clientele; the proprietor did attempt to discourage the riffraff and scum of the city from hanging about. Even so, Haram doubted that Saradon and his band would patronize this establishment. But then, not everyone had the high reputation of Saradon and his band. He followed Merrit inside.

They paused a moment to let their eyes get used to the dimness. The inn was lit, after a fashion, by oil lamps here and there about the common room, and the scent was a mix of ale, highly seasoned meat, and unwashed bodies. Merrit led them to a table in a corner where a small group sat. It was a quiet and watchful group, and it seemed to Haram that they had been keeping unobtrusive track of all that went on in the inn.

There was a tall, broad man with black hair and beard, wearing a chain-mail shirt. He had a sword belted at his waist, and a helmet sat on the table in front of him. Haram was too impressed with him to note much else, but a person of more experience would have seen that the surcoat was patched several times, and that the armour was also patched, with a few spots where rings had sprung loose and had not been replaced.

There was a woman also, who wore only a leather jacket, and carried a light sword at her waist. She wore her fair hair tied back, and was light of complexion, and when Haram met her eyes, he got an uneasy feeling that she had already measured him up and found him wanting. There was an air about her of one who might, for any insult, real or fancied, use the sword she bore.

The other man was light in build, with red hair liberally sprinkled with white. He wore a boiled leather cuirass and had a short sword at his hip. The long staff leaning against his chair had a glyph at the tip which Haram, for all that he lived in a great cosmopolitan centre, did not recognize.

The woman waved them over, but did not smile in greeting them. "So, you did come."

"I said I would, lady." Merrit answered.

"So you did. So, let us be known to each other. I am Astaran. My companions are Orizd," she gestured at the large warrior, "and Sagahan," she gestured at the mage. "And you are?"

"I am Merrit, son of the Tailor Yaharan, and my companion is Haram, son of the Leatherworker Kohan."

Orizd eyed them up and down. "You wish to be Venturers, then?" There was a hint of an accent in his speech.

He did not wait for them to answer. "I suppose you think you know what a Venturer is. You have some notion of wandering the world, hunting goblins, ogres, and the like, finding rich treasures and glory? Yes, I see you do.

"The life of a Venturer resembles that very little. There're some Venturers, men who are little better than bandits, who'll rob travellers and merchants if they can find nothing better. We are not that sort. But our life is a hard one, much travelling, mostly afoot, an occasional fight with a band of goblins or an ogre or whatever, when we risk our lives. And like as not, the treasure we find is barely sufficient to buy food for our next venture."

He pointed a large finger at them. "There have been times, not a few times, when we spent winter in small villages, earning our keep by protecting the sheep from wolves, four-legged and two-legged. So if you seek riches and glory, seek them somewhere else."

Haram knew the warrior was testing them to see if they could be frightened away. He clenched his fists. "Nevertheless, if you'll have us, we'll come with you."

Orizd gave a sharp bark of laughter. "So! Then never tell me I didn't warn you. Have you any skill with weapons?"

Haram hesitated. He and Merrit had practised sword fighting with sticks, but he had a feeling that mentioning such training would be worse than saying nothing.

"Ah! You have none, then? No, I'd expected as much. We'll train you as time allows, and we'll not expect you to fight at first unless the situation is desperate. Your duties in the beginning will be camp-chores, cooking, washing, and the like. Does either of you have a dagger? No? Well, that's another expense to be charged to you."

"But sir, we have no money."

"Nor did I think otherwise. The money will come from your shares of whatever we acquire."

"We get equal shares, then?"

There was another bark of laughter. "Not likely, boy! See, we divide our acquisitions up into ten shares. Three go to me as the leader. Astaran and Sagahan receive two each for their skills and experience. The remaining three go to the general fund, from which we draw for living expenses, repairs to armour and weapons, and the like.

"You'll be given your food and clothing while you remain with us, but no shares until such time as you've proven yourselves to be part of us. At that time, you will receive a half-share each. As time goes on and you become more experienced, your share will become larger. If you are not satisfied with that, then you may find some other band of Venturers to take you. But I warn you, most other Venturers treat newcomers the same way."

He stopped, watching them, waiting for their response. Haram looked at Merrit, then back at Orizd. "I will still join, unless you have changed your mind."

"And I as well!" said Merrit, somewhat defiantly.

Orizd stared at them for a few moments, then finally smiled. "Done, then. You are part of us, to become partners if you survive to please us."

They went out shortly after to buy a pair of daggers. As they went, Merrit whispered, "Did you tell your parents?"

"Yes," answered Haram.

"What did they say?" asked Merrit.

"They don't like it much. Only Mother finally said to Dad that it'd be best to let me go willingly, and let me come back home when I found what sort of life it was in the Wild. Your parents?" answered Haram.

"I never told them. I knew they'd do all they could to stop me, even perhaps call the Watch and accuse the band of kidnapping. Best they know nothing," said Merrit.

"But they'll find out when they talk to my parents!" moaned Haram.

"And by that time, we'll be far away," said Merrit in his usual tone that he used when trying to convince Haram of something.

The daggers Orizd bought for them were very plain, but in Haram's eyes they were little less in quality than the magic swords of legend. He held his in his hand, enjoying the feel of it, and gazed at his elongated reflection in the blade.

"Put it in the sheath and cease waving it about, lad. Someone might think you were about to use it on them."

Haram shot a quick glance at Orizd, then did as he was bid. They walked back to the inn.

On the way, Orizd said, "We'd best get you a pair of sticks."

"Sticks?"

"Aye, sticks. Do not be discounting them, lad. A man who knows how to use a stick properly can defeat a swordsman. And you can use the sticks, you and your friend, to practice sword strokes in the evenings. When the time comes to give you a real blade, you'll have a bit of an idea how to use it."

'Practice sword-fighting with sticks!' Haram thought. *'But I'm still glad I didn't say anything about our play sword-fighting!'*

When they arrived back at the Dog and Bones, the other two were ready to go. They had a pack-pony, which they had already loaded, and they were standing by the inn waiting. Orizd said, "I had thought to have one last cup of ale to say farewell to the town."

Astaran glared at him darkly. "One cup?"

"Yes, one cup. You think me incapable of taking only one cup?"

The frown on her face said that she had serious doubts about the matter, but she finally nodded shortly. "One cup, then."

She turned to the two boys who had been gawking at the entire exchange. "Listen, you two. Some day some person who fancies himself a master of jest will tell you that part of your duties include bedding me. And he will undoubtedly say that while I have not mentioned the fact, it is only out of a certain shyness.

"So I tell you here and now that the first one of you who comes to me with that suggestion is likely to go away a little sorrier and sorer. When I am bedded, it is not by some awkward child who fancies himself a man. Is that clear?"

Before her fierce gaze, the two could only nod their heads dumbly.

Orizd chuckled. "Look now, Astaran, you have frightened them out of their wits!"

"Huh! If they had a wit between them, they wouldn't have chosen to become Venturers! So come, let's have that one cup of ale and be away."

Chapter Two

Ifan Sor, the seat of the Kings of Aradair, is situated in the north of Wanahair, the King's Land. From it, roads lead in many directions. The company, five people and a packhorse, took the road to the northwest, into the Duchy of Sarasair. A day's travel found them still on the road, which seemed to cut straight through the middle of dark green hills.

As they set up camp, Haram looked around nervously. "Are there goblins in these hills?" he asked Astaran.

She laughed. "Within a day's travel of the King's city itself? Not very likely! By Tran and Viron, you're not much travelled, are you?"

Nettled, Haram spat back, "No, but that can be cured!"

Astaran looked at him, raising her eyebrows. "Ah, you have a temper, do you?"

Orizd broke in then. "Let be, Astaran. Better for them to be a little scared and over-wary than be careless and wake up one morning dead."

She glanced at Orizd, then nodded, smiling slightly. "As you say, best they be in the habit of being wary before we reach the truly wild country."

Sagahan, as was his nature, said nothing.

They carried on, day after day, following the road north-westward. Each day at about noon, they would stop for a short while, have some lunch, then rest for a while longer. Then Orizd would say, "Up, boys! Time for sword-practice!"

He would then demonstrate a particular sword-stroke or counter, which Haram and Merrit would practice while he stood back and gave comments and advice.

"Tran and Viron, don't close your eyes when you strike! No, your balance is all wrong, your left foot is directly behind your right. A little breeze could blow you over! No, don't catch his blow dead on your own stick! You might find yourself with one foot of stick and him with three, then where are you? And with swords, the matter is even as bad. You might find yourself with a broken stump of a sword."

"Well, if you don't move faster than that, you can expect even more than barked knuckles! You have to throw his blow off to your own right, preferably keeping your own balance, and putting him off his. Now again, and try to move like you meant it this time!"

In the evening again, after camp had been pitched and everyone had eaten, the two were set to practising again.

The boys eventually became discouraged. "We can't handle sticks," Haram said to Merrit. "how are we ever going to manage real swords?"

"We're doing better, even better than he wants us to. He just isn't in any hurry to give us decent shares in what we take."

But there came a time one evening when Orizd called to them, "Have done, lads! It grows too dark for this! Put up the sticks!" He got up and walked over to them, frowning. "So. It comes, it comes. Perhaps someday you might make passable swordsmen."

He turned and walked away.

Evenings were also the time when the senior members of the group would tell stories, stories of other Venturers who had become rich and retired, stories of others who had died, or turned bad, or simply disappeared. Even Sagahan, on occasion, would occasionally mention some incident of note.

Most of his stories were of ancient times. "It's said that when the Great Invasion was halted, there was a goblin wizard in the hills to the North. He gathered about him goblins and other unsavoury beasts, and maintained his hold for several years,"

"And what became of him?" asked Haram.

"Well, some say that Garan Blackhair slew him in combat, and his followers dispersed. Others say it was Gorval Greenmage, with his Wand of Crystal."

"But who was it, then?" Haram persisted.

"Ah, a very good question! I have a suspicion, just a suspicion, mind you, that there was a quarrel among his own band, and it grew to a rebellion, and he was killed in the course of it. Goblins are well-known to be a fractious lot, and hard to control."

Haram settled back, a little annoyed at the ability of Sagahan to spoil a good story by his "maybe this-maybe that" statements.

They always slept outdoors, even though there were towns along the way. At first Haram felt too diffident to say anything, but one cold and wet evening he said to Orizd, "Why do we not find an inn?"

The warrior gave him a look. "Inns, is it? By Tran and Viron, boy, you have an exaggerated notion of our status! I told you before you joined that there are some Venturers who become rich, some who make a bare living, and some who starve or turn bandit. We are not among the first group, nor among the third. But, if we spend money staying at inns, why we would soon find ourselves in that third group.

"And banditry, lad, is not a life I would choose. For one thing, the life is not likely to be a long one.

"So we horde our coin, we sleep outside, we get along and we make do. A time will come when we strike a treasure, when we come away from a goblin-hold with a mass of loot, and then it will be that we begin staying at inns."

Haram never brought the subject up again.

At the town of Rathahan, in the land of Saraster, they had a brief discussion as to the route. "Southwest to Ninantha, or straight on?" asked Orizd.

Haram, knowing that his opinion was not sought, remained quiet. "Straight on through, I think," Astaran said. "You recall what happened when last we passed through Ninantha?"

"It was not my fault! That fool began making remarks---"

"Remarks about Shondakranians, which you would have ignored if you had not had half a keg of ale inside you! But the fact still remains that it's too soon to risk going through Ninantha again."

"You think so?" Orizd's eyes were flashing as he towered over Astaran.

"She is correct, you know." It was a surprise for everyone when Sagahan spoke up. The two looked at him.

"It is still too soon; they will remember us in Ninantha, and that could mean trouble which we do not need. Let us go on northward."

"Northward it is, then," said Orizd, still scowling.

A little north of the town of Rathahan, they turned off the road towards some hills, which stood tall and green in the distance. "Where do we go, then?" asked Merrit. Haram would have asked the same question if he had been closer to Orizd.

"Where? Why we go hunting goblins, of course. And surely even you do not think that goblins wander freely along the roads of the kingdom, inviting all and any to slay them? We go up to the hills, where goblins may be found."

And so they went. A day later they were deep in the hills, the four of them travelling carefully along some near invisible path, while Astaran went scouting ahead.

The hills, which had been fair and green and inviting from a distance, proved rugged and uneven at close quarters. The trail, such as it was, wound in and among and up and over the hills, and off the trail, going was hindered by patches of low-growing thorn and jumbled rock.

They travelled much more slowly now, not merely because the trail was poor. As Orizd said, "There's always the danger of running unawares into trouble, be it goblins, ogres, or the dread Man-eating Mice of the interior." Haram was fairly sure the mice were a joke, but had long since learned to avoid allowing himself to be the butt of the Shondakranian's humour.

They also kept a watch during the night, something they had taken more casually on the more travelled roads of the kingdom. Deep in the hills, however, there was always danger. Everyone took a turn at the watch; even Haram and Merrit took their turns, clutching their sticks and shivering, starting at the least sound.

Astaran had a habit of coming back from scouting unannounced, stepping out almost into the midst of them from nowhere, or so it seemed. She came back thus in the middle of one day saying, "Goblins ahead, eight of them! Coming this way too, probably a scouting party for the main band."

Orizd looked around at the scattered brush and rocks on the grassy hillside. "Could we ambush them?"

She frowned. "There's not much cover between here and there. We could go back to that little stream we passed this morning."

"And take the risk that they might see our tracks?"

"None of these eight are tracker-goblins. A good thing, too; the trackers have noses like bloodhounds." She paused. "Still, you're right; the risk is too great."

Orizd turned to the mage. "Sagahan, what of you? Could you make us invisible for a while?"

Haram expected the mage to think for a while before answering, but he spoke immediately. "No, not a spell of full invisibility. True invisibility, you see, requires that one bend the eyesight around the object to be rendered invisible, and bend it from every angle. To spread such a spell over the five of us, six, if you include the horse, would be to spread my power very thin. And if the spell was spread so thin, it is likely that any little thing might break it, leaving us visible at just the wrong time. There are some who say---"

Orizd broke in. "Let be, let be, mage. We need no lecture on your art and its shortcomings, or on what some mage says about the possibilities and impossibilities of this, that, or the other. What we need is help! Is there nothing you can do for us?"

"Yes, I think there is. There is a spell, you see, not true invisibility, but a spell which will trick the goblin's eyes into seeing rocks, bushes, or hummocks of earth. We must all be very quiet and still, however. The spell would trick the goblin's eyes into missing the movements involved in breathing, but something such as scratching or turning the head would break the spell for sure. Though even there, I understand certain mages are able---"

"Yes, yes, but at the moment, we care little about what certain mages are able to do! They are not here, and we have to make do with you. Let us get on with this!"

"First," said Astaran, "a few warnings and instructions. As I said, I believe these are the scouts for a larger band. This means we must mark the place of the sun in the sky at the time the ambush opens, for after that, by the time the sun moves one palm-width the main band will either be on us, or be so near that escaping them will be a chancy thing."

Orizd was nodding his head. "Exactly. And you two lads, you'll leave the fighting to us. Goblins are trained from imp-hood to fight, and you are not. But it would be a help if you were to dance around, threatening them with your knives, to give time for the three of us to deal with them. You understand?"

"Yes, sir," they answered together.

They moved the pony a hundred paces back, far enough to keep him out of sight of the goblins. "It is difficult," Sagahan had said, "to keep an animal such as this still for sufficient time to trick the goblins into thinking it is anything but an animal. Mind you, it is rumoured that the mage Kaderrit is supposedly able to keep an animal still by a spell, but---"

Orizd cut him off. "Leave it be, mage! Let the spell work, as you say. What does it matter if some mage in Arzawa or Nithahar or the back of the moon is able to do?"

Orizd asked Astaran, "You don't think any of them will see your tracks, either coming or going?"

"I told you, none of them are trackers, and when the day comes that I leave traces for a common goblin to see, that day I will go to Shondakar and become a temple-prostitute in Mun-é-hiren!"

The prospect of a fight apparently made Orizd almost merry. "Quietly, quietly, little lady! I have no doubt of your abilities! Now, let us pick our places."

He took his bow from his back, a recurved bow which seemed to be about the thickness of one of Haram's wrists, and strung it with no effort at all. He looked around. "Now, this curvy lady is ready too. And all of you, we cannot let any of the goblins escape. The main band will be after us soon enough, but if one of this group escapes, he'll bring them that much sooner. So! To your places, then."

The Shondakranian looked around and assigned positions to each of the party. They sat down, and Sagahan spoke. Some sort of coolness trickled down over Haram, starting at the crown of his head. There was an itching along with it, but he dared not scratch, remembering the mage's warning.

The feeling subsided a little, and he continued to wait and watch the hillside opposite.

Haram sat as still as he could. He wished he could look around at his companions to see what they were doing, but Sagahan had cast his spell, and they had to sit still. All he could do was stare at his hand clenched around his stick, occasionally flicking his eyes over to where they expected the goblins.

After what seemed like a wait of three hours, he was sure that the goblins had gone some other way, or worse still, that they had seen Astaran's tracks and were circling around to carry out a surprise attack of their own! And the band dared not move their heads for fear of dispelling the magic that hid them.

Was that a movement on the hill opposite? Haram concentrated on it. Yes, it was a goblin head! It was soon accompanied by another, and another. Finally, all eight of them were visible, marching toward the hidden band.

The magic must indeed be working, for the goblins showed no sign of alarm as they marched down the slope, then up again toward the ambush.

Haram had ample time to study the goblins on this, his first sight of a live specimen. They were not a large folk, the biggest being only a little taller than Haram himself, but they were all squat and heavily muscled. Their arms were a little longer in proportion to their bodies than a man's, and their fingers, like the rest of their bodies, were thick and covered with dark hair. The faces were all large and round, ugly enough to be easily distinguished from a man's.

They were all armed and armoured. Two of them were wearing scale armour, overlapping metal scales sewn on leather jackets, several of them wore heavy boiled leather cuirasses, with metal plates sewn in strategic places, and the others wore plain leather. All had helmets, mostly metal bowls with nasals and ear guards, though two had only thick leather caps.

They had heavy recurved bows hung at their backs, and each had a round shield, also slung at the back. Haram guessed they must feel certain of their safety in this country, walking without shields.

Each had a belt at his waist, bearing a short, heavy sword on one side, and a dagger on the other. Slung here and there on the belts were little knives, small hatchets, pouches, and other accoutrements.

As they came even closer, Haram saw that each of them had at least one ear pierced, and from that ear hung a cord of leather bearing several decorations. There were several feathers, dyed and painted in bands of bright colours. Each also had small bones tied individually to the cords, and some had what looked very much like human ears also tied to the cords.

Haram was suddenly afraid; he'd heard stories of Goblin fights, and he had known that he would be fighting goblins at some time, but he was suddenly aware of the fact that he might be killed in doing so. The goblins were closer now, so close that he could see every hair on their faces, see the yellow eyes searching the hillside for traces of enemies. Would Orizd never give the signal? Was he perhaps also frozen with fright, like Haram himself?

There was a shrill whistle, and before he knew what he was doing, Haram was on his feet. In the same moment, he saw a black arrow in the chest of one of the goblins, saw him fall. Another arrow, one of Astaran's shafts, fletched with leaf-green feathers, struck a second goblin, and Sagahan was standing, pointing a finger. A bolt of light shot from that finger and struck a goblin, who fell like a stone.

Haram saw another bolt from Sagahan's finger strike a goblin, saw the goblin fall, but then begin to rise again. He had no more time to look, then, for one of the other goblins was bounding toward him, heavy sword upraised.

Chapter Three

Remembering Orizd's instructions, Haram jumped backward. The goblin came on. Haram moved backward again, keeping his eyes on the advancing foe. Suddenly something caught Haram's heel, and he stumbled, going down heavily on his back. Laughing triumphantly, his opponent leaped forward for the kill.

Haram flung up his hand, trying to ward off the sword with his stick. The goblin smashed down on him. Haram stabbed with his dagger again and again at the goblin's side, but the blade did not seem to penetrate the leather. He remembered how Orizd had told them that goblins were trained for combat from imphood. *'I'm doomed,'* he thought, but he gritted his teeth against a scream of terror, and determined to die fighting.

He was suddenly aware that the goblin was not moving, and in the same moment, he heard Orizd's laughter. Then the heavy goblin was thrown off him, and Orizd was chuckling at him. As he struggled to his feet, Haram saw the arrow, one of the Shondakranian's black shafts sticking through the goblin's neck. He also saw the scratches on the goblin's leather armour where he had struck with his knife.

Orizd was still smiling as he said, "A magnificent fight, lad!"

Haram was about to return a hot answer, but he controlled his embarrassment by taking a deep breath and said instead, "Well, as you've told us, any fight you can walk away from is a good fight."

Orizd exploded in fresh laughter and clapped him on the shoulder. "Ah, good lad! You might do yet!"

They then began looting the dead, with Orizd lecturing the boys as the group worked. "Goblins wear little of value in the way of jewellery, especially those whose rank is low enough for them to be assigned to scouting duties. Now here's a pair of copper bracelets, one with what looks like a gem set in it. This 'gem' is actually a bit of glass, but we'll keep the bracelets."

He called instructions to the boys as they continued to work. "Leave the shields. They're large and bulky, and worth little at the market. Leave the daggers and the tools; they aren't worth the bother of taking them away. Keep the swords, and anything that looks valuable."

In the belt pouches, they found money of various sorts.

"What are these coins, Orizd?" There were ten silver coins, with a king's face on one side and a tower of brick on the other.

Orizd looked over his shoulder briefly. "From Shondakar. Worth about as much as a silver pony."

The silver pony was the common currency of Aradair, so called because many years ago they had a horse on the reverse side, the symbol of the Kings of the land. There were three silver ponies in the loot from the goblins. In addition to these, there were fifty-two copper coins of several sorts, all unfamiliar to Haram. When he asked Orizd about them, Orizd answered, "Don't worry about it; copper's copper. If we can't spend them, we'll sell them for the metal."

When all the goods had been piled together, Orizd glanced at the position of the sun in the sky, then looked at Haram and Merrit. "Not the sort of treasure you had been expecting? Best you accustom yourselves to it; this is the sort of thing we usually come by. Oh, occasionally if we find a goblin-chief or a hobgoblin, there's a bit of gold, but not often."

Haram, who had been thinking that the gains were very small for the risk involved, kept his thoughts to himself, but said instead, "Do we share it out now?"

Orizd cast another glance at the sun. "Nay, not yet. And in any case, we seldom share out after one such skirmish; the shares are hardly worth the bother. We'll wait until we have a bit more. Now, pack this all on the pony and let us be gone."

As they were packing, Haram said to Orizd, "We've got some swords here. How be if Merrit and I take one of them each, to be paid for out of our shares as they come up?"

"By Tran and Viron, no!" Haram quailed back. Orizd went on a little more calmly. "Those swords are goblin swords, lad, and anyone who knows swords will see that they're goblin swords. We can take them to a smith and sell them, and the smith will be able to fashion them into other forms and sell them himself.

"But if you were to go about wearing goblin swords, there are those who would think surely that you were goblin-friends. Take my word, *'goblin-friend'* is not a name you want attached to you, if you hope to survive among humans. Best wait for your swords. Now, are we nigh ready to be gone?"

They did not flee back the way they had come, as Haram had expected, but rather went off at an angle. He took advantage of a short pause that afternoon to ask Orizd about this. "If we were to flee back along our path, the goblins would see it as just that flight and would strain to catch us up to have their revenge. If we go off as we have done, deeper into their territory, it will seem to them that we are not terribly concerned, and thus they may ask themselves if we might be beyond their abilities to fight. Perhaps we have some terrible magic or something such. Belike, it will make them a little less eager to come up against us."

Haram nodded. Altogether, the life of a Venturer seemed much different from what he had been led to expect. Not precisely worse, but different.

He was not sure whether they deluded the goblins or not, but that band never caught up to them. They saw no more goblins as they went up and down the brush-strewn rocky hills.

It was Merrit who asked, "Are there truly goblins in these hills?"

Astaran looked at him scathingly. "No, boy, we are wandering around out here for the sheer pleasure of it! If you look at the trail, you can see goblin-tracks aplenty, some older, some newer! But that's much to expect from a town-brat, I suppose!"

Haram could not see any tracks either, though he took Astaran's word for it. He thought, though he kept it to himself, that she ought to have been pointing out the signs of goblin passage for them, so they could eventually recognize them on their own. Should not all the party have some training in this?

He wondered about the possibility of hiding in ambush for the goblins, but he said nothing to any of the others. They were more experienced than he, and if they thought it a good idea, they would have brought it up themselves. On further reflection, he dismissed the idea. The goblins following them were estimated at thirty to fifty; against that, five people were too few.

Even after they left the hills, they did not slacken their pace greatly.

"When goblins are looking for vengeance, they can be persistent," Orizd said.

They slowed a little when they came to the road again, and soon came to the town of Sandaris, Three Ways, so called because three roads joined there.

In Sandaris they sold their loot. Astaran did the bargaining for them, and it was instructive to watch her deal with the dumpy little merchant with the wispy grey beard.

"A copper apiece for these bracelets? I have *'fool'* written across my forehead, perhaps? There's copper enough in the two of them to make six copper pieces. I'll take five coppers, and still know I'm being hard done-by."

"And I have *'rich fool'* across my forehead? By Tran and Viron, where would you get paid weight for weight of copper coins for plain copper? Three coppers."

"Give me four and it's done, thief!"

The merchant was not put off by the insult. "What else have you? The swords? Nicked and bashed around a bit, aren't they? Two ponies, the lot."

"Two ponies! Listen, I know and you know that you're not going to sell goblin swords to anyone, save perhaps goblins. They'll go to a smith for the metal, to be made into whatever he wishes. And that being the case, nicks and bashes don't count. Two ponies apiece."

"My wife and children starve, because I am so good-hearted. Three ponies for the lot."

"Six ponies, or I go down the road to Lisan Wer to see if there's an honest merchant there."

"Four robber-woman!"

"Four ponies and seven coppers, then."

"Four and five, or you can go to Lisan Wer."

"I take it, but only because there isn't an honest merchant in town."

And so it went, through all the goblin loot. At the end, Astaran came away muttering, "Ought to have gone to Lisan Wer."

Though he had no notion of the worth of the goblin swords or bracelets, Haram was quite sure that she had got the best price available. After they had left the shop with their money, Haram spoke quietly. "Do you really think we ought to have taken it to Lisan Wer?"

She looked around to see that no one was listening, then said, "No, not really. It is always good to convince them they have gotten the best of the bargain. It puts them in a good frame of mind for the next bargain."

At Sandaris they replenished some of their supplies, then set out westward. A little west of the town, they came to a river, flowing south to north across their path. Turning, they followed the river to its source in some hills. After the first day, Astaran shook her head. "No goblin tracks in these hills, not since the last rain."

Two days later, she said, "Still no goblin tracks. Very old ogre trace, that's all."

Astaran shot a few rabbits to supplement their rations, and she skinned them out and put the hides on stretchers.

"They'll be worth a silver pony each, though I doubt I'll be able to get that much for them." She looked up at Haram and Merrit. "You see what sorts of things Venturers do? Anything that can add a few coins to the purse and not leave the folk of a village angry with you. Not the sort of high adventure you expected, is it?"

"But it is still better than living all your life in the City of the Moon, knowing that each day will be like the one before it, and like the one before that," protested Merrit.

They moved south-westward out of the hills, striking the road and moving westward along that through the forest. Well within the forest they came upon the town known as Lisan Hawr, the Town in the Wood.

The people were dark of hair and complexion and seemed generally friendly at first. Astaran had sold the rabbit-skins, getting almost as much for them as she had thought they were worth, and on the strength of that, they decided to have supper at the inn in town. They had ordered their supper and were waiting for it when the door opened and five townspeople came in, sturdy tradespeople, all bearing cudgels.

They looked around, then came straight over to the table where the Venturers sat.

One of them, clearly chosen beforehand as a spokesperson, said, "Sirs and lady, this is a peaceful town. We wish no trouble here."

Orizd looked up in puzzlement. "We wish no trouble either. We want only to eat our supper in peace."

"Eating supper is fine. Even drinking a bit of ale is acceptable. What we frown upon is drunken brawling."

"And why would you expect us to be the sort to indulge in drunken brawling? We have come through this town a time or two before and have had no trouble."

"Stories have a way of travelling up and down the roads, Sir. Enjoy your meal, but drink carefully. If there is trouble, we will be able to deal with it."

They turned and walked away, leaving Orizd to continue glowering long after the door had shut behind them.

Chapter Four

Orizd sat quietly for some time, then slowly looked around. "Innkeeper!" he shouted.

The innkeeper, a pale and pudgy man, hurried over. "We will have ale, man, and much of it! Hurry!"

Astaran spoke. "Not so quickly, Orizd! You heard what they said; I, for one, do not want any trouble."

"Trouble? Who is making trouble? Not I! I merely want something to drink."

"So you do, and so do all of us. But I promise you, Orizd, at the first sign of drunkenness, I leave, and you will be left to your own devices. I will not be pulling you out of trouble any longer."

The two sat staring at each other for a while, then Orizd looked over at Sagahan. The mage nodded. "She is correct, you know.

When you drink too much, there is always trouble. And if we continue to help you out of trouble, there will soon be no town in all of Aradair that will welcome us."

Orizd continued to frown, then looked up at the innkeeper. "So. Go fetch us each a mug of ale, then. And have no fear, I shall be on my best behaviour."

Orizd was as good as his word all night, though toward the end of the evening he was showing some signs of the strain. Haram noticed this and was very careful to avoid antagonizing the warrior. When they left Lisan Hawr the next morning, many of the townspeople were still watching with distrustful eyes.

Astaran walked beside Haram for a little ways. "A lesson to you, boy. Offend too many people in too many towns, and no matter how successful a Venturer you may be, you will have nowhere to sell your loot."

She spoke quietly and Haram, very much aware of Orizd walking just ahead of them, could only nod his head in response.

The days went on, stretching into weeks, and the boys continued to train with the sticks under the critical eye of Orizd. He also began training them in the use of the sling. "It is a simple weapon, a piece of leather and two cords, but it is effective. And it has an advantage over the bow in that you are never out of ammunition so long as there are pebbles in reach. I know that some mould their own bullets out of lead, these having more range and accuracy than stones, but stones will do for now."

So they practised with their slings as they walked along, and the time came when they could hit a man-sized mark more often than not at a hundred paces. Orizd, of course, was not satisfied with that, and demanded continued practice.

Several times they found bands of goblins which they felt safe in attacking (and several times they found bands of twenty or more which they decided to leave alone). Eventually they had gathered a treasure of some ninety-three silver coins, of various sorts, and over two hundred copper coins, also of various sorts, all this including the money gotten by selling goblin swords and the like.

By this time, they had come to the town of Vas Kapadan. As usual, people watched them approaching.

A man, clearly one of the chief men of the village, stepped out to greet them. "A good day to you, sirs and lady. You are Venturers, then?"

"We are," answered Orizd. "Is there something we can do for you?"

"There's an ogre has moved into the hills hereabout, and he's playing hob with the crops and the flocks. Could you rid us of him?"

"Belike we could. But you must know that we have to eat as well. What would you pay us?"

"Surely your reward would be in the ogre's treasure, would it not?"

"Ah, but ogre treasures usually consist of broken sword blades, bits of bright glass, and the like. We must have more than that."

They set to bargaining, then, and eventually struck what seemed a reasonable agreement. If the treasure in the ogre's lair did not amount to at least twenty silver pieces, the village would make up the difference.

As they marched away from the village toward the ogre's lair, Orizd called the two boys to him. "I hope that you understood the lesson there. We would likely have sought out the ogre in any case, but if the village is willing to pay us for it, we accept their pay. Thus we make some profit, no matter whether or not the ogre has treasure. Thus do Venturers survive."

Haram said nothing. Some time ago, he had come to understand that there was more to the life of a Venturer than wandering the lands, seeking goblins or other beasts to slay. On occasion, he still dreamed of riding the land as a paladin on a magnificent horse, but he had told no one of those dreams, knowing it would only open him to ridicule.

Merrit nodded seriously. He had become a little more close-mouthed in the last months, having hinted once or twice at his own personal desire for glory and wealth, only to find himself mocked by the others. He kept his own counsel now, and even Haram did not know a great deal about what he felt or thought.

The ogre was laired in the highlands outside the town. As the band marched forward, Astaran went on ahead to scout out the situation. As they were setting up camp in the evening, she came back to make her report.

"He's up there for certain," she said. "When the wind blows right, you can smell the smell of an ogre's den. There are tracks as well; from the tracks I can say that he is four arm lengths or more tall, and not in good health. He drags his feet sometimes, as though he were weary."

"He is sick, then?" asked Orizd. "Will that sickness help us at all?"

She shrugged. "It will help us in that he'll be unable to put forth his full strength in the fight. On the other hand, an ogre of that size may well have strength to spare for all of us."

"Have you any suggestions as to how to fight him?"

"One way would be to wait for him along the way to his lair, and ambush him. But ambush or no, it's going to come down to sword-work before we defeat this one."

"So, we sit beside the trail for him for a few hours or a few days?" Orizd shrugged. "Best we get down to it, then."

Merrit spoke up then. "Why don't we go to the ogre's lair while he's away and take what treasure there might be and be on our way?"

There was silence. Finally, Orizd looked at him. "Aye, suppose we do that. Even supposing there is treasure in the ogre's lair worth more than what the villagers will pay. What then? If we come around through here next year, or the year after, what sort of welcome will we get? Don't be a fool, boy. When you make agreements, honour them, else they may come back to haunt you."

Merrit flushed, but remained silent.

Astaran found them a place to lay their ambush. So far as Haram could tell, it was no better than any other place, but he knew better than to argue with her or any of the others. He was no longer so terribly in awe of them as when they had left Ifan Sor, but he still respected the fact that they knew much more of this business than he did.

Before they took their places, Orizd spoke to the two. "This fight will not be like the other fights we've had, and this time we'll be needing you to take a full part. At the very least, you will be needing to use your slings. Nay, you would not be able to kill an ogre with two slung stones, nor even four, but even a hit with a stone will hurt him, weakening him for the time when we have to fight hand to hand.

"And when we are fighting hand to hand, if you see a clear chance, use your slings. He'll have too much reach for you to risk your daggers or your sticks, but even a stone or two in the midst of the fight may at least distract him for long enough for one of us to make good use of our swords. Have you any questions?"

They had none.

They had been sitting quietly since some time before sundown, and there had been no sign of the monster. Haram shifted slightly in his hiding place to ease a cramped leg. He wondered what good they could do now, since the light was so poor. He was unsure of his ability to hit the tree across the trail, let alone a moving creature. It was not for him, a very junior member, to make suggestions or complaints. Orizd would undoubtedly call them out of their places in a few moments, and they would go back to their camp.

There was a movement out on the trail. His first thought was that Orizd was coming out, as he expected, to call them from their hiding places. His next impression was that it was too large to be Orizd, then suddenly he knew what it was.

The ogre was huge, seeming twice as tall as he himself, and broad as well. It had features similar to those of a goblin, though there seemed less intelligence in the glance it cast at its surroundings. It had a hairy pelt of some sort wrapped round its loins, and a large club, little more than a tree-limb, broken off and rubbed smooth, clutched in its right hand.

Haram looked at the stone in his sling, a stone about the size of his fist, and wondered how much good a missile such as that would do against this monster. Orizd gave the signal, a shrill whistle, and in the same moment, bowstrings hummed and arrows flew.

A bare instant later, a bolt of some kind of fire streaked out from Sagahan's position, blinding Haram for a moment. Haram leaped to his feet; for the sling is not a weapon easily wielded on one's knees behind a bush.

His vision was returning, and he could see the ogre staring around, looking for whoever it was who had wounded it. As he whirled his sling, Haram suddenly realized that he would be the target for the monster's rage.

And so it proved. He released his stone at the same moment that the ogre saw him, and the ogre gave a roar of anger and lunged toward him.

In the same instant, two more arrows struck it in the chest, and some sort of glowing dart flew out to hit home in the same place. Sagahan had realized that though his bolts of lightning were effective, they also blinded friend and foe, and no one could afford to lose their vision, not even for a moment.

Haram jumped backward, moving around a tree as the ogre surged forward, covering ground at a terrifying rate. There were two more arrows in the ogre's chest, then another two of the glowing darts, but the beast was concentrating on Haram. As it rushed toward him, Orizd sprang out and swung his sword, a vicious chopping blow into its side.

It bellowed and turned to face this fresh attack, forcing Orizd to skip backward as it swung its club toward him. Astaran came in behind the ogre and struck with her lighter sword. Even wounded as it was, the ogre was quick. It swung a backhanded blow with its

45

club, which Astaran barely dodged, then brought the club around to where Orizd was moving in from the front.

Haram suddenly recalled Orizd's instructions, and put another stone in his sling, whirled it around his head, and let it go. With the dim moonlight and the noise of the battle, he could not tell whether or not he had hit. He took up another stone. The small bright darts were flying out of the bush where Sagahan hid; the mage carried a light sword, but he was no expert in its use, and in a fight such as this he would do best to employ his magic instead.

Haram threw stone after stone at the monster, and sometimes even saw them hit, once drawing blood from the ogre's upper chest. For all that, though, he felt he might as well have been tossing flowers. Even the Sagahan's darts seemed not to have any effect.

Astaran and Orizd leaped in and out, striking, thrusting, slashing, and by their agility avoiding the monster's return attacks. Even as he cast his stones, Haram realized that armour would give little protection in such a fight; a blow from the ogre's club would break bones, no matter how they were protected

The ogre's club swept backward toward Astaran, and though it barely seemed to brush her as she dodged, she went spinning backward to fall limply to the ground. Haram cried out and jumped forward, throwing another stone.

The stroke that felled Astaran had been a grazing blow, but the ogre felt it and turned full around. With a roar of triumph, he raised his club in both hands and stepped forward to smash the life out of his fallen foe.

Chapter Five

Haram fumbled another stone into his sling, knowing the futility of it. At the same moment, Orizd gave a loud shout and lunged forward, burying his blade up to the hilt in the ogre's back. The ogre straightened, whirled, and swung its club; Orizd jumped back out of the way. The force of the swing apparently threw the weakened monster off balance; it fell forward and sideways, crashing to the ground.

Orizd stepped forward and hacked twice at the thick neck, beheading the ogre on the third blow. That done, he rushed over to where Astaran lay.

Haram joined him as swiftly as possible, and Orizd was bellowing, "Sagahan! Mage, come here! She still lives!"

A moment later, they were all gathered around her, the three backing away a little to give Sagahan room to kneel down and examine her.

"Well?" demanded Orizd.

"I am not sure," said the mage. "She is sorely hurt, and I have used much of my power already. I believe I can save her, but it will require an effort on my part, such an effort that I will likely sleep for half a day after. And she herself will require much rest. It would be best if we were to move our camp somewhere nearer here for the time being."

"Haram! Merrit! You heard the mage; go fetch our gear from the camp, and I'll begin making a fire and the like."

Haram was a little startled. Orizd rarely called them by name; it was usually *'boy'* or *'boys.'* They set off, however, leaving Sagahan sitting cross-legged beside Astaran, eyes half-closed, breathing deeply.

When they returned with their gear and the pony, Sagahan was slumped on the ground beside Astaran. Orizd was standing watch over them. "What happened?" asked Haram.

"The mage has healed her, and in doing so has used up so much of himself that he is asleep. And I have been waiting for you two to return so that we can carry them to our new camp."

The new camp was not far away, "Just far enough," as Orizd put it, "that we need not have a dead ogre for a bed-companion." When they had settled the two into their bedding, Orizd held up a leather pouch.

"I took this off the body of the ogre. I doubt it contains anything worthwhile, but let us look."

Opening it, he poured the contents into his hand. There were three bright golden coins, golden crowns of Aradair, so called because they had a crowned head stamped on one side, with a gryphon holding a banner on the other. There was also a small handful of what looked like marbles.

"What are those things?" asked Merrit, pointing.

"Just what they seem, boy. Marbles."

"Marbles? In an ogre's pouch? Why?"

The warrior looked at Merrit. "You will learn, boy, that ogres are in general, unintelligent creatures, for all that they are shaped like men or goblins. But do not count on that, for there will be always one or two who can think as well as any man. In any case, ogres tend to like bright-coloured or shiny things, and sometimes things merely catch their attention for no reason that a man can fathom. Belike he merely fancied the smoothness of the marbles."

"Where would he come by marbles?" asked Haram.

"Where do you think?"

Haram grimaced and tried not to think of some child faced with a huge monster swinging a tree-limb. He could only hope that the boy had died quickly.

As he had promised, Sagahan slept for half a day, and Astaran woke about the same time. For a time she could remember nothing and no one, but eventually her memory began to return, though she never did recover any memory of anything that happened after they had left the town of Vas Kapadan.

It was a further hour from the time that she woke before she was able to stand up. When she could stand, one of the first things she said was, "Why are we all lollygagging around here? Don't we have an ogre's lair to search?"

As they went, Orizd explained to the boys the habits of ogres in regard to treasure. "It is the habit of ogres to take their prey and bring it back to their dens, eating it there. If the prey happens to be human, and happened to be carrying pouches, packs or the like, the ogre might or might not open them after eating, or might set them aside to be opened later, or might forget them altogether. And since what a man might consider trash might be attractive to an ogre, or vice-versa, valuable things might be dropped on the floor and trodden into the ground.

"In order to search for treasure in an ogre's lair, therefore, a person must go in with a torch to light the dimness, and spend as much time as possible turning over the trash in the corners, picking up what looks valuable, and also picking up whatever packs, pouches, wallets, or other containers have not yet been opened."

The lair itself was a dim cave beneath an overhang of rock, full of the acrid stench of ogre and the worse stench of rotting flesh. They made several trips inside, picking up anything that seemed worth a second look.

When the stench finally drove them outside, they would spend a while scrutinizing things picked up, and opening the containers to see what they contained.

After the last trip inside, the Venturers sat down to see what they had.

For the first time since they had joined the band, Haram and Merrit saw gold in the treasure they had gained. They even had occasion to handle some of it, finding coins in some of the pouches they were searching.

At one point Haram heard Merrit say "What is this thing? Some kind of copper amulet?"

Since he was busy at the moment trying to decide if the necklace he held was silver with a gem set in it or merely tin, with a false jewel, Haram did not look up until he heard Sagahan say "Let me see that!"

Something in the voice of the mage caught Haram's attention. Merrit was holding a flattened piece of copper, about as large as the palm of his hand, and on it were some kind of marks. Haram could not read, even the usual runes of Aradair, but he could see that these marks were different.

Sagahan inspected it, turning it over and over in his hand, and at last he said, "Boys, if ever you find such a thing, a flattened sheet of copper with writing on it, tell me immediately."

"Is it valuable?" asked Merrit.

"To the right person, it is very valuable."

"What is it?"

"I will tell you later, after we have dealt with the rest of this. Remind me if I should forget."

When they had finished sorting out the treasure, they found that they had eighty-three gold crowns, as well as five other gold coins with a picture of a man wearing a turban on the one face, while on the other was a rearing horse. They also had one hundred and seven silver ponies, along with twelve silver coins of a sort Haram had never seen, and two hundred fifty-six copper coins.

In addition to this was a finely worked brooch of gold, set with what appeared to be diamonds. Astaran looked this over carefully and declared, "This will probably be worth five times as much as the rest put together. Of course when we sell it, we'll be fortunate to get half its value."

The rest looked around at each other. Belike they were not rich, but they were much closer to being rich than they had ever been before. After a moment, Orizd spoke. "So let that be a lesson to all of us. Nine times out of ten when one loots an ogre's lair one finds nothing more than a handful of silver ponies, if that. But on the tenth time! Ah, the tenth time is like this!"

A little later, Sagahan told the boys a story. "Years and years ago, in another age of the world, there was a magician by the name of Drum-na-drum. He was a person of great knowledge, and he had discovered a secret to prolonging his life. He found, however, that his books and scrolls suffered from time, even if he himself did not.

"In order to spare himself from having to spend all the days of his prolonged life re-copying his magical books and scrolls, he set about finding methods to preserve them. After some time and experimentation, he hit upon the method of inscribing them on thin sheets of copper, and fastening these sheets into books.

"No one is entirely certain, but it is thought that there was a war, and war can take even artificially prolonged lives. Cities, nations, and peoples fell in that war, and Drum-na-Drum himself died. Some of his books, however, survived. Occasionally people would come upon thin sheets of copper with strange runes carved upon them. You will still see today people using these pieces of copper as amulets, to bring good luck.

"Some years ago a sage bent his mind to the deciphering of the runes. He learned how they read, and he eventually learned the language of the copper sheets, and thus discovered a source of knowledge. Since that time many have been searching for the copper sheets and the books, and they have been seen in widely scattered places.

"One of these pieces of copper such as we have found is worth a little money. A full sheet would be worth enough to keep us all for about a year. Several sheets, particularly if they are in sequence, would make us wealthy, and if we were to find a whole book, why we need never do anything again for the rest of our lives."

He paused and looked around at them. "So as I have said, be watchful. If you ever see anything such as this, let me know, and if you ever hear of a copper book, tell me."

When they went back to the village, the villagers stared at them with some suspicion. Haram knew, without having to be told, that the villagers were expecting them to come back falsely claiming to have killed the ogre, or belike claiming to have killed the ogre and hiding the true amount of his treasure in order to collect their wages from the village as well.

The three veterans, however, appeared to pay no attention to the expressions of the villagers. Orizd greeted them cheerily and said, "Well, we have met the ogre and slain him, and the treasure in his lair was more than the few silver ponies I had expected. We will therefore not be requiring payment from you. We have only come to tell you that you need have no fear of the ogre any longer."

The village headman, still wary, said :Congratulations to you, then. On behalf of myself and the village, we offer you our hospitality for the next few nights."

He hid his relief, though not well, when Orizd said "No, one night only, then we must be going."

"Not even two nights?"

He pressed no further when Orizd said, "No, one night only, We must be travelling again in the morning."

Before they left Vas Kapadan, Orizd bought two short swords. Haram, though he did not let on, was sure that this was proof that they had been accepted by the group, or at the very least were quite close to acceptance.

Now instead of sticks, the two used swords. Orizd trained them in drills, series of blows and parries to be done in order for so long as they could manage to stand upright. He had come to be approving, though sparingly, of their progress with the sticks, but now he was once again unsatisfied with their ability with swords.

In addition, Sagahan began to teach them the runes of Aradair, both reading and writing. "It may help," he said, "at the odd time, to know whether the label on a vial claims it to be a potion of invisibility or a poison."

They finally came to the city of Yath Hawr, where it was planned to spend some days in resting and buying fresh supplies before they left again. They found rooms at an inn, then Orizd looked at Sagahan and Astaran. "You will guard my armour and belongings again?"

Astaran nodded curtly. "And don't think to buy any drink with promises; I would like to buy horses for us all before we leave."

Orizd nodded with equal curtness and began to strip off his armour. Astaran turned to Haram and Merrit. "You two might also wish to have some money to spend. You can have ten silver ponies each, and if you're too drunk to come with us in three days, we leave without you."

"On ten silver ponies?" muttered Merrit, but softly enough so that Astaran did not hear him, or at least was able to pretend that she had not.

They took their money and went out. One of the first things they did was to buy sweet buns at the baker's shop nearby. They then roamed around the market to see what there might be to buy. The market was full of the sights and sounds of a market: fruit-sellers, bakers, leather-workers, rug-sellers, calling out the superiority of their wares. There were wine-sellers, jugglers, story-tellers, pipers, and all the sounds and colours of a market in general. The choices were so broad that they ended by spending nothing.

Finally Haram said, "Enough! We have three days here, and there is a bed back at the inn which, though it be no more than a straw mattress, is likely softer than anything on which I've slept for many months. I'm going to rest, and belike tomorrow I shall find a way to spend some of my ten silver ponies."

Merrit, on the other hand, was not yet weary, and decided to walk around and see a little more of the city before he went to bed for the night.

It was late at night and very dark when Merrit burst into the room to shake Haram awake. He was greatly excited, and it took a moment before Haram could understand what he was saying.

"Saradon's band is in the city, and they want me to join them!"

Chapter Six

"Saradon wants you?"

They were back down in the common room once more, as Astaran had sleepily threatened to strangle them if they continued to jabber while she was resting.

"Certainly. I've told you that already."

"But I had thought we'd stay together."

"I know what it is! You're jealous because I have this great opportunity and you don't."

"No, I do not feel jealous!" He paused, on the point of saying that he felt betrayed, but that was such a strong word.

"I have an idea, then," said Merrit. "Let us arm-wrestle for it! Here, take my hand, and the winner will take the place with Saradon!"

Before he could say yes or no, Haram was clasping Merrit's hand. He was about to say that this was foolishness, that Merrit could have the place with Saradon, but already Merrit had given the signal, and without really wanting to, Haram was pushing against Merrit's arm.

With half his mind, he noticed Merrit's left arm moving, then there was a stab of pain in his knee. Momentarily distracted, he felt his hand hit the table, and heard Merrit shout in triumph.

Then he saw Merrit putting his dagger away, and he knew what had happened. Merrit had pricked his knee under the table. Haram stood suddenly and Merrit stood as well, his hand still on his dagger.

"If you had thought of it first, you could have done it yourself," he declared in a defensive tone. "And if a Venturer stays to the rules all the time, he ends by being a pauper."

He paused and Haram, remembering that he had not really wanted the place with Saradon, relaxed a little. Merrit went on. "Look, I'll talk to them in Saradon's band, see if they'll take two of us. But even if they don't, think of what this means. It's a grand opportunity. There are five of them, two warriors, warriors who wear scale armour, and a scout, a dark man whom I think is half-Elf, and two mages, either of them more than equal to Sagahan. And they all have horses, and they will supply me with at least a pony until we raise enough to pay for a horse.

"In a while, I'll have enough money to begin my own band, and when I do, I'll look for you to give you the first choice to join me."

He paused again. "You see, it is better that I do this. What have we here, with this band? We have a warrior who is a drunkard, a scout who is a woman, and a mage who is third-rate at the best. We could go hunting goblins for the rest of our lives, always making sure that there are no more than ten of them, and picking up a handful of coppers each time. How often do you think we would happen upon such treasure as the ogre had? Now there is enough money to buy swords for us. When do you think we'll have enough to buy armour?"

He suddenly stopped. "I'm going now. Won't you wish me well?"

And despite everything, Haram realized Merrit had been a loyal friend up to now, and that he would be sorry to see him go, and that it would be churlish to send him off in anger. "I wish you well indeed, Merrit. And when you form your own band, do come and look for me."

Merrit smiled broadly. "I will. And may it go well with you too, Haram."

Three days later, Haram had cause to feel less charitable about Merrit. The other three had come back from their various pursuits, Orizd looking much the worse for wear, and Astaran demanded, "Where is your friend? Did he think I was not serious about leaving without him?"

At that point, Haram realized that Merrit had gone away, leaving him, Haram, to make explanations. "He will not be back. He has a position with Saradon's band."

She turned burning eyes on him. "What do you say?"

"He has a position with Saradon's band. I'd have thought he would have told you."

"And so would *I*! When did this come about?"

"The night we first arrived in the city, he came to wake me to let me know."

"And what of you? Did you not think to take the opportunity as well?"

Haram thought for a moment of telling her that there had only been one position open with Saradon, but realized in time that this would only increase her wrath. He shrugged. "I am still here."

"And the sword we bought him?" demanded Orizd, who had gradually realized the situation.

"I don't know. If it isn't here, then I suppose he has taken it, thinking it was his own."

"His own? Aye, his own when he'd earned the money to pay for it! Well, bad luck to him, I say!"

"I say we are well rid of him," said Astaran. "If he feels thus about our company, that he will leave it when he thinks he sees something better, might he not run to save his own skin if serious danger threatened?"

"Merrit is no coward!" said Haram hotly.

"No? He left in the night, leaving you to make the explanations, did he not?"

Haram had no answer for that. He was annoyed himself that his friend had taken off, with a sword that was not rightly his, leaving Haram to bear the wrath of the party. All he could do was say, "Merrit is no coward," a declaration that seemed weak even to him.

It was a difficult morning for the band. No one said anything against Haram outright, but Merrit's defection put him under a temporary cloud.

The band did not fret over the situation for too long, though. "I've looked around at horses, here and there," said Astaran. "I've sorted out a couple of horse-dealers where we can probably get reasonably good mounts without putting ourselves back on the brink of starvation."

The first horse-dealer Astaran had chosen was a tall spare man, with a shock of wild black hair on his head, and a nose that had clearly come from some Shondakranian forebear.

Though any of the three veterans were adept at bargaining, an unspoken agreement said that Astaran handled the trading for them. There was a great deal of description of the fine points of these specimens of equine magnificence on one hand, and analyses of the shortcomings of these broken-down nags on the other, but she finally bought three horses, all light horses with some combat training, and one pony for Haram.

With some hard bargaining, she arranged that tack should be included in the price, though the merchant insisted she would be the cause of him becoming a pauper, begging for bread in the streets with his wife and seven children.

When they had taken their animals away, she turned to the others. "The price I got was the best that could be had, I think, and even so, it was high. We are not quite back to the poverty we were in before we fought the ogre, but we shall have to be careful until we see what fortune we have. And mind, having horses means we shall need to look to provisions for them as well as ourselves. In the main they can feed on grass, but they will do better if they have a bit of grain as well."

"I am not unfamiliar with the care and feeding of horses," said Orizd stiffly.

She shot him a look. "Aye, a good Shondakranian. My apologies. In some circumstances, I tend to lecture like our mage." She flashed a fleeting grin.

Sagahan smiled briefly, but said nothing.

The animals all had been given names to which they would respond; Haram's pony was, ironically, Arkhwelt, the same name as the mighty charger of the ancient hero Ves-Tavor of the Nine Dragons.

Haram had thought that the day-to-day life of a Venturer had driven all capacity for imaginative daydreams out of him, but when he was mounted on Arkhwelt, he found he could envision himself as a bold paladin mounted on his warhorse. He said nothing to the others, of course.

Without Merrit, Haram found himself drawn more and more into the company of the three veterans. Without Merrit to practice with, for instance, he was forced to practice sword-work with Orizd. Having become used to Merrit, Haram found Orizd was an entirely different proposition. For one thing, he loomed over Haram like a large oak tree, and though the warrior held back some of his strength, Haram felt himself completely over-matched.

The shock of the Shondakranian's first blow almost tore the sword from Haram's hand. Orizd dropped back into guard position. "Tran and Viron, hold on to the thing! It won't do you much good lying in the dirt!

"Listen, boy, I am larger than you, and in the normal run of things, I would chop you out of my way as a farmer chops a pesky willow. But what I am intending here is to train you so that you will *not* be a willow-bush for the first big man you come against. Therefore, the first thing you must learn is not to let the size of an opponent, or his armour, or his fangs, or his fluffy pink bunny-tail distract you from *your* purpose, which is to chop him out of *your* way.

"Now, again!"

Orizd also possessed much more stamina than Merrit ever had, and was still calmly and quietly going through the sword-drills when Haram was ready to drop. He changed off occasionally with Astaran, saying, "For learning the balance of the sword in the hand, one opponent is fine. But for learning the finer points, you need variety."

He also had Haram drill with Astaran's sword, and with Orizd's sword as well. Astaran scowled at the thought of allowing another to handle her blade. Orizd said, "I know, and I understand your feelings, but it is for the good of us all."

He turned to Haram and said, "If you learn to handle your sword only, fine for you. But if in the midst of a melee your blade breaks and you must take one from a fallen foe, you will not be allowed more than an instant to find the difference in its heft and balance."

Astaran taught him as well, tricks of the wilds, knowledge of plants, and the like. "See this here, boy? Foxglove. You can brew up a deadly poison from it. And on the other hand, this willow? Its bark can be made into a tea, useful for treating pain, or even some fevers. You can even chew it for relief from pain, though the taste is not particularly pleasant. In fact, when making the tea, you might want to toss in a bit of that mint over there."

She also began teaching him the rudiments of tracking, drilling him in the knowledge even more relentlessly than Sagahan drilled him in the knowledge of runes.

After two weeks of all this study, as they travelled the hills of the interior of the Kingdom, Haram suddenly realized what the meaning of this new training, aside from more work for him. It meant that he was accepted as one of the Venturers.

This was confirmed for him one evening as they sat around their campfire. Orizd said, "Now that we have four members, we might be able to take greater risks." He waved a hand as though to wave away protests. "Oh, we won't be taking extreme risks, not for some time, but we might fight larger parties of goblins, for instance, and in doing so, we will find the gains larger."

"I hope you do not expect us to be rich by midwinter," said Astaran with a smile.

"No, not rich, but perhaps richer. Perhaps we might be able to think of other things than merely surviving. Haram, tell us, what is your goal in life?"

"My goal?"

"Aye. Surely you hope to be more than a hand-to-mouth Venturer for the rest of your days?"

"My goal---" Haram shut his mouth. However much he was a part of the band, there were some things he did not want to tell them.

"Ah, come, lad! Tell us. We won't laugh. But let me guess; you wish to be a paladin on a great horse, slaying evil monsters and righting great wrongs! Am I not right?"

And while Haram stared at him openmouthed, Orizd went on. "Aye, you need not tell me! What else is there for a young man? I, even I, when I was your age, I had the same dream. I would be a paladin. I would wield my sword only in the service of just causes. I would make the world a better place."

From somewhere, Haram gained the courage to ask, "And will you still become a paladin someday?"

Orizd turned blazing eyes on him, and Haram knew he ought not to have asked that question. Then the warrior's face softened, and he looked into the embers of the fire as into some far distance. "I, become a paladin?

Between the days of youth and the time of becoming a man, many things change, whether we will them or no. And sometimes a moment of foolishness will undo all the good intentions of past years."

He looked at Haram with deep sadness on his face. "We may have done you a disservice, lad. When you sought to join us, we ought to have sent you back home. For all the riches and gold you may find, none can compare to that, that you have a home to go to."

The same thing which had made him inquire about Orizd's desire to become a paladin prompted Haram to ask if he had no home to go to. He was about to speak when he saw Sagahan looking at him and shaking his head. He closed his mouth.

But the warrior looked quickly from one to the other and smiled bleakly. As though Haram had actually spoken, he said, "I might go home again, if I were ready for the welcome. Enough years have passed that many will have forgotten what passed, but there would be some whose memories will be long. If I were to come home with enough wealth and forty warriors riding at my back, they would not turn me out again."

He stayed silent for a time, then laughed sharply. "And yet I have been at this business for enough years to know that there is little likelihood of earning sufficient money for that. Our band is stronger, but not that much stronger, and it will be the rare time that sees us up against an ogre or any other creature with so much treasure. I must learn to curb my dreams; they only cause me pain."

They were in Halan Howrdas, a fortified town guarding the Shondakranian border, when they were accosted. The man was a merchant, clearly one of the town's wealthier citizens, as his clothing could attest. He was not fat, though he was clearly well-fed, and he came to their table as they were in the midst of eating their dinner.

"Sirs, might I beg a moment of your time?"

They all looked up at him. He was dressed in red and gold, with a gold ring in his ear which Haram suspected could pay for the week's lodging for the four of them. His eyes were hazel, and he had a grim look to his mouth.

"Be seated, sir," said Orizd. Haram remembered one of Orizd's many lessons. *'If a merchant approaches you politely, be polite in return. At least, until you find out what he wants.'*

"Have you any knowledge of the land across the border?"

Orizd smiled. "A little." There was no trace of sarcasm in his voice.

"Would you be willing to undertake a task in Shondakar?"

"Why, that would depend on the nature of the task, and the pay to be offered."

The merchant considered a moment, and it seemed he would give another careful noncommittal answer, but when he spoke, emotion got the better of him. "They have kidnapped my daughter; will you rescue her for me?"

Chapter Seven

"Now sir," said Orizd soothingly, "sit down, calm yourself. There is no telling who may be watching."

"You are right," muttered the merchant, sitting down. "Your pardon, I am overwrought."

"And well you might be. But if we are going to speak of this at any length, it ought to be in secret. Tell us quietly where you live."

The merchant did so, then Orizd said, "We will be at the back door after dark. See to it that the only servants are those to whom you would trust your life, or better your daughter's life. Now if you would be so good as to curse us as you leave..."

The merchant understood readily. He stood, flinging his chair back so that it almost fell over, and said hotly, "A pox on you, then! If you fear to do this, I will find people who are less fearful!" He stormed out.

"Well done!" muttered Astaran. "Did it fool anyone, you think??"

Orizd shrugged. "Was there anyone to be fooled? If so, we can hope that they were misled."

A tall, thin man, who seemed to be much the worse for ale, came unsteadily over to their table. "A mean man to get on the wrong side of, that one," he said.

Orizd shrugged. "We do not plan to be in these parts for long."

"He sought to hire you to go into Shondakar for his daughter, did he? Oh, that news has been around for some time. And you being Shondakranian, I suppose you know the country."

"I hail from Margarit-ja, and this borderland is not my country at all," said Orizd, a little stiffly.

"But you would be better able than some, if you were to accept the challenge."

"Challenge, is it? Why let me tell you, fellow..." And Orizd was off on a long tale of tracking goblins, detailing every arrow shot, every blow of every sword, until Haram began fidgeting with embarrassment. Eventually, the tall man excused himself and went away.

"Well done," said Astaran. "If he had any opinion of us before, it is less now."

"Good. The fellow was a rather clumsy spy, and if he tells his masters that this band is led by an old blowhard, and that we have probably turned down the merchant's request, all the better. Best have your enemy undcrestimating you."

"I was not arguing with your methods. I was rather admiring them."

"Fine. And if we can attract the attention of the Innkeeper, you can also admire my appetite."

During supper, the talk was of a number of things, of how the horses were holding up and such, including the usual jests regarding the name of Haram's pony. Even Sagahan joined in once, with a long play on words which could be fully understood only by someone well-versed in heroic lore. He was then forced to explain it, which he did at great length.

When they had finished their meal, Orizd leaned over toward Astaran. "Why do you not take a walk around the town? The rest of us will be leaving soon as well."

She nodded, then stood up, excusing herself from the table. Haram cast what he hoped was a surreptitious glance around to see if anyone appeared to be paying too close attention to her. Most of the men who were not too drunk to notice seemed to watch her, so he could not say whether or not there was a spy about.

The other three conversed in a desultory fashion for a while, though Sagahan took brief part, aside from acknowledging statements aimed at him. Mostly it was remarks from

Orizd, remarks with which the others could agree or disagree, and usually remarks intended to further Haram's education.

"If you're ever in an oak wood, lad, take care how you treat it. Most times, you'll be able to tell if you've come into a druid-grove or not; there is a feeling about such places, is there not, Sagahan? Yes. And if you ever come to such a grove, be careful. You may pick up dead branches from the ground for your fire, but touch the living wood at your peril!

"I've even heard stories of druids who will exact a price for green grass destroyed by a campfire. So be wary, lad."

"Are the druids magicians, then?"

"They are and they are not. From what I understand, their magic is the magic of the wild, the wood, and living things. They teach their lore freely to those who come to learn, though even such students must prove their willingness to study before they are accepted. I only know for certain that I do not wish a druid to be angry with me. Sagahan, what do you know of their magic?"

"Druid magic? I know little of it personally. As you say, it is magic of the wild, the wood, and living things. It is said that a druid with great power can cause the very land to rise up against his enemy. Of this, I have no personal experience, and of the many tales I have heard, there are only two or three which I think may have any large amount of truth to them. In magic, you see, there are---"

"Enough, enough, mage! We have no need for one of your disquisitions on the nature of magic and the true colour of blue! Come, let us go walking!"

They went out then, walking about casually as though only seeing the sights. As they walked down the street, Astaran joined them. "Is his house being watched?" asked Orizd.

"Yes, but not very carefully. We can dodge them if we use a little caution."

"Good."

Paying careful attention to the people on the streets, particularly any who might seem to follow them, they went to the merchant's house. Astaran led them by a somewhat circuitous route, and Haram never saw the person who was supposed to be watching the house.

The back door was opened for them by the merchant himself, and he led them to an inner room. There were four cups of wine poured already, and the merchant let them find their own seats. When that was done, he spoke.

"We have not yet been introduced. My name is Lavad."

Orizd introduced the party. "You realize, sir, that we have not agreed to take on this task, only listen to what you have to say?"

"Yes. I hope I can persuade you, however." He paused briefly, then went on. "Two weeks ago, my daughter Terrial was taken as she was travelling with one of my pack-trains. We received word that she was being held, and that if we did not pay a ransom, she would be sold into slavery."

"Pardon my interruption," said Orizd, "but did you not consider simply paying the ransom, or was it higher than you could afford?"

"No, the first demand was actually quite reasonable. We left the money in the place where we were told to leave it and went to the place where they had agreed to leave Terrial. Instead of sending her, they sent a message by a local peasant saying that they had decided that the money was not enough, and wanted as much again."

He looked around at them. "You see then what I face? What is to prevent them from raising the price again and again, and after they have squeezed as much out of me as they can, to sell Terrial into slavery too? It is for that reason that I approached you."

Orizd nodded. "Exactly so. You do realize, sir, that your approach to us in the Inn might well get back to the kidnappers?"

Lavad brushed a hand over his face. "Yes, I suppose so. I suppose desperation overcame my wits. But can you rescue her?"

"That may be. First, we must find out all that we can about these bandits. What do you know about them?"

"There have been raids on towns, farms, and pack-trains recently by bandits who shelter across the border in Shondakar. Our King has sent embassies to protest to the King of Shondakar, but the King of Shondakar claims the bandits shelter on this side of the border, and are thus none of his concern, unless they attack Shondakranian people."

Orizd frowned. "Very general information. Can you say nothing specific?

What part of Shondakar do they hide in?"

"You hurry me, sir," said Lavad with a wry smile. "I believe I can tell you exactly where she is being held. The *kattenasp* of the Shondakranian province of Haraiva just across the border has a son, Ksarsha. To keep him out of trouble, his father made him *harnasp* of the city of Shab-nazdig.

"Ksarsha has been making himself popular with the people by maintaining their taxes at a reasonable level. He is also maintaining himself in the state expected of a *harnasp* and the son of a *kattenasp*. The tale is commonly told that soldiers of his guard act as bandits, always careful to commit no crimes in his territory. And since he is responsible for the control of bandits, he assures his father and lord that there are none in his land.

"He has also discovered that the spoils of mere banditry are not large, so he has taken to kidnap and extortion. It is suggested his spies have familiarized his men with the faces of every person from every family of means on this side of the border."

Orizd frowned and looked at Astaran. "What say you? Can we fight the whole of a *harnasp's* guard?"

She shook her head. "No, but perhaps we need not fight them all. Do you know anything further, Lavad?"

"Oh, indeed. There is a low tower in the city of Shab-nazdig which I have had pointed out as the place where Ksarsha keeps special prisoners. No one is quite sure what makes the prisoners special, but one drunken guardsman said they were 'very valuable.' What think you?"

"Ah, much the same as yourself; that this is the place where he keeps the prisoners to be ransomed."

There was quiet around the table, then Orizd said, "We might at least go to the city of Shab-nazdig and see if it is possible."

"And what then?" demanded Lavad. "You come back to me, agreeing to take on the task, and go back again, during which time my daughter suffers?"

Orizd frowned. "Suppose we make an agreement now, and if it proves possible to free your daughter, we will do so? If not, we will come back to tell you."

"I like it not at all!" said the merchant.

"You may have little choice," said the warrior calmly. "There are few people enough who'd be willing to take a trip into Shondakar, and many of them would insist on being paid the bulk of their fee before they went."

"And what of you? What do you demand?"

"Five hundred gold crowns each," said Astaran.

The merchant's head snapped up. "Oh, aye! And you will rescue my daughter so that we can beg our bread in the streets together? Five gold crowns each!" Concern for his daughter did not entirely overwhelm his nature as a man of trade.

The end of the bargaining found them agreed on a price of one hundred gold crowns each, to be paid on the completion of the mission. Five gold crowns altogether were to be paid beforehand for necessary expenses.

As they walked back to the Inn, Orizd clapped Haram on the shoulder. "Ha, Sir Haram, see to your noble mount Arkhwelt! We are off to rescue a fair maiden in distress!"

Haram could only smile faintly, for he had been thinking much the same.

Chapter Eight

The three travellers came openly to the gate of Shab-nazdig. As Orizd told Haram on the way, "If we make too great an effort to remain unnoticed, we will likely only bring more suspicion on ourselves."

The guards at the gate wore leather cuirasses and greaves, with spiked metal helmets on their heads. They had long spears in their hands and swords belted at their waists. All wore dark moustaches as well, of varying lengths. They inspected the travellers, then waved them past.

"First of all," said Orizd, "let us find ourselves an inn."

The Inn they found, the Dragon Mace, was fairly clean and was reported to have good food. The prices were steep, however, and Haram had to keep himself from gasping when he heard the figure. As they moved to a table, Orizd said, "We might find a more expensive inn, but we would stand out clearly as people who do not usually frequent such places. They would generally leave us to our own devices, but when the alarm is raised, they would remember us. In the least expensive inns, there is always someone marking who comes in and who goes out, while the accommodations are less than comfortable. Here we are fairly safe from spies, and will generally be let alone to do whatever business we choose to do. It is expensive, but worth it."

"Do you think we have eluded Ksarsha's spies?" asked Astaran.

The warrior shrugged. "Much depends on whether they had any important news to report. What could they say about us? That Lavad spoke to us and left us in anger? Possibly if one of his servants talked out of turn, that he had a secret meeting with someone that same night? All very vague, not worth reporting by any spy, unless there was no other news and he felt it necessary to send along *something* to justify his pay.

"And even if he did send that news along, would they necessarily connect the secret meeting with us? We will not wait around to see just how safe we are, but I think we are safe enough."

"But if we were contacted by Lavad, and a week or so later we appear in Shab-nazdig, what is the natural thing to think?" the archer protested.

"But is the arrival of every group of travellers reported to the *harnasp*? I think not. And even so, we will not be in town long enough for the information to get through the channels and be acted upon. Now, let us eat."

They went to the marketplace and looked over the items for sale. At one point Sagahan sought out a herbalist and spent a good deal of money there. Orizd bought a small wooden shield for Haram, but cautioned Haram about using it. "If it comes to fighting, best leave it on your back. Fighting while using a shield is very different from fighting without one. When we have some leisure, I'll give you some training."

They returned to the Dragon Mace to dine, then went up to their room. Orizd looked at Sagahan and asked, "Now?"

"As good a time as any."

"Fine. Haram, guard the door. Put your back against it so that no one can open it without pushing you over. Keep your sword in your hand as well; if someone pushes their way in, it may prove necessary to kill them. Can you do that? Good. Also, whatever you see here, keep your mouth shut; Sagahan must concentrate on his work. Carry on, mage."

Sagahan sat down cross-legged in the middle of the floor, staring at the window, his palms upturned on his knees. For a long time nothing happened, then suddenly a small but bright blue flame appeared in each palm. Haram gasped, but since none of the others made a move, he assumed that this was a normal part of the spell the mage was casting.

For a long while, nothing further happened, then a bright blue spot appeared on Sagahan's forehead. After a moment, what looked like a thin filament of cobweb began to stretch out from that spot, moving straight toward the window and on out. It went at high speed, and once it had passed through the window, it turned and moved on out of sight, all the while connected to the spot on the mage's forehead.

After that, they could only wait in silence.

A long time later, the filament pulled back, the end suddenly appearing in the window and disappearing into Sagahan's forehead. The light on his forehead winked out, and almost immediately afterward, the two lights on his palms extinguished themselves. He toppled backward, and Orizd was just in time to catch him before he hit the floor.

"All seems well," the warrior said. "Now let us all go to bed and rest for what remains of the night. In the morning, we'll begin making specific plans."

Haram was awake early the next morning, and with some difficulty curbed his impatience, waiting for the others to wake up and begin planning. Even then, the first thing Orizd said upon rising was, "First of all, let us eat."

By the time they actually began to discuss plans, Haram was barely able to control his fidgeting.

"I have found her," said Sagahan. "She is indeed in the tower reserved for special prisoners. She is in a locked chamber on the second floor. The tower is guarded by two guards at the only door, with a guardroom just inside the door containing six to ten more. In the evening, there are no others around, and that would probably be the best time to act." He paused, wrinkling his brow.

"There was a feeling of something strange there, something which I could not identify. It was not something which interfered with my search, though I am uncertain that it could not if it had desired to. There may be more to this than we know."

"What was it?" asked Astaran. "Some other magician? A demon?"

The mage shrugged. "As I said, I could not identify it. It was not a magician. Whether or not it was a demon, I could not say."

A little after nightfall, they walked out of their room, carrying two full wineskins. As they neared the tower, there were fewer and fewer people on the street, until at last they were the only ones about. They paused around the corner from the tower.

"Are we ready?" asked Orizd. "Any last questions?"

No one spoke. "Then Tran and Viron be with us, and let us go."

He took one of the wineskins, sniffed its nozzle to be sure what it was, then sprayed it over Astaran, Sagahan, and Haram. That done, he handed it to Astaran, who did the same for him. He then nodded at Sagahan, who muttered something quietly. Then the liquid glowed.

"It is a matter of taking something which already has a propensity for shining, and only a minor spell is needed to accentuate the glow." Sagahan had said.

Haram looked at the others, and as much of himself as he could see. They were an eldritch sight.

"We hope not to have to fight at all," Orizd had said, "and we'll want some form of disguise. This way, they'll notice little more than that they were attacked by four shining figures. It will also probably give us an advantage in morale; what will they think we are? Perhaps demons?"

Haram held the second wineskin. They strode around the corner toward the door of the tower. The guards were shocked into immobility by the sudden appearance of the four shining figures. By the time they had recovered their wits sufficiently to do anything, the four were on them. Haram pointed the nozzle of the second wineskin at their faces and squeezed. Liquid splashed across their shocked countenances. They breathed in, and suddenly, in the act of presenting their spears, they fell.

"A powerful sleeping potion will allow us to deal with a lot of them, without the necessity of fighting," Sagahan had said. "But be careful all of you, and do not breath too deeply where the potion is being used."

Astaran took a ring of keys from the belt of one of the guardsmen. Haram held the wineskin ready while Astaran, holding her breath, applied one of the keys to the keyhole of the door.

"If there is to be little or no sword-work, why must I carry the wineskin?" He had asked.

Orizd had grinned wickedly. "Because if there is sword-work to be done, it will be desperate time, and it will need the best swordsmen to do it."

The door swung open. Haram stepped forward. Immediately before him was the guardroom, with six guardsmen inside. They were just beginning to look up in surprise when he sprayed the rest of the contents of the wineskin at them, then stepped back out of the way. The enclosed quarters of the guardroom kept the fumes concentrated in the one area, growing stronger around the guards as they moved. Those nearest the doorway had gotten the strongest dose and fell, obstructing the movement of those behind.

As Astaran and Orizd stepped forward, swords in hands, the guards hesitated a little, then surged forward. By this time, however, they were all suffering to some degree from the effects of the potion, and only one of them, a large man, reached the door. Astaran danced back from him, keeping his attention, while Orizd came in from behind and slammed the flat of his sword across the guard's skull. He fell, and did not move.

"Here," said Orizd. "Help me shift him back inside. It will preserve the illusion of something magical being at work."

Without a word, Astaran and Haram bent to work. They heaved him back inside the guardroom, laying him on his back. By the time they were finished, Haram was feeling a little dizzy.

"All that noise and clatter of metal, won't it bring someone to see what's happening?"

"Hah!" Orizd snorted. "In most civilized places, people who hear clashing metal go the other way. Eventually, the word may come to some city guard, though, so come along, quickly!"

After he had staggered up a few stairs, he felt a little better. Finally, Sagahan led them to a certain door. Astaran bent to the lock again, and a few moments later, that door was also opened.

Inside were a chair and a cot against the wall. On the cot was a small female figure. As the Venturers stepped inside, the figure on the cot sat up and stared at them. Haram's immediate impression was of a small triangular face with a mass of curly red hair above it. She opened her mouth to scream, and Astaran was there in that instant, a hand clasped across the mouth. It occurred to Haram that four glowing figures bursting into her prison would be terrifying to the girl.

"Hush now," Astaran said. "We've been

sent by your father to rescue you. I know we look frightful, but it is only a guise put on to help us in our work. Do you understand?"

The glow from Astaran's hand lit a pair of wide green eyes as the head nodded. She took her hand away and held a finger to her own lips. "First, we get you away, then after that you can ask all the questions you wish."

They hurried down the stairs and out the door. As they went out, Haram heard Sagahan mutter something, and the glow that had covered the party faded.

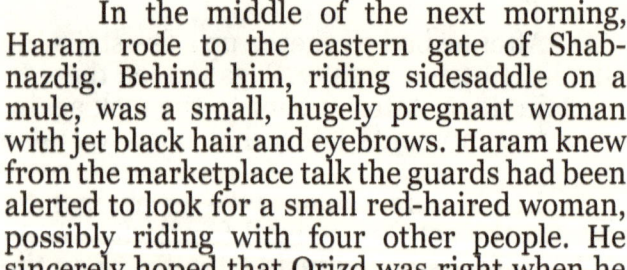

In the middle of the next morning, Haram rode to the eastern gate of Shab-nazdig. Behind him, riding sidesaddle on a mule, was a small, hugely pregnant woman with jet black hair and eyebrows. Haram knew from the marketplace talk the guards had been alerted to look for a small red-haired woman, possibly riding with four other people. He sincerely hoped that Orizd was right when he said that this disguise would prevent them from looking too closely.

As it was, the guards looked them over and sent them on their way with rude jests about Haram's virility. For all his experience as a Venturer, Haram's ears burned.

Terrial had said very little since they had brought her away, but she had spent a good deal of time looking over her shoulders, as though she expected a troop of guards to descend on them at any time to drag her away. When Astaran had explained the disguise, and the need for it, she had only nodded quietly and let Astaran dye her hair, colour her eyebrows and lashes, and take her aside to pad her so as to look pregnant.

After they had ridden some distance from the gate, he turned to her. "Are you well?"

She nodded quietly, but her eyes belied that agreement. "What is it?" he asked.

"The others, when do they join us?"

He felt a sudden anger. Was he then such an obvious tyro that she did not feel safe with him? Indeed, would Orizd have trusted her to his care if he thought him incapable of protecting her? He restrained himself from answering hastily, and instead said, "This afternoon, tonight at the very latest."

"Oh." The tone was one which said that the news was disappointing.

"I am sure you will be safe with me until they arrive!" He could not keep all traces of anger out of his voice this time.

She looked at him swiftly. "Oh, but there are things you do not know---" she broke off suddenly.

"What things?"

She shook her head. "Please, these are things I would rather not speak of carelessly. Wait until your friends arrive, then I will tell you all at one time."

"And if there is something special against which I should be on my guard, I must wait until they arrive? Surely that is not sensible!"

She shook her head again. "No! If it comes, I doubt whether you or anyone could protect us. Perhaps your friends will have some ideas about it."

And despite all his questions, she would speak no further.

They camped late that afternoon by an old grove of oaks, made a campfire, and waited.

Haram sat in sullen silence, occasionally glancing across the fire at Terrial, who said nothing at all. For a long while they sat thus, then Terrial asked, "How long do we wait for them?"

The possibility of the rest of the party not coming had never occurred to Haram. He considered the matter. "If they have not arrived by nightfall, I will assume that they have met with serious difficulty. In the morning, we will go on alone."

"In the morning? If they have met with difficulty, that almost certainly means that someone has found out who they are and what they have done, and there will be soldiers scouring the countryside for us! We would be best to travel immediately."

This only made Haram the more determined. "Think on it, lady! If, by some strange chance, they were come upon and captured five minutes after we left them, it would still require more than an hour to interrogate them and force them to tell where we had gone. And surely the soldiers who scour the countryside would do so by daylight, lest we turn off the main trail somewhere, and they miss our tracks.

"And as for ourselves blundering across unfamiliar territory in the dark, why that would be more dangerous than waiting until morning when we can see the trail, even if it should allow the soldiers a small start on us. Further, we are almost over the border, and I doubt they will follow us too closely, lest they meet with patrols from our side of the border."

It was the turn of Terrial to lapse into scowling silence, and they remained in that state for some time. Later on, Haram cooked up some supper for them, and passed her a plate without a word. She took it from him without a word and began eating.

Suddenly, she let out a gasp; Haram looked up, and she was staring past his head at the wood. He surged to his feet, drawing his sword and turning. An old man stood there, browned by the sun, white of hair and beard, wearing a brown robe belted at the waist with a plain brown cord.

Chapter Nine

The old man appeared to be all alone, and weaponless. There was a twinkle in his eye and a bit of laughter in his voice when he said, "Peace, put up your sword. I am no foe you need fear."

Haram looked beyond him to be sure that he had no confederates hidden in the wood. "Welcome to our camp, then. We have food to spare, if you wish to join us."

The old man smiled. "Thank you for the offer, but no, I have no need of food at the moment. I will sit with you a while, though, if you have no objection."

Haram, extremely conscious of the trust which the band had placed in him, thought for a moment to refuse, but in the same instant he saw what Terrial would see; his fear of an old, bearded man.

"Certainly not," he said. "Sit down and be comfortable. If you will not eat, may I offer you a drink? The ale is not of the best, but I'm told it is the best Shab-nazdig has to offer."

The old man took a mug of ale, nodding his thanks. "Shab-nazdig, is it?" He looked at each of them in a way which almost made Haram regret his invitation. "And how are things in Shab-nazdig these days?"

Haram shrugged. "Much as usual, I expect. It's not my city, so I could not say whether or not its present condition is normal."

The old man chuckled. "And could I be mistaking you for a Shondakranian, with hair like that and an accent such as you have? Oh, no, not at all!" He chuckled a little more. "I trust your venture in Shab-nazdig was successful?"

Haram stiffened and almost reached for his sword. It sounded as though the old man knew who he was and what he had done! But he had been with the band long enough to be careful of his conversation, even if he had not full control of his reactions.

"Well enough, well enough," he said, shrugging. "I may not be rich, but neither will I starve this week."

The old man's eyes were still glimmering with amusement. "Oh no, I ask no trade secrets, for you bear the look of a Venturer. I only make conversation. And if Shab-nazdig is not a safe subject for conversation, what else ought we to talk of?"

Haram grinned. "We might discuss the weather. It is fine for this time of year, is it not? Good for all growing things?"

The comment did not seem worthy of the great burst of laughter it brought from the old man.. "Very fine. Yet it is subject to sudden changes, you know. My name is Korennis; what may I call you?"

"I am Haram, and this is Terrial." Even as he spoke, Haram realized he was probably giving away information which Orizd would prefer him not to spread around. On the other hand, he reminded himself, their names would not be important unless the other three had already been taken and had confessed to what they had done. Even then, it was unlikely that the troops of the *harnasp* would pursue them before morning, and he and Terrial would be across the border before they could be overtaken.

But when he saw Terrial's look of disgust from across the fire, he was a little less certain of himself.

"Was there aught unusual happening in Shab-nazdig?" inquired Korennis.

For a moment, Haram was a little alarmed, certain that the old man was trying to pry slyly into what they had been doing. Being careful to keep his voice as normal as possible, he answered, "I have lived my life so far in Aradair, and this was my first trip into Shondakar; everything seemed unusual."

The old man seemed to accept that answer, though he smiled a bit. Then his expression grew a more grave. "There are things, you know, which even the best sword may not stop."

Unaccountably, Haram was reminded of the strange feeling Sagahan had gotten when he had traced down Terrial's place in the tower. But he smiled and said, "I hope to stay well out of the way of such things."

"Very wise. And if you accidentally put yourself in the way of one of them, what would you do?"

Haram was beginning to enjoy this banter. "Why, the best I could, I suppose. Is that not all a man can do?"

Korennis looked grave. "It is. Would you take some advice, young Haram?"

There was something about the question which prevented Haram from giving a flippant answer. He frowned and considered. "One who never takes advice can run into needless dangers, but one who listens to all advice never thinks for himself. I suppose it would depend on the advice."

The old man nodded. "Walk warily. There are strange things abroad, and dreadful things waking. Go back into Aradair and do not come near Shondakar again for a long while."

Haram frowned. "Is this a threat?"

"No threat, young man, only a foretelling. You have stepped into something, albeit unawares, which is much greater than you."

Across the fire, Terrial was staring at Korennis as though she found his veiled references entirely too clear. Haram felt himself sweating.

"Are we in immediate danger?"

Korennis shook his head. "I cannot foretell so accurately as that. There is great danger, though, and it would be best if you were to flee immediately."

Haram frowned. "I cannot. My companions expect to meet me here, or near here. Perhaps when they come."

"Then let us hope they come soon."

For a long while they sat in silence, then Terrial slid over toward Haram. "Let us do as he says," she muttered. "Let us pack up and flee. We can be over the border within a few hours."

He shook his head stubbornly. "The two of you keep hinting of great fear and dread on our track, but you won't be specific. Tell me who follows us, aside from the *harnasp*, and perhaps I will consider moving."

"Are you a fool? Do you think he won't hear if his name is called? Do you think that mere distance matters to him? If he knows my whereabouts, he will come for me."

Haram looked up at that. "Will he indeed? And if mere distance matters so little to this mysterious creature, what good to flee? He will certainly find us wherever we might go, so why go anywhere?"

She gave him a look of disgust, then moved back to her place and sat staring into the fire with the expression of one who has lost all hope.

There was a long time of silence, broken only by the sounds of the fire and the sounds of the horses. Arkhwelt neighed and stamped nervously, and Haram got up and went to him. Something was certainly upsetting him, and Haram patted his muzzle, looking at the jagged white blaze on the brown background, the blaze which intrigued him by its irregular shape, almost a bolt of white lightning.

"Well, that makes the three of you who seem to expect something terrible to happen. And maybe I'm a fool for not moving, but I'll wait here for Orizd and the rest." But he did not say so to the others.

A long while later, the sounds of trotting hooves brought Haram up suddenly out of a light doze, clutching at his sword. Three riders rode into the light of the fire, and he saw with relief that it was his companions. Astaran's eyes widened as her eyes fell on Korennis, and she leaped down from her horse to stand before him almost like a suppliant before a high priest.

"A good evening to you, sir. I regret the trespass on your land. Has the boy offended you? If so, he shall surely be punished."

A gleam of amusement came to Korennis' eyes. "No, he has been very polite, even when pressed, and the first thing he did was to offer me food and drink. And he has never hinted at causing destruction to my grove, though I doubt he knew it was mine. Do I take it that you are the companions he has been waiting for?"

Haram was suddenly aware that Korennis must be a druid and was ashamed that he had not deduced as much from all the evidence.

"Is there aught we can offer you, Lord, besides hospitality?"

The old man shook his head. "Nothing, now. It is too late." Her face fell, but the druid laughed. "No, no, you need not fear me. You ought to fear rather the confrontation which comes. I had hoped it would not, but I feel it approaching."

Sagahan broke in then. "You feel it yourself? Since first I saw the young lady, I have felt something slightly wrong. The wrongness has been increasing throughout the day, and I still cannot guess what it is."

"Nor will I tell you, lest talking about it should bring it more quickly. My power is not without limit, but I will try my best to give you what protection I can."

"Ought we to flee this place?" asked Orizd.

"The time for flight is long past," answered the druid. "Even the fastest could not outrun what comes now."

He walked away from the fire, then stepped a careful circle around them all, including the horses. Three times he walked the circle, speaking no word, but Sagahan went suddenly pale. "I hope he means us no ill, for his power is well beyond my own."

Korennis walked back to the fire again and looked at them. "I have done what I can. Now we must wait and see."

As though those words were a summoning, there was a sudden humming in the air, and a feeling of oppressive heat. A pinpoint of light showed before them, a point which gradually grew into a large ball of roiling sulphurous light. Suddenly, the light turned into a manlike figure, which towered above them.

It was broad and heavy-looking, with large muscles rippling in its arms, and it wore no clothing save for a short kilt. The face was large and round and bald, with sharply pointed ears and sharp carnivorous teeth showed when it smiled.

Orizd muttered something that sounded to Haram like, *"Drauh!"*

"Give me the girl," the flaming being hissed. "She is mine."

Haram found himself thinking that they should indeed give up the girl, and was immediately ashamed of himself. Not that his thoughts or feelings mattered, for Korennis spoke.

"She is not yours to have."

Fierce eyes turned on the old man. "You would rob me of what is mine, druid?"

"She is not yours, else you would not be here trying to take her from us."

"You play with words, druid! She is mine, she was promised to me, and I will have her!"

"No."

"You think this circle will protect you? Fool! I can crack it like a walnut if I wish!"

Korennis merely shrugged. The glowing being raised its hands above its head and brought them down swiftly. Orange flames leaped and crackled around the circle, and despite its protection, the five inside felt uncomfortably warm. The horses neighed in fear, rearing, and Korennis shouted "Control the animals! Do not let them run loose!"

Haram and Orizd leaped for the halter-ropes and managed to calm the horses somewhat. The flames died around the circle, but the flaming being was still there.

"Will you give her to me?"

"Never!"

"Old tree-loving fool! You cannot keep her from me forever!"

"Perhaps not, but I can try."

"Take this, then!" He raised his hands again and brought them down sharply. Lightning flashed and crashed around them, striking against the circle and rebounding. Once again, Haram and Orizd had to hold the horses to keep them from bolting.

The lightning died away, and the fiery entity stood glaring at them.

"I will have her yet, and you shall all suffer!" he shouted. Korennis made no answer.

Chapter Ten

The flame-being prowled around the circumference of the circle, occasionally flinging himself with a scream at the people inside. "By Tran and Viron!" whispered Astaran.

The prowling entity turned his eyes on her. "Ah yes, call on them by all means! But one day I shall be more powerful than they, and I shall rule supreme!"

He continued to prowl. Haram eased up beside Korennis, and whispered, "Could he actually break through the circle?"

"Oh yes, he could indeed. But to do so would require that he put forth enough power to attract the attention of his more powerful enemies. His best hope is that one of us will break the circle; if that happens, he will deal with us all in the blink of an eye. So make sure the horses are under control and remember yourself that we are safer here than anywhere."

It occurred to Haram to ask who their adversary was, but something told him that was not a good idea. Instead, he whispered to himself, "Tran and Viron be with us."

The stalking foe turned to look at him. "You, boy, why should you be caught up in this? You have a life ahead of you; go away, leave these obstinate fools to their fate."

He spoke so earnestly and persuasively that Haram could almost believe that he would be let go. Even worse, he looked down and saw that he had taken an involuntary step toward the circle; he remembered what Korennis had said about breaching the circle and forced himself to stop.

"Come, boy," said the sweet reasonable voice again. "I will not harm you. Come out, take your horse, and go away."

There was some sort of magic in the voice, and this time Haram was not aware of moving until he felt something holding him back. He looked down, and Korennis was holding his arm. He looked up into the druid's eyes, heard him murmur, "Hold firm, lad, hold firm!"

Exerting all his will, Haram held himself still, kept his feet from moving. The adversary glared at him and at the druid, and with a throwing motion of his hand, he cast a roaring gout of fire at them. The fire splashed harmlessly off the barrier around them, and the flaming being took to prowling once more.

From time to time, he would stop and talk to one or the other of the party, trying to persuade them to come out of the circle. The only one he did not speak to was Terrial, and Haram suspected that this was because she knew enough about him that she would not believe any of his promises. The only other one who moved, or nearly moved, was Astaran, and a touch on her shoulder by Orizd brought her back to her senses.

Haram suddenly noticed that the sky was beginning to pale. The effect was to dull the brilliance of the flames and make the adversary less fearsome. He finally approached the circle one last time and said with a snarl, "Be on your way, then, but remember that there is nowhere where you can hide from me! I shall always remember you, and I shall find ways to be revenged!"

He disappeared in flames, and the flames gradually shrank down into a sphere, into a ball, into a tiny dot, and were gone.

Korennis breathed deeply. "He is gone. Do not go out beyond the circle yet, until the dawn is fully up, but I think we are safe for the time being."

Haram suddenly felt free enough to ask, "Who was that?"

"Ah, he has many names. Mostly he is known by his Shondakranian name of Drauh, the Master of Lies."

"And what would the *harnasp* of Shab-nazdig want with him?"

"Power, just as anyone wants who goes to serve the Master of Lies. He can provide great power to his servants, but he is untrustworthy; make a bargain with him and you will usually find he has twisted the wording of the bargain so that you come away the loser. That means that you become his slave, doing whatever he wishes, suffering whatever he lays upon you. But there will always be those who feel that they are shrewd enough to make a bargain he cannot subvert. They always lose in the end, for often if he cannot twist the bargain, he merely breaks it.

"But the *harnasp* might well feel it worth the risk to deal with him, and gain whatever power he can gain, increasing his stature and prosperity. Dangerous business, but there you are."

He turned to Terrial. "When you come home, best have your father visit a priest and buy the most powerful amulet he can purchase for you." He looked at her surprised face and chuckled. "I am a druid, but I still hear the news. And such news as the disappearance of Terrial daughter of Lavad has come even to this part of the country."

He looked at the four Venturers. "Best you should get amulets made as well, and also probably best you should not come too close to Shondakar for a while."

"And what of you?" asked Haram. "Will you be safe here?"

"Here in my grove, I will be as safe as anywhere. And if I must come out of my grove, I have the means to make myself safe."

"I'm sorry we brought such trouble on you," said Haram.

"Aye, well, and so am I, but it is much too late to concern ourselves with such matters. At least he did no damage to the trees, though the area around this camp will not be the same for some years."

They were riding in a southerly direction, roughly parallel to the Shondakranian border. They had stopped in Halan Hawrdas for their pay, and Lavad did not seek to cheat them or make a new bargain, so happy was he to see his daughter back.

Orizd had taken the druid's warning seriously, and they had stopped in Halan Hawrdas long enough to have very powerful amulets made, though the making of these amulets had taken much of what they had earned from Lavad. Despite this, Orizd felt fairly satisfied. "The word of this deed will get around. We may even find people seeking us out to slay monsters for them, and the like."

Orizd continued to drill Haram in the use of the sword and the shield, and Haram found indeed that it was much different than the use of the sword alone. He also continued to study reading and writing from Sagahan, and trail-craft from Astaran.

From time to time, he considered his parting from Terrial. In the morning, as they were about to mount their horses to leave the neighbourhood of the druid's grove, Haram had approached her and said, "I apologize. I was wrong to insist on camping here for the night."

She turned and looked at him. "Yes," she said, "you were."

For a moment he was on the verge of shouting at her, justifying his actions, but instead he closed his mouth firmly, turned on his heels, and walked back to Arkhwelt. He did not attempt to speak to her again.

When they were dismounting in front of her father's house, however, she turned to him. "Haram?"

"Aye?" He was prepared for whatever insult she might cast at him.

"I'm sorry. I was rude to you before. You were doing what you thought was the best, and I could not tell you truly what pursued us. My apologies."

And before he could say anything to her, they were all walking to the doorway of the house where Lavad himself stood. He had no further chance to speak to her alone.

"We're in fairly safe country," said Orizd, looking around. "We're unlikely to come across goblins, or even bandits, here. Just the same, we'll set watches."

So they continued on their way, setting watches at night, but never seeing anything more dangerous than a wary wolf or two.

One night Haram unrolled his bedding under a low overhang of brush to be protected from a threatening overnight rain. Later on, when he had more time to think of it, he realized that this saved his life, putting him right out of sight in the early dawn. He was wakened by a scream.

He was sitting up, reaching for his sword before he was even aware of what was happening. His first impression was that there were a thousand goblins in the camp, all snarling and shouting and hacking with weapons.

As he sprang to his feet, he realized they were probably no more than thirty, but that was enough, and more than enough. He bent down to pick up his shield, but in the same instant a goblin came shrieking at him, sword raised. He parried the first blow and the second, then got in a stroke of his own, which took the goblin in the side of the head and dropped him to the ground.

He looked around; Orizd was standing in the midst of several goblins, bleeding from a half-dozen wounds while swinging his sword and shouting war-cries in what must be Shondakranian. There were also flashes of lightning, which Haram took to mean that Sagahan was giving some account of himself. Astaran was lying on the ground, covered in blood, but still trying to defend herself against several attackers. He started to run toward her.

Three goblins suddenly interposed themselves, two with swords and one husky one bearing a spear. He noticed idly that the spearman's ear decorations included two golden coins as well as the usual feathers and bones, at the same time as he realized he had never had any lessons on fighting against more than one opponent. Fear grasped him, but he remembered Orizd saying, *'Master your fear, else it may kill you.'*

His first parry was automatic, and in the midst of it he found he had to jump away from a thrust of the spear. Frantically, he twisted around to see what the third goblin was doing, and parried a blow from that one and deliver a return stroke that hit only the goblin's shield.

He whirled again to parry a thrust of the spear; in mid-thrust, the goblin stepped forward with his other foot and swung the iron-shod butt of his spear up like a staff. It hit Haram just above the right eye, and he staggered away, not even feeling himself hit the ground.

Chapter Eleven

When first he woke, he knew he had had a nightmare about being attacked by goblins. Then he felt the pain in his head and knew it had been no nightmare. He sat up, groaning, then saw to his horror that the goblins were still about. They had plundered the camp, and were apparently having discussions as to the division of the plunder. One of them noticed Haram and stepped over toward him.

Before Haram could move, the goblin had grabbed a fistful of his hair, pulled his head back, and laid a knife at his exposed throat. At that moment, there was a command in the goblin language, and the knife-wielder released him. The goblin-chief swaggered over to him and leaned down to look at him.

"Hah! Not much to you, is there?" he asked, in horribly accented language.

Haram, stiff with fear, made no answer. The goblin chief cuffed him on the side of the head. "You answer when we talk to you, boy!"

Haram gathered his wits as best he could. "Yes, sir." It seemed the safest thing to say. He heard one of the goblins mutter two words, then the whole band broke into raucous laughter. The leader turned to look at his followers, then looked back at Haram. "So, boy, at least you got hard head, eh? I think maybe we keep you a while."

"Yes, sir." Again the goblin translated, again the other goblins laughed.

"Now, you stand up and come along with us. And be careful. We have little need of slaves, and it would make no matter to us if we had to slay you."

"Yes, sir."

The first thing Haram learned was that he was always wrong. If he walked slowly, he was beaten for lagging. If he walked quickly, he was beaten for trying to run away. If he hurried to serve when he was ordered to do so, he was beaten for "presumption." If he did not hurry, he was beaten for laziness. Any order given to him was reinforced by a cuff or a kick.

He was the least of the least among the goblins, and the lesser goblins found this out quickly. They were delighted to find someone one whom they could vent their frustrations. When the leader put forth orders that only he should be able to injure the slave severely enough to hinder his walking, they rapidly learned how to deal him lesser injuries. Haram was never without a bruise or wound somewhere on his body.

As the days lengthened into weeks, he also learned never to try to retaliate, even for the grossest unfairness, for that only earned him more beatings.

He learned some of the goblin-tongue, much of it through being beaten for not understanding. He learned not to speak too well either, for that was also "presumption."

He learned not to think beyond the next few moments. There was never a time when he could have escaped, for all the beatings he received for supposed attempts at it. When they marched, he was in the midst of the column, surrounded on all sides. When they camped for the night, he was chained by the ankle to a wooden peg driven into the ground. Even if he were somehow to break the wooden stake without awakening everyone nearby, flight with half an arm's length of chain dragging noisily at his ankle would be impossible.

He learned all of their names. There was Orgatha the Chief, and Grohak the second-in-command, and Haraga, who was in charge of scouting. And there was also Vrakga. Vrakga was not one of the officers, nor was he one of the lower goblins, but he took delight in making life miserable for Haram. He would invent errands for Haram to do, errands which invariably ended with Haram receiving a beating for something.

Early in his days with the goblins, Haram was approached by Vrakga. "Go to Grohak," he commanded, and tell him *'Nishmat ul-fwada.'*"

Worn-out and weary, Haram merely did as he was told. Approaching Grohak, he said, "*Nishmat ul-fwada.*"

Grohak roared in anger. He began bellowing at Haram, all the time battering the boy with his great fists. All Haram could do was try to tell him, "Vrakga told me to."

Grohak finally quieted down enough to listen to him, then gave him one more clout. "Vrakga!" he shouted. "The slave says you sent him to me with insults!"

And Vrakga, of course, beat Haram for trying to shift blame. He used variations of the same trick from time to time, always with success, for Haram could not escape a beating, usually two. If he refused to go, he was beaten until he changed his mind. Once he had delivered the message, he was beaten again. He learned not to admit that anyone had sent him, for if he was silent he would be beaten longer, but if he admitted to having been sent, someone else was always called to give him a further beating for shifting the blame. It was during one such episode that he suddenly caught sight of his sword.

One day, after Vrakga had played his trick again, Haram found himself again admitting that Vrakga had sent him. He already knew it was futile to hope that he would escape more beatings.

"Vrakga!" roared Grohak. "The slave says you sent him to me with insults!"

"Hah! Again he tries to escape the blame for his own misdeeds!" Vrakga strode over to beat Haram again, and Haram suddenly recognized the sword at the goblin's hip, the sword which Orizd had bought, the sword with which he had learned all he presently knew of swordplay. He had never before taken notice of Vrakga's sword, but he saw it now.

Somehow, it made a difference. There was no possibility that he could wrench the sword from its scabbard and escape, but it gave him something to hope for. There might come a time, an instant's chance, when he might recover his sword. He might not escape, but he would kill some of them and force them to kill him.

Of course, he could force them to kill him at any time, he knew that. But he wished for more than mere death; he wished for some sort of revenge.

He had already learned to hide his thoughts; anything that could be construed as a sullen or angry look was reason for a further beating. But within his mind, as Vrakga was beating him, he formed a resolve. He would survive, whatever they might do to him. One day, when the chance came, he would take his sword from Vrakga and wield it.

He kept that thought in his mind from then on. He felt that eventually they would come to see him as harmless, a mere object there to be beaten for any reason or no reason at all. They would then become careless, and at that time he would find a chance, an opening.

Day followed day, and much of his time was taken up with avoiding beatings as far as possible. He was always aware of Vrakga and his sword, wherever they might be in the column, but he was careful not to allow that awareness to lead him into careless offence.

He wondered, once, if in seeking to lead the goblins to consider him as harmless, he might indeed turn into that harmless thing he was emulating. When the time came, would he merely stand by, staring at the sword-hilt, fearing to touch it lest it mean another beating?

He shut that thought out of his mind. If he indeed felt that, he would run screaming madly now, clutching at the nearest goblin's throat until they cut him down. And all that would remain was a laughing memory in a few goblin minds.

No! When he made his attempt, he would be sure that the goblins did not remember him with laughter, but with silent dread! However long it took, he would not forget!

They travelled a long way. Haram had asked once where they were going to and was beaten for presumption. He never asked again. He heard, after he had begun to understand the goblin-tongue somewhat better, that they were under orders from the King of the goblins, who seemed to live off in the north somewhere. Exactly what those orders were was not clear, though it seemed to be a far-ranging scouting expedition.

They stayed away from towns, though they were not averse to raiding an occasional isolated farmstead, particularly when they were in need of fresh meat. Haram himself seldom accepted meat from a goblin, unless he had actually seen the carcass from which it had originally come.

He would occasionally eat plants which he recognized as edible from Sagahan's lessons. This was a source of great merriment to the goblins. The younger ones would elbow each other and someone call to him, "Cow-slave! There's a fine patch over here! Only a few nettles!" Then they would laugh uproariously.

Haram, intent on surviving, ignored them as best he could.

Occasionally, as they wandered their way amongst and around and up and down the green-covered hills, Haram thought he recognized a part of the country. He had to admit, though, that he had not travelled extensively enough in Aradair to be sure of recognizing anything. He was only sure that they were still in Aradair by the look of the farms and houses that they saw.

One day they were toiling up the slope of a hill, brown grass hissing under their feet, the afternoon sun beating on their backs. They were going up the hill rather than taking the easy way around it on account of a few goblins who had been grumbling a little too much about always having to work so hard.

"Hard work, is it?" snarled Orgatha. "Let us see about hard work, then! Up the hill, all of you, and five lashes for any laggards!"

Haram knew that this meant ten lashes for him if he lagged, so he worked at keeping up. Orgatha strode on at the head of the column, demonstrating to any and all that he was the equal of any goblin under his command. Haram staggered on, carrying his burden of odds and ends which Orgatha and Grohak had loaded on him. His eyes were fixed on the heels of the goblin in front of him, and he concentrated on taking one step at a time. His lungs were bursting, but he knew what would happen if he paused for a moment, so he forced himself to go on.

There was a sudden strangled shout from the head of the column, then the sound of several goblins crying in terror. He forced himself to look up and saw that Orgatha was no longer leading them. There was confusion ahead, goblins milling around, and he heard the goblin word for *'ambush'* being repeated through the ranks.

Hoofbeats sounded ahead, and three riders came over the hill, just to the left of the head of the column, loosing arrows into the goblins. There were shouts of pain and fear now, though somewhere Haram thought he heard the sound of Grohak's voice bellowing orders, attempting to reorganize the goblin force to meet the threat from ahead.

Haram knew suddenly this was the opportunity he had been waiting for. Vrakga had been ahead of him in the column, but the column was turning into a seething lump of goblins, despite all Grohak's angry shouting. Haram cast the bundle off his back and looked around; there were goblins running past him, afraid for their lives, but there were others ahead who realized that their best hope was in standing to fight. He pushed his way forward, looking for Vrakga; there was no sign of him. Had he gotten away already, or was he perhaps dead further ahead? Then, suddenly, he caught sight of the sword. It was still in its sheathe, and Vrakga was bending a bow, aiming a shaft at one of the horsemen. Haram leaped.

Vrakga was hardly aware of Haram's hand on the sword-hilt, but when Haram pulled it free, Vrakga half-turned to see what was happening. Frantically, Haram swung the sword at the goblin's face. Vrakga partially interposed his bow, but so strong was Haram's blow that it cut through the bow and halfway through the goblin's head.

For a moment, Haram stood looking down at the dead goblin. Then he felt more than heard a movement next to him and barely brought the sword up in time to parry a stroke from a goblin on his right. He was too slow to return the blow, and the goblin was striking again. Haram was surprised to find that his hand had not forgotten all the moves Orizd had drilled into him, and his parry was automatic. The return-stroke this time was also automatic, and though the goblin parried in his turn, there was surprise on his face. He had forgotten that they had taken Haram after a fight. He had forgotten that Haram had ever been anything but the Cow-slave to be ordered about and beaten for any reason, or no reason at all.

In fact, that surprise slowed the goblin sufficiently that Haram was able to strike again, and this time the goblin's parry was too slow.

Haram looked around again. The goblins who remained in the vicinity were dead, and the rest were fleeing away back down the hillside. There were six men in various sorts of armour standing nearby, and one of them stepped over, extending a hand.

He spoke in a heavy accent. "Give us the sword, boy. 'Tis part of the plunder."

"It is my sword. It was taken from me when I was captured."

"Aye, and 'tis no longer yours, for it passes from the goblins to us. Give it over."

His hand was still extended, but the smile had left his face.

Chapter Twelve

A hollow feeling crept into the pit of Haram's stomach. He had recovered his sword. He had ceased to be the thing the goblins had tormented at will. Now he was being told to give up the sword again.

"No," he said. The words came hard to his tongue after so long with the goblins, when silence had always been safest. For a moment he thought to explain more, then decided that it made no difference.

The man frowned. He was slightly smaller than Haram and a little broader across the shoulders, with dark hair and a lumpy nose that looked as though it had been broken at least once. He put a hand on his own sword.

Haram brought his own blade up to a level with the other's stomach. "No," he said again. Then, forcing the words to come, he said,

"It is my sword. I have taken it back from the goblins, and I will not give it up again."

The man looked at him, looked down at the blade, back at Haram's face, then turned on his heel and walked away. Haram went back to Vrakga's body and unbelted the sheathe. As he was putting it on, another man, a taller and slender one, came up shouting at him.

Haram drew the sword and held it ready. "Let me be, fellow. You can have all the plunder; all I wish are the sword and the sheathe." He felt a strange beleaguered sensation, not at all the way he might have expected to feel on the day of his liberation from the goblins.

The man looked at him and backed away. Haram stood quietly. The little broad man was coming toward him again, in the company of the one who was clearly the leader of the band. This man wore chain armour well-made and well kept, and a blue surcoat over it. He had a long sword sheathed on his back so that he could draw it across his shoulder and strike in the same motion.

He was keeping his hands clear of the sword, though. His face was clean-shaven, tanned, and he had a pair of piercing blue eyes. "My name is Vorath, and I am captain of this band. Tanno tells me you claim that sword."

"Yes."

"Only 'yes?' No explanations?"

Vorath was smiling and seemed friendly enough. Haram strove for an answering smile, but was uncertain as to what degree he was successful.

"I have already explained." The words still came with difficulty. "Did Tanno not tell you?"

"Ah, but will you not tell me yourself? Please?"

"The sword was taken from me when I was made prisoner by the goblins. I have recovered it today."

"You have recovered it through the work of my lads and myself. Does that not give us some claim on it as legitimate spoil?"

Haram shrugged. "It happened to be today, but I would have taken it one time or another."

"And you recognize no claim of ours?"

"No. It is my sword, and I will not part with it again."

Vorath was still smiling, though a little forced. "We could take it from you."

"You are no fool. You could only take it from me by killing me, and I assure you it is a mere sword, of great value only to me, and not worth fighting for." The words came easier now, though only a little.

"What of clothing?"

"What of it?" Haram looked down at himself, clad only in the ragged remains of a pair of trousers. "Do you think to offer to trade me clothing for the sword?"

The captain laughed. "No, not hardly. I will give you some clothing freely. And we will not fight you over the sword; as you say, we are not fools. Come, let us have a bite to eat, and you can tell us your story."

So they prepared their food and ate. The

captain gave Haram some clothing to put on, and they all listened as Haram described the early morning attack which had ended with him being a prisoner of the goblins.

"And you," he asked, "How was it that you happened to be at the top of the very hill the goblins climbed?"

"By Tran and Viron, that was mere chance! You see, our scout had warned us that the goblins were marching our way. We had no real desire to fight so many, so we moved aside, up to the top of the hill, keeping the crest between ourselves and the goblins. When they began to climb the hill, we were certain that we had been seen, so we made ready to fight. We aimed our first arrows at the leaders, then rode to the attack. And why do you smile so?"

"The goblins climbed the hill not because they were aware of your presence, but because their officers were punishing them for slacking."

Vorath laughed out loud. "Ah, a fortunate turn of events for you, then!"

"Yes indeed. May I travel with you at least so far as the next town?"

Vorath hesitated for a moment, then smiled. "Of course."

He had not been able to keep count of the days with the goblins, but he now discovered that he had been with them for a little over a year. Having spent so much time with the goblins in watchful silence, he found it difficult to regain the habit of casual conversation. The initial argument over the sword had placed a further barrier between himself and Vorath's band, so he was left fairly much alone.

Tanno had still not forgiven him for the sword and muttered under his breath whenever he was near Haram. One evening as he walked by, he muttered, "Any real man would die rather than be slave to goblins."

Haram looked up. "You said something?"

"I said any real man would die rather than be slave to goblins."

"Ah. I thought as much."

For a moment Tanno was dumbstruck. He had been expecting a fight, or at least an argument, but not this. When he spoke again, it was to curse Haram in very imaginative terms, as several sorts of coward. Haram got to his feet.

"Are you quite done?"

Tanno stood there sputtering.

"The next time you speak so to me, have your sword in your hand, Tanno. Do you understand me?"

Tanno stared at him a moment, then spun on his heel.

"Tanno!" Haram made his voice snap out. The man turned back. Haram had his sword in hand already. "I asked you a question, Tanno. Do you understand me?"

Haram was quite sure that Tanno would draw his own sword and was also quite sure that Tanno was the better swordsman. But on the other hand, he found he cared little, that death or life were all one to him. Tanno looked at his face and paled.

"Yes," he said with a gulp. "I understand."

"Good," said Haram, and felt a little disappointed that the matter had ended so easily.

Somewhat later, Vorath approached him. "Go a bit easy on the lads, will you? They are not sure what to make of you."

"I should go easy on *them*? Let them leave *me* be, and I will leave *them* be."

"Aye, I know, I know. But when you look at Tanno with a look that says you care note whether you live or die, and practically dare him to draw his sword, it upsets the lads. What will you do now?"

"I hadn't thought of that," answered Haram, and found that it was perfectly true. He had not thought of anything in the future. He had no money at all, and little prospect of earning any immediately. "Could I not travel with you?"

Vorath shook his head. "Not that I doubt your courage or skill, but the band has no need of more members as yet. We have had a long spell of little plunder, and what we took from the goblins was not great. To take on another member under these circumstances.. ." His voice trailed off, and he stood looking at Haram embarrassedly.

Haram dealt with the band mostly through Vorath. The day after they had discussed Haram's joining the band, Haram asked, "Vorath, could you get me a piece of leather about the size of the palm of my hand, and a couple of pieces of cord, abut the length of my arm?"

"I think I might. What do you need them for?"

"I want to make myself a sling."

Haram remembered Orizd's comments on the sling as a simple but effective weapon. He picked up a few pebbles from the ground and began practising as they walked. He found that, just as his arms and hands remembered the use of the sword, so they remembered the use of the sling. In fact, Haram was able to knock down a quail or two from time to time for supper.

The men of Vorath's band were still hesitant about accepting him, though they appreciated his contributions to their larder. All save one were men of the red or black-haired stock of Aradair, Vorath, Tanno, Hwerul, Coron, and Drevin. The last one, Afal-kayyon, was shorter and swarthy, with jet-black hair. Haram understood he was from the island of Rahasin to the East.

Haram did not ask where they were going, and it was only when they arrived at the town of Sanda that he realized he was in the habit of asking no questions. He walked along quietly beside Vorath's horse, patiently going wherever the band was going.

When they came to the Inn, an establishment which went by the name of The Bull's Head, Vorath leaned down to speak to Haram. "You will be our guest until we leave the inn. No, no, I insist! We are not so penurious as all that!"

Haram quietly acquiesced.

While they were seated at the supper table, a man came in. He was well-dressed for a villager, and a little stout, and he carried in his hand a heavy staff. He approached the table.

"Good evening, sirs, I am Chrosso, mayor of this town."

"Good evening, mayor. What can we do for you?"

"Ah, exactly, exactly! Sir, there is a band of goblins in the neighbourhood who have been raiding the local farms. Lately they have taken to raiding the houses on the edges of town, and we wish to have them dealt with."

"What of the local baron? Has he no troops to deal with such matters?"

The mayor shrugged. "Three times in the last two years, messages have been sent, to no effect. The baron assures us that he has our difficulties in mind, and that he will deal with them as soon as may be. We cannot wait any longer."

"So then." Vorath took a sip of his wine. "How many goblins are there?"

The mayor shrugged again. "Between twenty and thirty, we think."

"Arms?"

"The usual. Swords and maces and spears, several bows and arrows."

Vorath frowned. "And what would you pay us for this, if we were to fight the goblins on your behalf?"

"Pay you, sirs? One would think that the plunder to be had from the goblin lair would be pay enough."

"It might be, and it might not be. Suppose we find the goblins, but we never find their lair, then what? We would put our lives at risk for a handful of silver ponies? No, we must do better than that."

So they discussed the matter, offer and counter-offer, and Haram, very much reminded of Astaran, felt a twinge of something like homesickness.

The bargaining ended. "Agreed, then," declared Vorath, "a bounty of five silver ponies for every goblin head, with a bonus of eighty if the total number of heads exceeds twenty."

"Agreed." The two clasped hands to seal the bargain.

After supper, Vorath took his band apart and talked to them. Haram was almost certain that the discussion involved him, but since he had not been invited, he paid no attention. After a while, Vorath left the band and approached Haram. "You heard how many goblins they believe to be present. We would not wish to encounter twenty or more in an open fight. My plan is to whittle away at their numbers in ambushes and the like until we have a better chance against them in an open fight.

"But there is a risk even in such a plan; we may meet up with numbers of them in a place where we cannot run away. If that were to happen, an extra sword would be a good thing to have. Would you join us, for the time being?"

"And what would my share be?"

Vorath looked a little shamefaced. "I talked to the lads, and I talked to them, but the end was the same. A flat five silver pieces, however much we make. They are not willing to see you given a share, even a beginner's share. They say that whatever you may have done with Orizd's band, you have not yet proven yourself with us, and do not merit a regular share."

Haram remembered the days with Orizd and remembered that five silver pieces was never something to be sneezed at. And at present, he had only his sword and sheathe and a suit of clothing borrowed from Vorath. "I accept," he said.

"Ah, good, I will tell the others." But Vorath was looking at him curiously. Haram realized that his acceptance had sounded little less than overwhelming. Perhaps Vorath was even regretting his offer a little now. Then the leader turned to go back and inform the band.

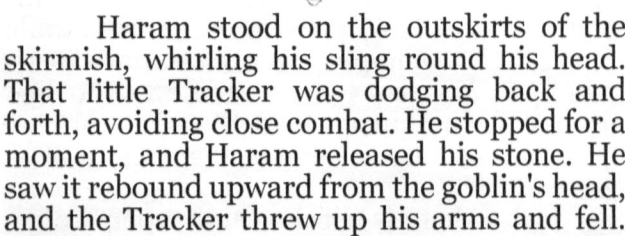

Haram stood on the outskirts of the skirmish, whirling his sling round his head. That little Tracker was dodging back and forth, avoiding close combat. He stopped for a moment, and Haram released his stone. He saw it rebound upward from the goblin's head, and the Tracker threw up his arms and fell.

Haram put another stone in his sling, but by now the last of the goblins were dead.

There had been seven of them on the path when Vorath and his band had come roaring out of the brush at them. Now the band were tumbling the slain and searching for anything that might be of value.

That evening around the campfire, Vorath addressed the whole band.

"We've used the same trick twice, hiding along paths where goblin traces are clear to be seen, and ambushing them when they come. Goblins are not highly intelligent, but though we might count on using the same tactic again, I'd prefer to do something different."

"Had you some other plan in mind?" asked Tanno, rubbing at an old scar on his forearm.

Vorath rewarded Tanno with a smile. "Ah, just the question. I had something in mind, but it requires a bit of a risk from someone. So here is my thought."

So it was that Haram found himself walking along one of the goblin-trails late in the evening of the third day after the last ambush. He moved carefully, stopping occasionally to listen for sounds of movement ahead of him. As he slipped quietly along the trail, he wondered how he had allowed himself to be convinced to take on this task. Even as he wondered, he knew the answer. "An extra five silver ponies," he muttered. "A wonderful inducement for a man whose only clothing belongs to someone else."

He paused again, then moved off the trail into the shadows. It was entirely possible that the goblins had already heard him coming, and were waiting in ambush for *him*. Though he had lived with them for a long time, he had no illusions about his ability to out stalk a goblin. He waited, all his senses alert.

There was a sudden movement up the trail; a small goblin, half-hidden in brush, was peering down the trail. Haram smiled. "And I know what you're thinking, Goblin. *'Are they waiting in ambush for me up ahead?'* Come along and find out."

At the same moment, he realized he was in a tricky position. He was not properly in hiding, and the goblin had only missed him so far because Haram was standing perfectly still. Even if he continued to stand perfectly still, it was not at all certain that the goblin would continue to overlook him. But there was little else he could do now. Breathing slowly and quietly, he watched and waited.

The plan had called for him to find a hiding place well up the trail and ambush the goblin scouts. This would enable them to take the main body unawares as they came along the trail. He had warned them of the danger of this manoeuvre; if he met a large party of goblins, the plan might fall apart there and then, with him in the point of great danger.

"Ah, don't fret yourself!" Vorath had insisted. "We will be close behind you all the time. Only give the signal, and we will be there in moments."

The goblin was moving again, coming along the trail quickly and silently, moving like an illusion made of smoke. This was another of the Tracker goblins whose skill Astaran had spoken of. His eyes flickered from one side of the path to the other, passing over Haram in his hiding place without a sign of recognition. Closer, he came, closer and closer. In three more steps, he would be close enough that Haram would be able to draw his sword and strike.

Then the goblin's eyes passed over Haram's hiding place again and suddenly flicked back. He was seen! The goblin spun in his tracks and began to run back down the trail.

Haram followed; the instant it had taken for the goblin to turn had been enough for him to leap out in pursuit, and his longer legs gave him the extra speed to be able to catch up. He drew his sword as he ran, and a moment later, he struck the goblin down. As he fell, the goblin gave a loud squawk. Haram wondered how far back the main body of the goblins might be; if they had heard that noise, there might still be trouble.

He wiped off his sword and sheathed it, then dragged the goblin off the trail. The tracks left by the goblin's heels would be visible even to the least wary of goblins, but with any luck, they would not notice until it was too late. As he was settling the goblin into the shadows beside the trail, he heard a sound of tramping and trampling. A moment later, the trail was full of goblins.

He was not sure how many they were, but he was sure that it was too late to run. He took the whistle Vorath had given him and blew three long blasts on it. A moment later, the goblins were surging toward him. He raised his sword and charged.

He was dimly aware of shouting at them in the goblin-language, "May the demons feed on your ancestors," a particularly insulting phrase. He was also aware of striking with his sword at a large goblin who bore a resemblance to Vrakga. Then he saw only a red haze in front of his eyes.

Chapter Thirteen

He was standing against a tree with a reddened sword in hand, and around him were the corpses of several goblins. He looked up. The other members of Vorath's band were standing about, looking at him with strange expressions. A small fire had been lit, painting everything with a flickering reddish tinge.

'Why have they lit a fire already?' he wondered. *'And why has it become twilight so soon?'*

He looked up at them and tried to speak. He found his mouth and throat so dry that he could only make a hoarse croaking noise. Afalkayyon hastened over with a waterskin in his hand. As Haram took it, he noticed his hands were shaking, and that his arms were cut and nicked, and that he was generally covered with blood. He took a swallow of the water. "How went it?"

"How went it?" Vorath asked, astonished. "You do not know?"

He shook his head. "I remember nothing of the fight. What happened?"

Afal-kayyon turned to Vorath. "I warned you it would be thus, Vorath," he said, his Rahasin accent tinged his speech. "After the battle-madness, they seldom remember what deeds were done."

"So what happened, then?" Haram pressed his inquiry. "By the looks of things, you arrived in time."

Vorath smiled thinly. "We arrived in time, but only barely. By the time we arrived, you had already dealt with nigh half of them. We believe we have killed most of the goblins now."

"Ah." There seemed little or nothing to say.

"Sit down, Haram. Let Afal-kayyon tend to your wounds."

Haram looked down at himself. "I think I have suffered nothing serious, only a few nicks and scratches."

"I have told you that as well, Vorath." Afal-kayyon spoke up again. "In the battle-madness, often they suffer no wounds for all the fighting they do."

"All that blood---"

"Probably belongs to goblins, Vorath. But all the same, Haram, sit down and let us clean you up a little, make you fit for company again."

A few minutes later, Haram was seated against the tree, half-watching the others as they stripped the bodies. He was not paying particular attention, since he would not be involved in the sharing out, but he noticed when Tanno took a bit of leather cord from around a goblin's neck, looked at the irregularly shaped bit of metal hanging on it, and tossed it aside.

"Tanno!" he called. "Don't throw that away! It could be valuable!"

Tanno looked up at him in annoyance. Then, as he remembered Haram's part in the battle, his expression changed to wary watchfulness. "That? It's only a torn and ragged bit of copper with strange markings on it."

"It may be a fragment of one of the copper books of Drum-na-drum. Ask Afal-kayyon if he can tell."

With a skeptical expression still on his face, Tanno took the bit of metal to the magician. He spoke hesitantly. "Ah, Haram says this may be valuable. What say you? He spoke of someone named Drum-na-drum."

Afal-kayyon took the piece of copper and looked it over. "It is difficult to say in this light." He snapped his fingers and a ball of light appeared behind his head and to the right. He studied the metal and the writing carefully, then said, "Yes, I think it may well be a part of the writings of Drum-na-drum. I am not especially familiar with them, but this seems to bear all the marks of his work. It may indeed be valuable, to the right person."

He turned to look at Haram. "What do you know of Drum-na-drum?"

Haram shrugged. "Very little. The mage of Orizd's band, Sagahan, talked to us about Drum-na-drum and his writings once when we found a similar scrap of metal. Other than that, I know nothing."

The next day found the party back at the village, once again having dinner at the Inn. Once again, Mayor Chrosso came in and approached them diffidently. "As to the matter of your payment, sir," he said to Vorath, "there is a little difficulty."

Vorath looked up at him. "What sort of difficulty?"

"Twenty-six goblins at five silver ponies per head equals one hundred thirty, plus a bonus of eighty for over twenty, for a total of two hundred and ten ponies. Sir, there are not two hundred and ten silver ponies in the whole town."

Vorath frowned. "Then you made a bargain, which you had no intention of keeping?"

The mayor waved his hands hastily. "Not at all, sir, not at all. But we never expected you to kill over twenty, and certainly not twenty-six. As I said, there is not so much silver in the whole town."

"What would you suggest, then?"

"We have gathered one hundred thirty ponies' worth, though some of it is in copper. In two month's time we could gather the rest, though it would leave the village nigh destitute for years to come, putting us into the hands of the moneylenders. On the other hand, if you come back in a year's time, we will give you the rest, along with a payment of an extra ten ponies as a penalty for late payment. Would you accept that?"

Haram watched as Vorath considered this. The plunder taken from the goblins was mediocre, though the scrap of copper might be very valuable if they could find the right person to whom to offer it. Aside from that, they had taken about twenty ponies worth of money, much of it in copper, and a jewelled pin from the goblin chief, which Vorath had said was worth about a gold crown.

Vorath nodded. "Done, then, Mayor Chrosso. Bring us the present payment, and we shall stay the night. In a year's time or so, we shall return. Let us say that if we do not return within three years, then we will not be returning. Agreed?"

"Agreed." The Mayor looked much relieved. "I thank you, sir. There are many who would have taken what money we have and looted the town as well to make up the lack."

Vorath smiled. "And the word would get around, and such people would find scant welcome in any town throughout Aradair. All I ask is that you take this as a warning, and do not make bargains which you may not be able to fulfil."

The money, as Mayor Chrosso had warned, was not all in silver. Vorath paid Haram his fee first of all, then Haram went to another table while Vorath shared out the proceeds with the others. When that was done, he joined Haram. "Where do you go now, lad?"

Haram opened his mouth to speak, then found that he had nothing to say. Just as he had not thought beyond getting his sword from Vrakga, he had not thought beyond dealing with this band of goblins.

For a moment, there was a picture in his mind of a triangular face framed by yellow curls, but he set his mind against that. Terrial would not want to see him; all he could do was to remind her of a terrible experience.

After a moment he said, "I suppose I will go to the nearest city. Perhaps I will find a band there to join with."

"Ah. Would you wish to accompany us to the city of Yath Dar Lantam?"

Haram looked at the other members of the band, who were busily spending some of their new wealth on ale. "I think your men would not wish me to accompany them."

Vorath waved a hand. "For a time, they were not sure that being a slave of the goblins had destroyed you as a fighter. Now they are a little wary of you; battle-madness is a strange thing, and there have been some who use the threat of battle-madness to get their own way, to bully their companions. If you were to try that, I think we would not let you stay with us for long. For the time being, at least until we reach the city, we might all benefit from being together."

Haram nodded. "I will travel to the city with you." In his own mind, though he had spoken of finding a band to join, he was not at all sure what he wished to do. Perhaps by the time they reached the city, something would occur to him.

On the first night out of Sanda, Haram dreamed. Something was pursuing him, something large and dark, something which he could not outdistance no matter how hard he ran. He woke gasping for breath, reaching for his sword, though he knew that against what pursued him, the sword was useless.

Even as he was reaching for his sword, he saw the camp was surrounded. There were a dozen or more small man-shaped figures, all glowing red, with grotesque features, large noses, sharp teeth, and pointed ears.

He saw also that he was not the only one awake. Afal-kayyon was standing up, running a hand through his dark curly hair, and Vorath was standing beside him. The others were also either awake or waking.

"Are they dangerous?" asked Vorath.

Afal-kayyon frowned, pursed his lips, and shook his head. "I always put a protective circle around the camp at night, not a powerful one, but enough to keep out most things. These cannot break the circle."

"What do they want?"

"I was just about to ask that," answered the mage. He looked at the small capering figures, selected one, pointed a finger, and spoke a word in some strange language.

The mannikin stopped and looked at him. "What do you want here?" demanded Afal-kayyon.

"Ssend out Haramm!" It was not a request, it was a demand. "Yess! Yess! Yess! Haramm! Haramm!" shouted the others.

Both Vorath and Afal-kayyon glanced sharply at Haram, then looked back at the creature. Afal-kayyon shook his head. "No, we cannot do that."

"Ah! Grreat dangerr iff you do not! Grreat dangerr! Ssend out Haramm!"

"Yess! Yess! Yess! Haramm! Haramm! Haramm!"

"What has he done to you?"

"He hass done an ill turn forr the Massterr! Forr thiss he musst be punisshed! Ssend him out!"

"Yess! Yess! Haramm! Haramm! Haramm!"

The mage appeared to consider this for a time, then said, "No, we cannot send him out. Begone!"

The mannikin stamped his foot hard on the grass and snarled. "It will go harrd with you iff you prrotect the one whomm the Masster wantss!"

"And it will go hard with you if you stay too long here to bandy words with me. I will not send him out, and that is my final word. Begone!"

The imps danced around the fire shouting and screaming, and occasionally in their shouts Haram could hear his name. Afal-kayyon finally spoke again.

First, he said a long sentence in some strange language, then he said "Again I say to you, begone!"

And suddenly they were gone, as though their light had been extinguished. Vorath looked at the mage. "What were those, and what did they want with Haram?"

"They were imps, messengers from Drauh, and what they want with Haram. I think only he can tell."

All eyes turned to Haram then. "When I was with Orizd's band, we rescued the daughter of a merchant who had been taken by the *harnasp* of Shab-nazdig. As it turned out, she had been promised as a gift to the God Drauh, and he pursued us. We were protected by a druid when the god came upon us at night, and later we had amulets of protection made. Mine was taken by the goblins, so I suppose I am open to attack by the god at any time now."

Afal-kayyon frowned. "And yet we are far from Shondakar; one would not think he could reach so far. You must have angered him greatly, Haram."

Haram shrugged. "When he came to our camp, he seemed very angry. And yet, why should he be so angry over one girl the less?" The mage shrugged in his turn. "Who can tell with gods? It may well be that he had planned a special use for this girl, and you have set back his plans. He might well be unforgiving of such."

Tanno, who had been listening to all this, spoke up. "He is god-hunted? We have let a god-hunted among us? By Tran and Viron, are we fools? Vorath, send him away, ere he lead us all to ruin!"

Vorath glanced at Tanno, then turned back to Afal-kayyon. "What can be done about this?"

"Easiest would be to do as Tanno suggests, and cast him out from among us. On the other hand, we are far from Shondakar, and the power of Drauha is weak in these lands. I can make an amulet to protect him. And even a god will not likely be willing to extend too much power merely to be revenged on a mere man."

"And if we were to go back toward Shondakar? Would Drauha seek revenge on us for sheltering one on whom he seeks revenge?"

The mage shrugged. "Who can say about gods? If and when we travel toward Shondakar, I can make amulets for each of us to give us sufficient protection."

"And I say again that it is foolishness to have a god-hunted man among us!" shouted Tanno.

Vorath spoke to Tanno sharply. "Tanno, I offered to Haram our company to the city. And I will not break my word now."

"But he lied to us, or came as near to it as makes no matter, hiding this from us!"

Vorath looked at Haram.

"I had given it no thought at all. I had the amulet until I was taken by the goblins, and while I was with the goblins, the god troubled me not at all. Now he seeks me again. But I swear to you I did not purposely conceal this from you. If you wish me to go, I will go." He stood up, preparing to leave them, and was surprised to feel so little concern over the matter.

Vorath waved a hand. "No, no, there will be no need for that. I could wish you had mentioned this before, but I will not go back on my word. You may accompany us to the city. Afal-kayyon, how long will it take for you to make an amulet for him?"

"A few hours, no more. I will begin to work on it in the morning."

"Good. Do so." So they went back to their beds, though it was clear that Tanno was not completely happy with matters as they stood.

About the middle of the next day, they were coming up to a small stand of willows. The road ran straight through the willows, and Vorath said, "A good place for an ambush. Usually in such places, the brush is cut back by a bowshot on either side of the road. The local baron seems to have ignored his obligations."

"Have we anything with us to interest bandits?" muttered Tanno.

Afal-kayyon was seated on his horse, his eyes narrowed. "There is something there," he said.

Vorath turned to him. "What is it?"

"The lightest and easiest of spells tells me that there are people hidden there. If we wait too long, they will know that we are aware of them, and perhaps change their plan. If we continue as we are, we might be able to surprise them when the time comes."

"And if they have bows?"

"So do we."

"And to be obviously stringing our bows here would be to warn the ambushers that we know of them. I have a plan. One or two men could probably go by without risk; they want to trap us all. Those who go through could then circle back and take the ambushers in the rear."

"A risk for those who go through the

trap. Who will you send?"

Vorath said, "I will send no one unwilling. Haram, will you do this for us?"

Haram hesitated, then smiled. "I would be the best to send, would I not? No horse, only a sword, not enough to tempt a bandit into loosing an arrow. And yet, if I am clearly a scout, will they not have someone to watch me as I go?"

"Yes, but we will have an argument, you see. Point at the bushes and shout, though not loudly enough to be heard by the people in ambush." He himself pointed a finger at the bushes and shouted, "The rest of you, gather in a knot here, point at the bushes, talk to each other, move around and each of you string your bow while you are hidden from the sight of the people ahead!"

"And what would you have me to do next?" shouted Haram, pointing up ahead.

"Stalk off as though leaving us to our own devices!" shouted Vorath.

"Done!" Haram shrugged, turned, and walked away. After he had gone a few paces, he turned. "Do not tarry too long!"

"We will be close behind!"

He stalked along the path, walking as an angry man, and strode between the bunches of willows. There was a slight bend in the path ahead, and it was entirely possible that someone might shoot from ambush there, hoping to pull Haram's corpse out of sight before the others came close. Haram surveyed the willows carefully, without seeming to do so. There was no sign of anyone nearby.

Coming round the bend in the path, he

made a sudden dash for the side of the trail. No arrows followed him. Perhaps there was no one waiting to deal with him, or perhaps he had merely moved before the ambusher was ready. He picked up a few pebbles from the ground and took out his sling. With his sling hanging from his hand, stone ready for the throwing, he crept through the brush.

As he went, he tried to remember the lessons in woodcraft and trail craft which Astaran had given him. That brought back memories of the goblins howling in the morning, of the slaughter of Orizd's band. He felt like weeping, but no tears would come, and he wondered why.

There was a slight motion in front of him, and suddenly he saw a man in a ragged jerkin kneeling behind a bush, short bow in hand, with an arrow on the string. The man was peering down toward the trail, where Vorath's band was now coming among the willows.

Haram looked closely around him. He could now see two others off to his left on this side of the trail, and there were probably more across the trail, along with some he could not yet see. Whirling his sling three times around his head, he released the stone. It struck the man behind the ear, and he slumped forward into the brush behind which he was sheltering.

The nearest man, hearing the sounds, turned to look. He was still gaping when Haram loosed a second stone at him. It caught him in the chest, and he staggered back and down. The third man was now looking at him, and just as Haram was readying another stone in his sling, he heard a sound from behind. He turned to see a ragged man charging at him, brandishing a large battleaxe, rusty and nicked, but deadly for all that.

Dropping the sling, Haram drew his sword. For some reason, the war-cry he had used in the battle with the goblins came to his lips, and he shouted as the bandit came at him. "May your ancestors be eaten by demons!"

Chapter Fourteen

As the man came at him, Haram could almost hear Orizd's voice growling in his ear, "If it is not carefully used, an axe can leave its owner open for a moment at the end of the swing. Watch for that."

The axe swung, and Haram stepped back, then stepped in again while the man's torso was pulled round by the weight of the axe. Before the bandit could pull himself back into position, Haram struck.

Now there came an increase in the shouting; Vorath's band was on the attack. Tanno and two others came to the aid of Haram, while Vorath and the rest went into the brush on the other side of the trail. They had left their horses standing; in thick brush, a horse may be more of a hindrance than an advantage.

The man Haram had hit in the chest with the slung stone was just getting back to his feet when Tanno struck him down, then went down to help Drevin deal with the other bandit. Two men on this side of the trail had already been dealt with before Vorath's band arrived, so Haram rushed across the path to join Vorath.

It was a scattered fight, and he could hear sounds of battle, but he could see little. Vorath appeared in front of him, fencing with a burly man in a ragged mail shirt. Suddenly, the burly man was falling, and Vorath was turning to deal with another bandit armed with a heavy spear.

But the burly man was not done yet. His right arm hung limp as he got to his knees, then lunged to his feet, scrabbling for his dagger with his left hand. Haram was already leaping forward. The burly man staggered toward Vorath, dagger poised; just as he was about to stab, Haram was on him, striking one quick and accurate blow with his sword.

In the meantime, Vorath had dealt with the spearman. Turning, he saw Haram and the burly man lying on the ground. He smiled at Haram but said merely, "Good work."

In the end, it was not much of a battle. The bandits had been surprised by Haram's attack, then Vorath's attack had demoralized them completely. They had been ten in number, and eight of them were dead. The other two fled, and were not pursued.

Drevin was dead. No one was quite sure how, for none had been close to him when it happened, but they found him lying there in the brush with a gaping sword-wound in his chest.

"Why would they ambush us?" asked Coron. "One would think they would seek easier prey than seven armed men."

"Do you not think that the village of Sanda was full of the news of our band slaying dozens of goblins and being rewarded by the village with thousands of silver coins? And we did not hide from anyone the fact that we were on our way to Yath Dar Lantam. Such a temptation would be enough to bring them to risk attacking armed men. We were careless," was Vorath's answer.

The booty from the bandits amounted to twenty-three copper coins, along with five daggers and three swords, judged worth carrying to the city to be resold. The only armour among them was the chain-shirt worn by the burly man, but it was discarded as well. "You see where it has been cut several times, and repaired with wire? We might sell it for scrap, but even so, the work of carrying it would not be worth the price it would fetch." This was Vorath's verdict.

He also spoke to Haram. "For this day's work, we will give you a share as well. It will be the share of a beginner, but still a share."

Haram considered. "Look, one of the bandits had a shield, a round wooden one with a metal rim and metal boss. I will take that, and if it is worth more than my share, I will pay the difference."

"That shield? It is not worth the trouble to take it to the city to sell it. If no one objects, it is yours. And you will receive a share as well. Are there any objections?"

He looked around at the band carefully, but none said anything. "So be it, then."

The next evening, they reached the city of Yath Dar Lantam. It was an inland city unlike Ifan Sor, with no seaport, but otherwise greatly similar, being a centre of commercial traffic from many quarters. Vorath led them all to an inn, the Laughing Wyvern, where they took quarters for the night. Haram stayed with them, since the sharing of the booty would come only after they had sold what they could to the smiths and dealers in arms, which could not be done until morning.

After they had all dined and drank, most of the others went out to see what the city could offer for entertainment. Vorath asked Haram to say a moment.

"Lad, would you wish to join us?"

Haram thought a moment. "What of the others?"

Vorath shrugged. "I have spoken to them. Some do not like it at all, some think we would do well to offer you a place. It is not merely that you saved my life with the bandits, though that is a part of it; it is not merely that Drevin has died, leaving a place open, though that also is a part of it. You have shown yourself, in several instances, to be worthy of membership in the band. Taken altogether, there are enough reasons to offer you a place."

"What of Drauha?"

"I have spoken to Afal-kayyon about that. We are far enough within Aradair that he will not be able to reach us, and you have the amulet Afal-kayyon made for you. Afal-kayyon says also that Drauha must be wary himself, for if he threatens too many people outside his own territory, he will find that his fellow-gods will retaliate against him. They may allow him to seek you out, but if he spreads his net wide enough to include us, he may find himself facing Tran and Viron, and Afal-kayyon doubts he has the strength for that just yet."

Haram nodded. "In that case, I accept." Inside himself, he was wondering why he did not feel more happy at this. Being part of Vorath's band was better than being by himself, but despite Vorath's words, he did not feel he was really one of the band. *Perhaps I do not yet feel quite human? Will I forever in my mind be toiling up and down the green hills of Aradair, fetching and carrying for the goblins?*

Vorath was not unaware of Haram's mood. "Ah, lad, you do not seem overjoyed at the prospect of joining us."

Haram forced a smile and wondered what his smile looked like. "I apologize, Vorath. I seem to have lost the way of dealing with humans. Yes, I thank you very much, Vorath; Orizd used to say, *'Bare is the back with no brother.'* Today I have gained a band of brothers."

But though Vorath smiled at that, Haram could see that he was still concerned.

After Vorath left him, Haram took his

money and went out to look at the city.

"If I go out," he muttered to himself, "where people are so many, perhaps I can make myself be a little more like them and less like a goblin."

As he was wandering the streets, Haram suddenly heard a small voice from beside him. "Please, Sir."

He looked down. It was a young boy about seven or eight years old, wearing a red jerkin. Haram wondered at first if he might be a beggar, but his clothing was too new for that.

"Aye?"

"Please, Sir, are you a Venturer?"

"Aye, I am."

"Are you one of Saradon's band?" There was eagerness in the voice.

"Nay, I am with Vorath."

"Oh." The boy sounded a little disappointed. "They say that Saradon is in town, staying at the Flowing Pitcher."

Saradon's band was in town? Haram had a sudden urge to find them, to talk to Merrit again. He dug into his pouch and pulled out a copper coin. "Here, boy. Show me where the Flowing Pitcher is."

He tossed the coin; the boy caught it and set out at a fast pace. Soon they were in front of an inn, the signboard of which showed a pitcher of ale overflowing. "Here we are, Sir."

He smiled at the boy and went inside. The inn was larger and more comfortable than any that Orizd had ever stayed at, and seemed well beyond the purse of Vorath as well. It was well lit, though there were some dim corners, and in one of these corners Haram caught sight of Saradon.

He could see no sign of Merrit, however. Of course, Saradon's men were probably scattered about the city, just as Vorath's were. He walked over to the corner.

Saradon seemed to know he was approaching well before he arrived, for he looked up to survey Haram as he crossed the floor. Saradon himself was slender and wiry, and Haram could see that if he were standing, he would be quite tall. His skin was browned by the sun, there were crow's feet in the corners of his eyes, and his hair was beginning to go grey, but there was something about him which told Haram that this was a man who ought not to be underestimated.

"Good evening. My name is Haram. You are Saradon?"

"And if I am?" said the other cautiously.

"I have a friend who is one of your band, a friend I have not seen for some time. His name is Merrit."

"Merrit is -- no longer with us."

Haram caught the pause and wondered what it meant. "What happened to him?"

"Oh, he is not dead. At least the last word I heard was that he was not. He left us some six months ago."

"He did?" Haram realized that this was a stupid thing to say, but it seemed necessary to say something.

"Aye, it seemed best to all of us. Nay, we did not cast him out, we all agreed, he as well, that it would be best to part company. He did not agree with our ways."

Haram nodded. He remembered Merrit pricking his knee during the arm-wrestling contest, and defending himself by saying that Haram could have done it if he had thought of it first.

"Do you know where he is?"

Saradon shook his head. "Nay. I heard last that he was joined with someone named Zilva, a name I do not know. But if you are his friend, then you must be with Orizd's band. How is Orizd?"

"He is dead." For a brief moment, Haram was back at that morning full of the screams of goblins and the clashing of metal, with Orizd bleeding from several wounds, still fighting fiercely, then it faded. "We were attacked by goblins last year. All were slain, save myself. I was taken as a slave, and rescued a few weeks ago by Vorath's band."

"So Orizd is dead? He was a worthy man. Sit down, Haram, and have a cup of ale with me."

Haram sat. The ale came, and they each drank a bit, then Saradon spoke again. "Orizd taught you the use of the sword?"

"Aye, he did. He was teaching me the use of sword and shield when we were attacked by the goblins."

Saradon nodded. "Orizd was a good teacher. So. Would you like a place in my band? We have room for a man who knows which end of a sword to hold on to."

Haram paused for a moment. He meant to agree, but was surprised to hear his own voice saying, "Nay, I thank you, but I have a place with Vorath."

"Vorath? Aye, he is a worthy man."

He had said the same thing of Orizd, Haram realized, and wondered idly if he said as much about any leader of Venturers. But no, he had not said that regarding Zilva. Zilva was *'a name he did not know.'*

Saradon had had several cups of ale before Haram had come in, and he was now growing talkative. "So, lad. If you have been a slave of goblins, you will know a little more of the life of a real Venturer than some. There are still, and I suppose always will be, those who take to the wilds as a means of growing rich.

"In recent years, fewer and fewer even bother to present themselves to the King to ask for a royal Warrant, as was the case in the years after the Great Invasion had been turned back.

"And you know what that sort of thing leads to, don't you?"

Haram knew fairly well, but he had little chance to say so, for Saradon continued. "It leads to folk going off into the Wilds, finding that the life there is hard and the riches amount usually to a few silver ponies. and when they discover that, they often take to mere banditry."

He paused to drink some ale. "Nor would I claim that all who truly have the King's Warrant are honest men. A piece of paper with a fancy seal is no more than that, and has no power to make a man honest if that man has greed in his heart to begin with. There have been times before when kings sought to suppress the Venturers, seeing the bulk of them to be little more than bandits. When that happened, the evil creatures in the Wild increased, so the Venturers were left alone to do the work they had chosen. I wonder, though, how long it will be before another King of Aradair decides Venturers are little more than bandits."

Haram found himself in no mood for this sort of morose conversation. He stayed out of politeness long enough to buy a mug of ale for Saradon, then he went back to his own inn for the night.

The next day he clasped forearms with the men of Vorath's band, then they all hoisted a cup of ale to brotherhood.

"No fancy ceremonies and great oaths for us," Vorath said. "My feeling is that if a man won't stand by his fellows, then no great oath sworn to whatever gods is going to change him."

Then they were off.

Chapter Fifteen

Before they left the city, Vorath dropped several silver ponies in Haram's hand. Haram looked up at him in surprise.

"Afal-kayyon took that scrap of copper to a man in the city. It was, indeed, a part of one of the books of Drum-na-Drum, and the fellow paid us five golden crowns for it. This is your share."

Vorath waved away Haram's thanks. "If not for you, the thing would have been tossed away. Our fine sorcerous partner is a little chagrined to think that he never thought to warn us of such a possibility, and everyone else is racking their brains to remember if they ever tossed aside such a worthless scrap of copper before."

They travelled far in the next few weeks.

Their luck, however, seemed to have turned completely around. They found nothing, not an ogre, not a goblin, not even a were-beast plaguing some village where they might earn a day's keep hunting the creature down.

"Six weeks!" declared Tanno one night around the campfire. "Six rotten weeks, with not a bent copper piece to show for it! I tell you, Vorath, this is the kind of thing to be expected if you take on a god-hunted man as a member of the band!"

"We've had stretches of bad luck that lasted as long before, Tanno. You remember the winter we were forced to take on the job of guarding old Fradraz' warehouse in Gawn-e-kif? What would you blame for that?"

"Mock me if you will, Vorath, but I've said what I said."

"And if you're wise, you won't say it again. Haram is a member of our band now. He has taken risks for us; he has fought for us, and he has been a good help to us in many ways. And because he did a noble deed by pulling a young maid out of the clutches of the God of Lies of Shondakar, I refuse to believe that all gods have deserted us. What do you say, Afal-kayyon? You are more likely than any of us to have information on this matter."

The mage shook his head. "The doings of the gods are the doings of the gods, and not for men to sort out or regulate. It seems that, in general, they do not trespass on each other's territory, so that at a distance from Shondakar, Drauha will not likely have much power. The moment one says that, however, one is forced to admit that things will happen to the contrary.

"The most likely thing, however, is for Drauha to send his hirelings against Haram. It is said that the goblins, for instance, while they do not actually revere Drauha himself, might be willing to undertake a task for him. Then there are his human worshippers, who might undertake a deed for his service.

"As to our bad luck, though, I would venture to say it has little or nothing to do with Drauha."

"But you cannot be certain, can you?" demanded Tanno. "Even you admitted that much."

"*'Certainty'* is not a word to use when speaking of the gods. I would, however, wager that our bad luck had nothing to do with Drauha and his anger with Haram."

Haram, for his part, discovered that he could not become truly part of the band. Though he did, on occasion, take part in their banter and jesting, it seemed that there was some part of him that always held back. He was closest to Vorath, though even that was due more to the leader's persistence than any effort by Haram.

It was Vorath who spent time practising sword and shield work with Haram, aiding him to become more and more proficient. Haram never quite came to blows with Tanno, but he knew that whatever happened, the two of them were not likely to become friends.

Finally, they came upon the tracks of a band of goblins.

"At least twenty of them, or I'm a horse-loving Shondakranian," said Tanno.

Haram looked at him. Was he likely making a dig at Haram, knowing that the leader of Haram's original band had been a Shondakranian? Yes, likely so, in which case, the best response was to ignore him.

"Twenty," said Vorath, half-musingly. "Could we catch up to them, do you think?"

"Belike we could. And what would the five of us do against twenty goblins?"

"Oh, we ought to be able to come up with some devious plan to even the odds. And we do need the money very badly, don't we?"

What they did was a variant of the last tactic they had used on the large band of goblins, for which Mayor Chrosso and his village still owed them money. Haram and Hwerul rode into the goblin camp, as though blundering on them unawares.

Haram volunteered to go alone, but Vorath had forbidden that. "Twenty is too many for a single person to hold off for any length of time. We need one more." And Hwerul had nodded his head.

So they came riding, apparently carelessly, into the camp of the goblins, who had been alerted by their own sentries.

The goblins surged up around them, and Haram drew his sword. He remembered shouting, "May your ancestors be eaten by demons!" as a red haze descended over his eyes.

When he came back to himself, he was seated against a rock with a bloodied sword in hand. The rest of the band were pillaging the goblins' belongings. Haram could count fifteen dead goblins. The rest, apparently, had fled.

Haram cleaned himself up as best he could and put his sword away. It occurred to him to wonder how many goblins he might have slain himself, but it was not something he greatly desired to know. And particularly not as the others were, casting wary glances in his direction as they worked.

Unfortunately, this band of goblins had been nearly as poor as Vorath's band. When everything had been added up, Vorath announced, "Five silver ponies, along with twenty copper coins, and only two swords worth carrying to the nearest town for sale."

"What is the nearest town to here?" asked Hwerul.

"I think it would be Halan. What do you say, mage?"

"yes, probably Halan. We're near to the coast where the strait separates Aradair from Rahasi."

"Ah, the Dark Country! Do you feel a little homesick, Afal-kayyon?" asked Tanno.

Afal-kayyon shrugged. "I have wandered far, but perhaps it might be nice to go home sometime. That can wait, though."

They sold the swords, and even all Vorath's bargaining- skills gained them little more than living expenses for a few days.

The inn, known as the Albatross, was reasonably comfortable and inexpensive. The band decided to stay there for the night while they still had the money to do so. "Besides," said Vorath, "It will give us a chance to hear the gossip, to find out if times are more prosperous elsewhere for those in our trade."

There was precious little gossip of interest to Venturers. The price of fish was down, the price of bread was up, and taxes were nigh more than a man could bear. Such were the general themes of conversation in the common room of the inn that night.

Sometime later, however, a fisherman came over to their table. "May I sit, sirs?"

"Certainly." Vorath did not look eager, Haram reflected, but then in such a situation an eager look could well be misconstrued, leading to a heavy charge for information sold.

The fisherman was short, thickset, with sun-yellow hair and beard, though the hair was now somewhat crusted with salt from the sea. Large, powerful hands were lying flat on the table. "Belike ye have come for to fight the Drake of Bavian?"

"That may be as it may be."

The fisherman laughed. "Aye, it may be as it may be, indeed, and belike I am prying into private matters, but if you have come to fight the Drake, you will need transportation across the strait."

"Well, we had considered fighting this dragon, but the news we get inland is oft so puffed up that one cannot tell if it is a mere dragon we fight, or a world-destroying monster."

The fisherman laughed once more. "*'Mere dragon,'* is it? I must remember that! What would you consider a 'mere dragon' friend?"

Before he answered, Vorath called to the innkeeper for more ale, including ale for the fisherman as well. "Now, what is your name?"

"I am called Thraxas. And yourself?"

"I am Vorath. Now, Thraxas, the stories we here in the inland have this drake the size of the Grand Palace of the King in Ifan Sor, with eight heads. Some of the heads spit fire, some spit poison, and it can fight in all directions at once. This close to the situation. Surely, the news is more accurate?"

Thraxas threw back his head and guffawed, slapping his large hands on the table. "The news grows a handspan for every footstep it travels, they say! Now you will understand, Vorath, I have not seen the beast myself, though I have seen some of the devastation it has caused. But from what I hear, the dragon has a body as long as two horses, with a neck and head half as long as that, and a tail longer than the body. It is winged, though it seems to fly seldom, and while it has only one head, it does breath fire."

Vorath nodded wisely, and all the members of the band looked on without expression.

"So, will you go fight the dragon?"

Vorath frowned. "Has no one sought to kill it before?"

"Some have, but none have been

successful."

"Were these single warriors, or in groups?"

Thraxas shrugged. "As to that, I could not say for certain, though they say that it slew a captain and ten men sent out by the vinu of Arzawa."

Vorath frowned again. "So, then. What would you charge to take us across the Strait?"

"Two gold crowns for the lot of you, including horses."

"Nay, nay, Thraxas, I did not offer to buy your boat, merely use her for a short time! One copper for each, including the horses."

"And if I take time away from my fishing, will I not need to earn enough to make that up? One gold crown for the lot of you." The ending of it all was that they agreed to pay one silver pony each, with two coppers extra for each of the horses. After this had been done, Vorath said, "If you will excuse us, Thraxas, I must talk to my men."

Immediately that Thraxas was out of earshot, Tanno spoke. "A dragon! Vorath, are you mad?"

Vorath shrugged. "A little, perhaps. But consider; the dragon's size will have been increased by rumour even as near as here. The dragon is, therefore, according to the tale we have heard, a fairly small one. Being a small dragon, it is likely a young one, which allows us a slight advantage. As dragons get older, their hide becomes thicker and harder, until even the underside is as strong as a coat of chain armour. The hide of a young one, on the other hand, may well be vulnerable to a well-aimed blow anywhere.

"And even a young dragon will have treasure of some sort, and more than we have seen so far. Look, all of you, one reason we have been suffering so long in poverty is that we are too cautious. We go about seeking fights which we know for certain that we can win. And what do we get? A handful of silver ponies, if we are fortunate, with perhaps one or two swords which we can sell for another few ponies.

"And aye, I agree that to attack a dragon is a risk; but the risk if worthwhile if there is a treasure to be had, a treasure which by itself equals the sum of all the other treasures we have ever found. And certainly some or all of us may die, but what of that? Do we continue to seek the safe and easy battles, dooming ourselves to continual penury, or by one great battle, make ourselves rich?"

They were all silent for a little while, even Tanno. But Tanno finally spoke up. Have you ever fought a dragon, Vorath?"

"I have. Have you?"

"Aye, I have." Tanno sat staring at the far wall of the inn as though there were something pictured there, something he did not like. "Fighting a dragon is a tricky business, even one without eight heads."

"It is. What of you others? Are you all willing to make this attempt?"

Haram surreptitiously looked around at the others, wondering what their feelings were. He knew that for his own part it seemed to make no matter; he might as well die fighting a dragon as anything else.

Hwerul and Coron spoke almost as one.

"I will go with you, Vorath."

Afal-kayyon nodded. "As you say, the risk may be well worthwhile. I will come."

"I will come as well," said Haram, suddenly realizing that they were waiting for his response.

"Good, then! Let us talk again to Thraxas and see what is the best time for sailing."

The land was desolate and wasted. They travelled past the remains of houses and farms, burned heaps of ashes and charred wood. They went through what had been forests, now bare blackened stumps standing up amid the ashes. In the open country, even the grass had suffered sizeable areas of it being blackened and shrivelled.

As they travelled, they discussed the situation; what they had learned so far, and what tactics they might use. Tanno was far from sanguine about the matter.

"I do not like this at all, Vorath! You see all this destruction? And we go to face the monster that caused it!"

"Indeed, we do, Tanno, and we do not go carelessly either. But consider, all this destruction is the result of years of work by the dragon, not mere days."

"Even so, the dragon has destroyed a captain and ten men; we are only six."

"Aye, that is true. But consider the habits of soldiers, Tanno. Their usual method it to go marching in to confront the enemy face-to-face and fight or die. That is not our plan."

"Aye, and what is our plan? So far, it seems our only plan is to ride in to find the dragon. Is that so much different from the way soldiers act?"

Vorath shrugged. "It is foolish to try to make plans until we know the ground on which we shall have to fight. We know now that we are coming closer to the centre of the land, which the dragon claims. Once we see the lie of the land, we can make better plans."

"And while we are approaching him, suppose the drake comes flying over the ridge to approach us?"

"Then we must make plans very quickly. By Tran and Viron, Tanno, perhaps you ought not to have come with us!"

Tanno gave a small sour smile at that. "And if I did not come, who would there be to pull your chestnuts out of the fire? So be it, then, I will question no more. Only let us walk warily."

They had asked questions of the people in the surrounding area, but stories of the dragon seemed to be so varied that it was not really possible to achieve a proper description. Few of the people had actually seen the dragon, and those few still remembered it with terror, a terror which coloured their narration.

Vorath still insisted that these descriptions upheld his own contention that this was a small dragon, and thus a young one.

As they went, they made tentative plans for most eventualities, first and foremost, being what to do if they found it in its lair. These plans consisted mostly of spreading out immediately, surrounding the monster if possible, and showering it with missiles while they advanced to sword-distance.

They had not considered a plan for what they should do if they rode over a hill and found the dragon below them, eating a sheep. The sheep must have been taken from somewhere outside its territory, but none of the band had seen it in flight. Had it perhaps brought the animal some hours ago, then lay down for a sleep before dining? They could not say. All they knew was that as Vorath topped the hill, he suddenly held up a hand, then gestured for them to come, cautiously.

Down below, the dragon was tearing at the sheep with enormous jaws and sharp claws. Vorath had been correct about its size; it had a body about the size of a horse, though a large one, and its tail was twice that long, while its head and neck were half again the length of the body. Its hide was green, ranging from dark green on the back to a bright green on the sides and a pale yellow-green underneath. The claws were long, curved, and sharp, ivory-white where the blood of the sheep had not stained them and the rows of teeth in its long jaws were sharp and vicious.

It was facing half away from them, but Haram could tell from the movements of the head and neck that it could change directions quickly as needed. Vorath apparently saw this as well, for he gave his orders quickly and in a low voice. "Tanno, Hwerul, Coron, to my right, Haram, Afal-kayyon, to my left. Ready bows."

Haram readied his sling, though he was not at all certain how much good a rock would do in this case, no matter how hard it was thrown.

"Spread out and move. Do not shoot until you have a clear shot, or unless it sees you first. Go, now!"

They went down the slope, quickly and carefully. They were well within bow-range from the top of the ridge, but the closer they could come, the better it would be for them. Suddenly Haram saw the beast turn its head on the long snakelike neck. It was turning away from him, but in an instant it would be looking at Hwerul and Coron.

He gave a shout, whirled his sling twice round his head and let go. The rock rebounded off the front shoulder of the drake with the same sound as if it had hit a boulder. He dropped another stone into the sling and whirled it again. The dragon roared, and sent forth a blast of flame, missing Coron by a handspan, but causing him to flinch from the heat.

Even as he whirled his sling, Haram was rushing down toward the dragon. He noticed as he went the others had loosed their arrows, but that the horses were unwilling to approach the monster closer. After that, he had no time to notice what anyone else was doing, for he was too busy fighting for his life.

The drake used front legs, head and tail to fight with, and it required great agility on the part of the men of Vorath's band to avoid being hit or trampled. One of the first things Haram noticed as he came in closer was that an arrow was embedded in the dragon's shoulder, and his first thought was that Vorath had been correct, and the beast's armour was not fully proof against weapons. His second thought was that it was unfortunate that the arrow had not struck somewhere more vital.

He approached the monster's side at a run, noticing out of the corner of one eye that the head was turning in his direction. He could thrust his sword home, but in the time it would require to withdraw the blade, the dragon's jaws might well reach him. Instead, he took a slashing cut and danced back.

It was rather like slashing at an oak tree; the sword opened a wound, but even Haram could tell that the wound was superficial. The great jaws opened, and Haram dodged sideward, feeling the heat from the dragon's jaws as he moved.

It was a long and difficult battle, and they discovered that so long as they stayed in close to it, the dragon did not use its flame. For all that, it was still dangerous. Not a one of them escaped unscathed, scratched or gashed to some degree by the great claws. Once Haram found himself a little too far from the great green bulk and caught a blast of flame on his shield. The wood of the shield burst into flames, and he tossed it aside, rushing forward.

By that time, the dragon's attention had been claimed by one of the others, and Haram was unhurt save for some charred patches on his clothing where the flame had licked around the shield.

So the battle went, a constant leaping in to cut or thrust, evading the claws and the mighty swinging tail, and most of all the jaws which could either bite or breathe flame. When the beast felt itself beginning to weaken, it tried to take to the air. Vorath shouted at his band to take their bows again, and they did so. As the arrows pierced its tender underside, the drake turned back to strike at its tormentors.

They dodged aside as it breathed its flame, then closed in again as it landed. There was no telling who had struck the killing blow. Indeed, there may well have been no single killing blow, only a cumulative effect of numerous blows; however, it was. The dragon suddenly roared once, then again, more weakly, then its massive head dropped forward to the ground. Vorath stepped forward, raised his sword, and slashed at the neck. The head rolled free.

Chapter Sixteen

Afal-kayyon checked all their cuts and scratches. "The wounds of a dragon's claw are often envenomed," he told them. Any cuts he washed out with a special potion of his own devising. For their burns, and all of them had some burns, large or small, he provided salve. They gathered up such of their equipment as was still of any use. For instance, nothing remained of Haram's shield save the metal fittings and a couple of scraps of charred wood.

"Now," said Vorath, "to find the dragon's lair."

The dragon's lair was not easy to find. They crossed the withered landscape, seeking some clue to where the dragon might have set up his home. Finally Tanno burst out, "Tran and Viron, Vorath, how long do we ride from east to west to north to south and back again? A day and a half we've ridden, and we seem no closer now than we were at the start!"

Vorath was slow to answer, and a look at his face told Haram that their leader was in little better humour than the rest of them. As for him, well, he would continue to go with them, and maybe they would find the dragon's den and maybe not.

Afal-kayyon spoke up before Vorath could respond. "There may be a way of finding the dragon's lair without all this going to and fro."

"A spell?" asked Vorath.

"Aye, a spell."

"Why did you not use this spell long ago, then, and save us this useless tramping up and down?" demanded Tanno.

"It is a powerful spell," answered the mage calmly, "and to use it will take much of my strength. If we meet anything dangerous for a half day thereafter, I will be little use to you."

Vorath looked around at his worn and weary band, then back at Afal-kayyon. "Best you use the spell, and we all take the chance of your being weary. What will you need?"

"I have everything I need. But I will require that all of you stay fairly still while I am spelling; not too much walking to and fro, no hasty movements of any sort."

"Done."

It was difficult to stay still and quiet while the spell was being cast, but everyone did their best. After the first few minutes, however, it became more and more difficult, and as the time stretched toward an hour, it became a real trial.

Eventually Hwerul got up carefully, and trudged to his horse, took down a waterskin, and drank. When he had drunk, he passed it on to the others, who took it gratefully. Afal-kayyon was still chanting the strange words of his spell.

On it went. Even Vorath was squirming slightly. But Haram was used to sitting quietly for long periods; among the goblins, remaining quiet and unnoticed had meant less chance of a beating.

Then, with no warning of any sort, the chanting stopped. The mage straightened his back, faced to the west, and said in a hoarse and weary voice, "It lies about a half-day's march that way."

"Can you ride?"

The mage looked around at the others and grinned wearily. "I had better be able to, or the lot of you will go on without me."

So they rode, keeping as close as possible to the direction which Afal-kayyon had pointed out. It was nearing evening when they finally arrived.

There was no mistaking where they were; there was a large cave in the hillside, and nothing grew round about it for about a bowshot in any direction. All trees, bushes, plants, and grasses had been burned off by the dragon's flame.

They dismounted and approached.

They paused while Tanno lit a torch. Then he held it up and looked at the others. "Who goes first?" asked Vorath.

"You, of course," said Tanno. "You are the leader, you it was who believed in this so strongly. It is fitting that you should look first on the treasure."

The rest agreed, so Vorath took the torch and led the way into the cave. It was a wondrous sight. There were many swords, broken and whole, spears, again broken and whole, and various other items of clothing and armour. There were also numerous bags, leather and cloth, some broken open to reveal their contents. Gold, silver, and precious stones glittered in the torchlight.

For a long while, no one spoke. "By Tran and Viron," said Hwerul. "I did not think there was so much gold and silver in all the world!"

"How will we carry it all?" wondered Tanno.

"Ere we begin considering loading it and hauling it," said Afal-kayyon, "there are other things to think of."

"What things?" demanded Tanno, suspiciously.

"It would be best to talk of all this outside, where all this glitter cannot sway one's attention. No, come; none of it is likely to walk away while we talk, is it?"

So they went out into the twilight and Tanno asked, "What is it, then?"

"You all know of dragons, do you not? That they are creatures of evil? And you have probably heard of treasures taken from dragon-hoards which caused bad luck to the takers? It is true. Dragons are creatures of evil, and often the evil of the drake is transferred to the treasure it hoards and upon which it makes its bed. This was a young dragon, as Vorath promised us, and perhaps the curse may be weak, or non-existent, on certain items in the hoard. I think it would be best for us to try to find which pieces can be taken safely, and take only those."

He held up a hand to still the voices of protest. "Did I not hear someone wondering how we could take the whole lot away? Listen, we can still take enough to make us all rich! No, we cannot take it all by any means, but be assured that trying to take it all would be dangerous in many ways. The curse on some of it will be so strong as to bring trouble of various sorts, even fights and arguments among us. And if we take too much, how could we hide it from the people of the towns through which we must travel? And remember the bandits who ambushed us for a few paltry pieces of silver?"

"He is right!" Vorath spoke up. "Listen, all of you! We won the fight against the dragon with the loss of no lives! That was a piece of luck, the like of which I doubt we could equal in years. Should we then press our luck so far, taking along with us treasure which *promises* evil? No, let us be careful, let us be rich, but not open ourselves to whatever danger would come through being greedy!"

"Well, then," asked Tanno, "how do we tell what is cursed and what is not?"

"After a night's rest, I shall be able to go to work. I have a spell which is able to detect such a curse where it exists."

Tanno nodded shortly. "So. Ought we to guard the treasure tonight, then?"

"Do you not trust your fellows, Tanno?"

"Nay, Vorath, I trust them in most situations. But what we have in that cave may be a temptation beyond what a man might be able to stand."

"So? Suppose someone decides to load down himself and his horse in the night and creep away, heedless of the curse. You saw the hoard; there is sufficient for each of us to do so, and still leave much behind. I will set no guards."

In the morning, Afal-kayyon went to work. He seated himself cross-legged outside the cave with a square of leather in front of him. He muttered a few words, then indicated to the others that he was ready. They went into the cave and brought out things, one at a time, and set them on the leather. If they glowed with a blue glow, they were put aside as cursed. If they did not, they were set into another pile for possible sharing out.

For some time, the stack of safe goods grew and grew, so that it became clear to all of them that there would be no shortage of treasure from this venture. Then more and more items were revealed as cursed until Vorath called a halt.

"Clearly, we have come down to the parts of the hoard which have been with the dragon for a long while; I doubt if we will find anything more without the taint of evil upon it."

Hwerul spoke up. "Is it possible to

remove the curse?"

Vorath looked at Afal-kayyon, who shrugged. "From individual items, perhaps. Much depends on how long they have been in the dragon's hoard. But it would take a very powerful mage to remove the curse from the whole hoard. And besides that, we have enough here that is not cursed that none of us will go short."

"True enough," said Hwerul, "but I have seen a thing or two inside which I would very much like to have, if the curse could be removed somehow. And considering the size of the treasure, I would be quite willing to pay for the removal of the curse."

Afal-kayyon raised his eyebrows. "The payment would mean little, for how much of this will we be able to carry away in any case? If I am paid an extra hundred gold pieces, how would I carry that? But for the sake of our companionship, I will undertake to remove the curse from three items for each of you, if you wish. That is subject to my abilities, of course; if the curse is too strong, I may not be able to lift it."

So those of the band who wished to do so sought out things which had the taint of evil from the dragon still on them, and brought them to the mage. Hwerul brought only a silver drinking-cup which had caught his eye, and Afal-kayyon was able to remove the curse in a moment. Haram found a shield, a better one than the one he had lost, and found to his relief that it had no curse at all. Probably, he considered, a shield belonging to one of the soldiers who had recently come against the dragon.

Tanno found a brooch, gold inlaid with gems, and Coron found a pair of finely embroidered leather slippers, but Vorath did not bother, stating that he felt that with his share of what had been already certified as safe, he could buy whatever he might want.

In the meantime, he had been placing the treasure into six heaps. "There is no need for making unequal shares in this instance," he said. "Each of us can take as much as we can carry."

The various piles consisted of mostly coins, gems, and jewellery, and each sufficed to make any one of them wealthy. There were several other items left over, such as three small ivory tubes with strange inscriptions on them. Afal-kayyon inspected them. "The writing is not familiar to me, but these tubes clearly contain small spell scrolls, scrolls on which a spell is written. It requires no magical training to use them, merely the ability to read the writing on the scroll. They may be very valuable, or they may be worth only a gold piece each."

It was agreed by all that Afal-kayyon might as well take the tubes and their scrolls, since he was most likely to be able to discover the use of them. After all this was done, Vorath spoke to them all. "We had best be wary coming out of here. Many know that we came in to seek the dragon, and when we come out, they will wonder if we were successful. If we admit to them we were successful, then they will wonder what we have brought out. Even if we admit to nothing, there will be those who would ambush us to see what we might have.

"It would be best, I think, if we were to strike for the coast quickly, go to the town of Bavian and try immediately to find a ship to take us across the strait. And while we are in the town, spend only silver, and that sparingly---"

"By Tran and Viron, Vorath, are we children that we do not know all this?"

Vorath smiled briefly. "My apologies, Tanno. I worry perhaps a little too much."

They passed through the town of Bavian almost unnoticed, and Vorath bargained as rigorously for boat passage as if they were down to their last few coppers.

After they had disembarked on the beach near Halan, Vorath said to the others, "Keep quiet about our next destination, but if pressed, admit that we are going up along the north coast. With a little good fortune, we will be able to delude any who seek to wait for us on the road."

They stayed again at the Albatross, which appeared to be empty save for one man, wearing chain armour, and with his sword hilt poking above his right shoulder. He was asleep at one of the tables, his face resting on one arm thrown across the table-top.

When the innkeeper asked how had gone their battle with the dragon, Vorath said, "Well, we wandered back and forth across the countryside, and though we picked up a few silver pieces, I do not know how much we will have left after this night's lodging is paid for."

"That was not quite a lie," he muttered

to the others after the innkeeper had left, "I have not made an exact count of what we have, and am not certain what the cost of tonight's lodging will be."

They had just finished their meal and were settling back with a mug of ale when the man sleeping at the table suddenly woke. He looked around, wiped his eyes, and got to his feet. A little unsteadily, he stumbled across the room to the door. As he went, he bumped against Haram. He uttered a vile curse, then shouted, "Stumble-footed bumbler! Get out of the way when a true man walks by, will you?!"

He reached back over his shoulder and brought his sword hissing out of the scabbard and down in a vicious stroke at Haram's head.

Chapter Seventeen

Haram, his knees under the table and his torso half twisted around, was not in any position to mount a defence. Without a thought, he flung himself off the bench, not onto the floor, but into the swordsman's stomach, causing the attacker to stagger back a few paces. From the way the man regained his balance, Haram could tell two things: he was not drunk, and he was an expert swordsman.

Still wondering why this man should choose to kill him, Haram ripped his own sword free from the scabbard. Watching the man approach, Haram could see that he was outclassed. In a match of pure sword-craft, Haram would be dead in moments. How to keep it from being a match of pure sword-craft?

Haram leaped straight into the air, brandishing his sword, shaking his fist, and shouting in the goblin-tongue, "May your ancestors be devoured by demons!"

Then he went to the attack.

As he came, he continued to shout whatever goblin-phrases came to his head, such as "Form line, you lazy sods!" and "Sword inspection now!"

The other was too experienced to let his guard drop even for this, but for a moment he went on the defensive, parrying Haram's slashing blows.

Haram jumped back out of sword-range, then scooped up his mug of ale from the table and took a mouthful. He watched his opponent out of the corner of his eye and saw him approaching warily. The man was clearly wondering what sort of adversary he was fighting, what sort of trick he would try next.

Haram placed the tip if his sword on the floor and leaning on the hilt, surveying the man over the rim of the ale-mug. The man lunged. Haram brought up his sword in a quick parry, barely in time, then as the lunge brought his opponent closer, he screamed again in the goblin-tongue, cast the remnants of his ale into the man's eyes, and kicked at his groin.

The fellow was experienced enough to turn his thigh to catch Haram's foot, and to jump back, wiping at his eyes, sword presented to take Haram's next attack. And the attack came. Eyes staring, screaming curses in the goblin tongue, Haram sprang forward. The man went on the defensive again, parrying

Haram's succession of fierce slashes. Either he had had experience with battle-mad opponents, or Haram was not deceiving him.

Haram knew enough of sword-work to know that in a moment the fellow would be back on the offensive, that he would parry one of the slashes and come in with an attack of his own, and that the fight would not last much longer after that. In desperation, he tossed the ale-mug at the man's face, then lunged, reaching for his dagger.

In a swift movement, the swordsman batted the mug aside with the palm of his left hand, but that same movement blocked his own sword for an instant. In a further instant, it was all over; Haram was body-to-body with him, grating swords locked above them, while his dagger was buried to the hilt in the swordsman's side.

The man slumped, almost dragging the dagger out of Haram's hand. Haram pulled his dagger free, looking down at his opponent. The innkeeper came hurrying up, expostulating about the reckless drawing of swords and committing of murder in his establishment. Haram turned to him, trying to think what to say.

Then Vorath was beside him. "Be easy, innkeeper. This fellow picked a fight, and our companion could only defend himself." He dug into his change purse and withdrew a silver coin. "Perhaps this will pay for the difficulty, and for this fellow's burial."

The innkeeper viewed the coin with suspicion at first, then nodded. "So be it. I thought he was a friend of yours."

"A friend of ours? What could make you think that?"

"He was asking about you, wasn't he? He was making arrangements to be ferried across the strait to try to find you, wasn't he?"

"Was he indeed?" Vorath looked down at the dead man. "I do not know him. You others, do you recognize him?"

The others viewed the man, then shook their heads. "It may be that one of your enemies has hired him," said the innkeeper. "I would imagine that folk in your business make enemies from time to time."

"But none who would wish to kill us. Let us see if he has anything on him to say who he is or why he sought us."

He opened the man's change purse and emptied it out onto the table. It contained four gold coins, twelve silver ponies, and a number of copper pieces as well. In addition, there was another bit of metal, a piece of iron in the form of a single shaft, forking at the end to become three sharp tines.

Afal-kayyon was leaning close over the table. "The four gold coins are from Shondakar, but the silver and copper are from Aradair. He has come from Shondakar, and has spent a bit of Shondakranian gold in Aradair, hence the silver and copper. And that bit of iron, that is a symbol of Drauha, the God of Lies. It symbolizes his nature, that his word may mean two or three things at once."

"The God of Lies!" Tanno was looking at Haram. "Then he has not forgotten you!"

Afal-kayyon shook his head. "Nay, he

has not forgotten, but neither does he send demons or other beings. He is working through human beings to try to destroy you, Haram."

"So it would seem."

"Is that all you can say?" demanded Tanno. "A god seeks your death, and you accept it calmly, as though someone had offered you a drink of water!"

"What should I say? Should I begin quivering in fear, starting at every shadow? I suppose that this means that I shall have to be careful in any group, but what else can I do? Vorath, in light of this, would you wish me to withdraw from your band?"

"Certainly not! You are part of the group, and you shall stay with us so long as you wish, whatever happens."

"Thank you, Vorath. I appreciate your confidence."

"I think we ought to train you more rigorously in the use of the sword. You will be needing it."

They rode out of town as though they were going to follow the coast road, but after having gotten well out of sight of the town, they rode cross-country until they struck the road for Ifan Sor.

They travelled along, stopping in villages overnight, and admitted when pressed that they had had a little luck. "Denying it too strongly will have the same effect as admitting that we have riches," said Vorath. "People will become certain that we are lying."

During the evenings, and from time to time during the day, Vorath would train Haram in the use of the sword. "You know you were lucky back there? He was a much better swordsman than you. Your tricks ought to have done no more than delay your death. But you did so many strange things, the screaming, the attacks as though under the effect of battle-madness, the calm pausing for a taste of ale, throwing the ale in his face, then throwing the mug as well. All those slowed him down a little, put him just a little out of his timing, so that your final attack succeeded. But if there are more such coming after you, you cannot count on being able to deal with them all as you did with this one."

The trip to Ifan Sor was uneventful, save for one small hamlet known only for its inn, the Ox and Boar. The people of the town were rather standoffish, occasionally glancing at the Venturers with dark suspicion on their faces.

The innkeeper, though he served them, waited to see their money before he lifted a finger, and then seemed to grudge of any service rendered.

"What's wrong with this town?" Vorath asked. "They seem to hate us without having seen us."

"Aye, and so they might." The innkeeper was grudging with his words as well as his service.

"And why might that be?"

The innkeeper lifted his head and gave Vorath a surly look. "We had Venturers in here last week, a band headed by one called Zilva." The name immediately caught Haram's attention.

"They spent some money on goods, this lot, but in the morning attempted to slip out without settling their score here. "We raised a shout, and some likely lads came round with cudgels, and there was quite a scrap. Some of our lads took a cut or two, one of them very badly gashed, and though this Zilva and his lot went away without paying, they took some bruises along.

"So you shouldn't wonder that we look a bit harsh on your sort here."

Vorath nodded and led the band to their quarters. "No use trying to talk him around," he said later, "with the memory still so fresh. Like as not, we'd just end up in an argument, which would only confirm his attitude."

They came at last to Ifan Sor, and set themselves up in one of the better inns, the Dancing Gnome. They spent a day selling some of the plunder they had brought back, and changing some of the foreign coins for coins of Aradair.

Haram bought himself a shirt of light chain mail, and considered visiting his parents. He realized, however, that they would ask questions about Merrit, questions he didn't want to answer just now. He decided to leave that visit for another day.

The next night, they were seated around the table after supper, enjoying a mug of ale and talking about what they would do now, now that they were no longer poor.

Vorath took a long drink of ale and said, "Well, lads, I have been thinking about all this, and I have come to a conclusion. I have too much money to continue this wandering in the wilds, hunting and being hunted by goblins and the like. I think I shall buy myself a little inn here in the city and settle down."

There was a long silence. Tanno finally spoke. "Vorath, that is a noble idea. If you'll allow it, I will put my money with yours, and join you in the enterprise."

Vorath smiled. "Certainly, Tanno, and welcome."

Hwerul spoke slowly and thoughtfully. "I was a younger son, you know. My father did not want to see the farmstead broken up, so he left it all to my brother. Of course, my brother was a generous man, and I could have stayed with him. He would not have grudged me a place in his home. But there would be little chance for me to marry, and I would be forever the younger brother by the fire, then the kindly old uncle by the fire, but never have anything of my own. So I set out as a Venturer.

"But with this money, I could buy myself a farm. I would be able to marry and settle down and not be beholden to my brother for anything. It is a fine thought."

Afal-kayyon looked around at them all. "You know, I have always wished for time and leisure to study my art. I suppose you will all say that I do well enough, and so I do, but I could do better. I shall spend most of my money on books and equipment, and set up a small shop. In the times when I am not working at my shop, making my living, I shall be studying and practising."

Then Coron spoke. "Ah, if this be the way of it, I shall go buy me a ship. We were fisher-folk, you know, along the south coast. Had I stayed, I should have inherited my father's boat, and should have been able to live quite well by fishing. But my mind was on other things, on the faraway lands and places, and I thought at first to become a seaman on a merchant ship.

"But when I talked with seamen, I saw that such was a hard life, with little to show for it. So I decided to become a Venturer until such time as I could save enough money to at least buy shares in a ship. Now I have enough money to not only buy a share, but have a good say in where we go and what we carry."

Haram said nothing. He felt a sudden raging anger that he had just discovered this band of friends, and now they were deserting him! That realization surprised him; why should he be angry at his friends' good fortune?

He realized they were all looking at him, waiting for him to say something. "Me? I will continue to wander here and there, see what I can find. I have nothing better to do. Vorath, I will leave some of my money with you to use as you see fit. All I ask is free lodging when I pass through Ifan Sor."

Vorath looked at him closely. At last, he nodded. "So, then. Good fortune follow you,

Haram."

The next day, Haram still felt troubled. He spoke little to the others in the morning, going out into the city to wander about and see what news there might be. He bought a short bow and arrows. While it took a lifetime to train an expert archer, if he practised diligently, he might at the least be able to hit a target half the time, which would be useful.

He decided not to visit his father. Perhaps the next time he was in the city. He spent some time sitting and talking with other Venturers. He found the tale was already going round about the exploit of Vorath's band in Rahasin. They had slain four dragons, or was it five? They had taken away seven wagonloads of treasure, and it seemed they intended to set themselves up as Lords, perhaps even attempting to topple the King of Aradair.

Haram heard all this news in silence, saying nothing. Finally, a short squat man, one who might almost have been a Dwarf, looked at him and said, "Eh, lad, so quiet and careful, who be you, and with whose band?" Haram thought for a moment of dissembling, but considered that doing so could only make matters worse, if someone ever found out which band he truly belonged to.

"I am called Haram, and I'm with Vorath's band," he whispered.

Silence fell over the whole group as they all looked at him. He could see that some did not believe him, while others were wondering if he might have some of the fabled riches with him. "It was not so much as stories make it," he said. "We slew a small drake, indeed, and we took away a bit of treasure. But if you ask how much, I can only tell you that I shall be on the road again tomorrow."

There was another long silence, then another fellow, a slender, fair-haired man who might have been half-Elvish, spoke up. "Any of you hear of this ogre in the mountain country up north? I hear tell he's gathering up a band of ogres, and they're raiding the countryside."

"Now, there's a load of old turnips if I ever smelt one!" objected another of the group. "Nobody's ever heard tell of ogres banding together. Maybe they go in pairs from time to time, but not more than that!"

"You doubting me?" inquired the first speaker.

"No, not you. But you did tell us you'd just heard of these ogres. Did you see 'em yourself?"

"No, but I trust the man I heard it from!"

"And who did *he* hear it from? I'd wager it's nothing but a band of goblins, maybe a bit bigger than usual, that's all."

"Ah, but she could might be indeed!" called out a man whose heavy Rahasin accent was not improved by the amount he had had to drink. "Him was, back on the Island, it were known of three ogres wandering about, damaging."

"More old turnips! You see these ogres for yourself?"

"Not. Though brother of mine, seeing had was the tracks of their, and some of the damagings. Call not brother of me a lying-er!" The Rahasin stuck his face across the table pugnaciously.

The doubter made to say something in answer, but a friend caught his arm and pulled him back. "I won't doubt you, but I will say I've never seen the like of it, and I'd wager that goes for most of us here. And in any case, it isn't worth a fight and a fine from the magistrate, or worse!"

There was a short silence, then someone else asked, "Anyone heard any news of Zilva and his band?"

Somebody spat in disgust, and others muttered about dirty dogs making life the harder for the rest of us. Haram remembered the village to the north, but never even considered mentioning it. He still felt just a little out of place.

"When last I heard," the slim, fair man said, "they were on their way up to the land of Trethision, seeking Elvish loot. May they find loot, and more Elves than they wish to see!"

Chapter Eighteen

Haram listened carefully. Saradon had said that Merrit had gone with Zilva, but Saradon had also said that the name of Zilva was one he did not know. It seemed, however, that in this group, practically everybody knew or had suspicions about the name of Zilva.

"You know about Kohindath's Train?" asked a tall, slender man with a bow slung at his back.

"Old stuff!" jeered the man who had been so mocking about the notion of ogres banding together. "Where you been? Out on the plains of Shondakar? Everyone knows that one."

"I don't know it," said a moustachioed Shondakranian, "And I *haven't* been out on the plains of Shondakar. So, what is this story?"

The bowman, with at least one person for a new audience, told his tale. "Seems this merchant Kohindath had taken a very special shipment of pottery, headed for Ifan Sor. He never arrived, but about six months later, his partner in Ifan Sor saw some pieces on sale in the market that were supposed to have been in the lot. It seems one of Zilva's band had been selling them. When they talked with Zilva, he was a bit vague. He had gotten the stuff raiding a bandit camp off in the woods. The only evidence was the pottery, so they couldn't do anything to him. But a few other things have happened, and pretty well everybody now feels certain that he and his band wiped out Kohindath, somewhere along the way."

Now the man who had sneered at this as old news spoke up. "There was this town up on the northwest coast, across from Rahasin. Actually, it wasn't much of a town, just a few houses, some fishing boats, and a shack they called *'The Inn.'* Someone wiped it out. Men, women, and children, near fifty souls. Wasn't the work of goblins, though that kind of slaughter usually is, and they couldn't trace it to anyone for certain. But it's said that Zilva's band was in the neighbourhood somewhere near that same time."

"Why would he bother? Place like that, there'd be no money in it. Way I hear it, Zilva doesn't do anything but for profit."

The other shrugged. "No way of knowing how it went for sure, but I could make a guess. There was an argument over the price of beer or the like, and the words got hot. The innkeeper reached for a club under the bar, and somebody else got a weapon in first. And after the first one was killed, there'd be nothing for it but to kill everybody, leave no witnesses at all. No, I'm not saying it was right, or anything like that, just that it could have happened so."

The Shondakranian nodded. "So it could."

Haram pulled himself out of the group shortly after, having several things to think over. He disliked the thought of his boyhood friend in such a party as Zilva's seemed to be, and he absolutely hated the thought of Merritt involved with people who could be accused of robbing caravans or slaughtering villagers.

But he had to decide what to do with himself; one thing was certain, he had no intention of settling down.

He made some enquiries, and found a man named Gorr, a squat, broad-bodied veteran of the King's armies, who taught weapon-skills for a fee.

Gorr looked him over from head to foot, appraising him. "You're no boy of the streets who's never held a blade in his hand, nor one of the lordlings who wants to learn enough to be able to issue challenges for any real or fancied slight. So what do you come to me for?"

Haram answered honestly. "There's someone has a blood-feud for me, and while I can handle a sword a bit, I need to know more in order to survive." There seemed no need to go into the details.

Gorr nodded his head. "So. My fee is one silver pony per lesson, and I don't haggle. Anyone who can't or won't pay the fee can look elsewhere for their lessons."

Haram nodded in return. "Unless all I've heard is a weave of moonshine and starlight, the lessons will be worth it. I'll be coming three to four times a week."

A week later, he came back from his sword-lesson to find the rooms at the inn near empty. Afal-kayyon was packing up a few last things into a bag, and smiled when he saw Haram.

"Ah, Haram! Coron and Hwerul left their regrets, but they had to leave already. And if you had come much later, you would have missed me as well; I've purchased a shop over on Sailmakers' Lane, and have been making arrangements for the acquisition of various supplies. Drop by to see me when you can."

"Of course." Haram's response was mechanical, but inside he was angry enough that his fingers twitched, and he felt a desire to draw his sword and smash the furniture of the room to splinters. He was alone again!

His bad mood lasted until the next day, when Gorr halted him in mid-lesson.

"Ach, lad!" he exclaimed. "This plunging and bashing and smashing will not do! Anger is good betimes, to power your attacks, but when you let it cause you to forget all your lessons, it can get you killed. Who is it has angered you so?"

And Haram, knowing that he had no real reason to be angry, could only hang his head and mutter. The arms-master looked at him sharply. "So be it, then. I doubt I can teach you much until you have overcome your anger. It would be well for you to remember that. That fury might well kill you if you come to a serious fight. Go on, go have a good mug of ale, see if you can think of the reason for your anger, and be rid of it. Come back again tomorrow, and we will go on with the lessons."

Reluctantly, Haram went out.

After a further week, his swordsmanship had improved greatly and his anger had faded a little more, but he continued to feel uneasy, as though he had something to do. For the life of him, he could not think what that might be.

He took to wandering about the city and, in the course of his wandering around the city; he came upon some merchants who had just arrived. They were Shondakranians, distinctive by their robes and turbans and swarthy features. This reminded him of Orizd, particularly his last view of Orizd, bleeding from a number of wounds but still fighting against the goblins.

He wondered if any of these were followers of Drauha, and that brought to mind the thought of Terrial. What might have become of her in the time since he had seen her last?

He remembered her cutting remarks to him, but also remembered the apology she had made later. What might she be doing now? Belike she was married and on the way to raising numbers of little merchants somewhere. "Well," he muttered to himself,

198

"at least it'll give me something else to do rather than sitting around Ifan Sor."

Afal-kayyon was quite surprised to see him, and that surprise showed in his eyes as Haram walked through the door of his dingy little shop. "A good day to you, Haram."

"And a good day to you as well, Afal-kayyon. I will not waste your time, but come directly to the point; this amulet, would it protect me from Drauha if I go nearer to Shondakar?"

"How much nearer?"

"On the border of Shondakar itself."

The wizard folded his arms across his chest and looked up toward the ceiling of his shop. "It was made quite strong," he began. "Yet the strength of the god will increase as you come nearer to his home territory. Still, you ought to be safe under most circumstances." He paused to think again.

"Just to be safe, let me have the amulet. I will increase its strength so that you need have no fear."

As Haram slipped the amulet off and handed it to him, the mage spoke again. "You realize that nothing I might do would be infallible? It may well be that the protection of the amulet will fail, for reasons having nothing at all to do with the making of it."

"No, I had not known that."

"So. Now you are warned. But I believe that you will be in more danger from the assassins sent after you than from the god himself."

Gorr was not happy to see Haram going off. "You have done well, and you show promise, but you ought to have more training."

"I suppose I ought to, but there are other things I must do," said Haram.

Gorr frowned darkly. "Do not fault me, then, if you end up dead in a ditch somewhere."

Haram almost smiled at that. "No, I will not."

When Haram came back to Afal-kayyon's shop the next day, the mage brought out his amulet from the back of the shop.

"Here it is. It should keep you safe, but remember my caveat."

Haram inspected the talisman. "It looks no different than before."

The magician grimaced. "Please, Haram, do not be one of those naïve townsmen, for whom I have to add some sparkly stones to make them believe the magic has changed."

Haram grimaced in his own turn and felt himself redden. "Of course. Sometimes I can be a fool. How much do I owe you?"

"Nothing at all. I do this for the sake of our companionship on the trail."

Haram felt a momentary surge of anger, but quashed it immediately. Afal-kayyon spoke again.

"There is one other thing. You recall that I said that the amulet would not protect you against the assassins sent by the God? There is something I could supply which might help you against such, if you wish."

"What sort of thing?"

"It is a little charm to be recited, and it works on the bond between the assassin and the God. The result is a very small hesitation in the movement of the person, just enough that an accomplished swordsman might take advantage of it. It will not work on any ordinary attacker, or if one of the assassins hires some common street tough to put a dagger in your back. But against the assassins themselves, it will serve you well."

"And the cost?"

"Merely a silver pony. And perhaps you might mention my shop to others you meet." The mage was smiling slightly.

Haram nodded. "Good, then. I will take it."

"So then. It goes like this: *'Trrik trrak Drauha vrrak.'*"

The mage smiled. "I will give you a piece of advice along with it. Do not depend on it alone; depend also on your wits and your good sword. Many a man has gotten a charm from a magician, and used it so much and so often that he forgot to use his wits, and found one day that the charm failed him. Be careful."

"I will," said Haram.

The opportunity to test the charm came very quickly. He had gathered all his goods from the inn, save for most of his gold, which he had left with Vorath as promised, and went out the front door. A voice called out, "Haram?"

He turned. The man behind him was tall and broad, dark of face and hair, clearly a Shondakranian. He wore a helmet, a plain metal cap, and a shirt of chain belted at the waist, and he had a shield in one hand.

"You are Haram, once of Vorath's band?"

"I am."

The brown hand grasped the sword-hilt, and the sword came out and struck with amazing speed. But Haram, seeing the man for a Shondakranian, had been immediately alert, and spoke.

"Trrik trrak Drauha vrrak!"

Did the man hesitate briefly in his movement? Haram could not say for sure, but he was able to draw his own sword and evade the other swordsman's first blow at the same time. The attacker looked faintly puzzled, as though wondering why his first attack had failed so badly, then he struck again.

But Haram had been practising sword-work with Gorr for some time, and his reactions were quick. After a little fencing, he could tell that the man was as good as he was, probably a little better, and that he was stronger, and that if Haram allowed it, his opponent would wear him down and kill him.

There was little time to frame careful plans. He moved backwards, and the assassin bored in. Haram disengaged, springing backward, then turned to run. He heard a shout of triumph behind him, then three steps later he stopped, whirled, and thrust. The assassin had no time to interpose his shield or sword and was taken through the stomach. As the man collapsed, clutching his pierced belly, Haram withdrew his sword and slashed it across the assassin's throat. This was not so much an act of kindness as a matter of convenience; just to assure himself, he went through the man's change purse. Aside from several coins, there was what he had expected; the forked bit of metal which was the symbol of the God of Lies.

Haram looked up and saw several large armed men hurrying in his direction. Either someone had called the City Watch, or they had heard the rumpus themselves. The whole episode had been witnessed by several people, though most could only say that the two had drawn swords and gone at each other.

The innkeeper, however, made his statement firmly. "The dead man, he called to Haram, made sure of his name, then drew his sword first. Haram only defended himself."

The Captain of the patrol, a square-jawed fellow with the beginnings of a beer-belly, looked at Haram curiously. "Was that the way of it, then?"

"Yes," replied Haram.

"What was it he had against you?"

Haram had no desire to describe his doings with the God of Lies. "He did not say. He appears to have been a hired assassin, probably engaged by someone who imagines he has a grudge against me."

The captain frowned. "We do not care for people bringing their grudges and blood feuds within these walls, and settling them on the streets of Ifan Sor. It might be best for the magistrates to deal with this matter."

"Captain, I am on my way out of the city, and I would prefer not to be delayed. Perhaps I might pay the fine to you, and you could convey it to the magistrates?"

The Captain's eyes lit up; he understood Haram completely, now it was only a matter of asking no more than Haram could pay. "Usual charge for brawling's three silvers."

"Three silvers? I was born and brought up here, Captain, not in the far plains of Shondakar. Brawling is two coppers, brawling with edged weapons is five. But suppose, just to make things easier, I give you the five coppers, and two for yourself, and one each for you and your squad, for your trouble?"

But the Captain pressed harder. "You want a good deal for a few coppers."

Haram sighed. "Captain, you have my offer. I *do* wish to leave the city soon, but if necessary, I will stay to be brought before the magistrates."

And the Captain, knowing that if the case went to the magistrates, he would get nothing out of it, gave in. "So, then, give us the money and begone. And be careful how you tread in Ifan Sor."

So Haram handed over the money, including the fine, which he was certain would never come closer to the magistrates than the nearest wine-shop, gathered up his goods, and was on his way.

He rode along the most direct route toward Shondakar. With the money he had available, he did not concern himself with making more. Much different from his time with Orizd, or with Vorath. He felt a smile twist his lips slightly. For a little while, at least, he need not be concerned every day about finding something, anything, to make a few coppers!

In the evenings, he spent a little time practising with his weapons, bow, sling, and sword. Orizd had taught him some drills, and Vorath had taught him some more, and Gorr still more. He would go through these, time after time, with the voices of his memory telling him *'Too Slow,'* or *'Too quick,'* or *'Too jerky,'* and rarely *'That's better.'*

The God of Lies had hired good swordsmen thus far, and he'd beaten them both with trickery. *'You can't always depend on that, Haram,'* he told himself, as he pushed himself through another round of drills.

To make up for the vulnerability of being alone, he stopped at a village along the way and bought a length of cord and some tiny bells. He cut the cord in length and tied a bell to each length. When he camped at night, he strung the lengths of cord at about ankle level, between small bushes or tufts of grass, or, occasionally, small wooden stakes that he cut and trimmed for the purpose. With his campsite surrounded by these, it might not be impossible for anyone to approach him while he slept, but it would be difficult.

He came up to the dusty grey walls of Halan Howrdas just before sundown, about a week after setting out from Ifan Sor. He went round to the same inn where he had stayed as a member of Orizd's band that evening. A little less than two years ago, and already it seemed to be in the distant past.

The innkeeper looked at him closely, and Haram could almost feel him trying to recall when and in what circumstances they had seen each other. Haram did not bother to enlighten the man. The rescue of the merchant's daughter would have been a nine-days' wonder in those parts and, if reminded, the innkeeper would surely know who Haram was. But he would probably also inquire about his companions, and Haram did not wish to talk about that at the moment. Indeed, he did not wish his presence too widely known, for fear it should come to the wrong ears.

After supper, he walked down to the merchant's house. He pulled the cord at the door, which rang the bell inside the house, then waited. Eventually, a servant came to the door, looked him up and down, and said, "Yes?"

"Is the merchant Lavad at home?"

"He is, but he does not hire caravan guards; his caravaneers do that themselves."

"Nor am I interested in hiring as a caravan guard. It is actually the young lady Terrial who I have come to see."

The servant looked him up and down again, then said "Yes?" once more. The tone of his voice said as clearly as words might, "And what would the likes of you have to do with the lady Terrial?"

Answering that unspoken question, Haram said, "I was one of the band that rescued her."

The servant's eyes widened, and sudden recognition flooded in. "One moment, sir! Have a seat, sir, and I will be back in a moment!"

The servant closed the door, saw that Haram was seated, then went rushing off. True to his word, he was back shortly, with the merchant Lavad preceding him. The merchant had clearly rushed ahead and was practically out of breath. "What is it? What do you know of Terrial? Where is she?"

Chapter Nineteen

Haram stared in bafflement. "She is not here?"

Even as he spoke, he realized he was speaking foolishness; Lavad's reaction said as clear as shouted words Terrial was not there.

The merchant, irritable at the disappointment, responded sharply, "Nay, she is not here! And if you have no news of her, why have you come? Hoping to talk another reward out of me, I'll be bound!"

"No such thing! They'll tell you at the inn that I'm not short of money! I came merely to pay my respects, out of politeness." He emphasized the last word, but realized as the words were coming out that he did not know for sure why he had come.

Lavad, at the reference to politeness, took a deep breath. "Yes, of course. Come in. Let me at least offer you a glass of wine."

They sat round the table, eyeing each other uncomfortably, until the wine was poured. When the servant had retired, the merchant stretched out a long-fingered hand, raised the cup, and took a sip. Haram did likewise. After sitting in silence for a while, Lavad finally spoke.

"After you brought her back, she insisted on learning to defend herself. I finally gave in, to the extent of buying her a sword and having a man come in to give her lessons. Last year, she left. In the middle of the day, while no one was about, she called a servant to her. Said she was off to become a Venturer, and the servant should tell me not to worry. Before the servant could have word brought to me, she was far down the trail. I sent out men to track her and bring her back, but she evaded them. I don't know how, and we have not seen nor heard from her since.

"There was one time, three months ago, that a merchant brought back a rumour from over in Rahasin, that a young woman named Terilee, as he heard it, had been involved in the slaying of some monster or other. Perhaps it was her, perhaps it was not. And you have heard nothing of her?"

Haram paused a moment to try to remember all the stories and rumours that had gone around in Ifan Sor regarding Venturers and their adventures. Some women had been spoken of, but none with a name even similar to

Terrial. He shook his head. "Nay, I have heard nothing. But I promise you I'll make a point of seeking out news of her, and if I hear anything, I'll send word to you."

"The thing is," said Lavad, "that I am not certain how I feel. At times I am angry that she could do such a thing to the one who loves her best, and at other times I only wish I knew that she was in good health, wherever she is. Perhaps that makes no sense to you."

Thinking of his own ambivalent attitudes to his comrades' good fortune, Haram nodded. "I understand, perhaps better than you might think."

"If you do see her, tell her that her father misses her. Tell her to come back, even if for a day or two, simply to comfort an old man's heart."

Haram's own heart was heavy as he went back to the inn that night.

In the morning, he tried to think about what to do next. Why had Terrial gone off so? She did not need to become a Venturer! Her father was a wealthy merchant. He could buy her whatever she wished. And now she was gone, just as Orizd, Sagahan, Astaran, Merrit, and all the others were gone.

He sat musing on this, becoming more and more morose, until a whole day had passed. He noticed that the innkeeper and his staff walked carefully around him, and he wondered what they were seeing in him, what seemed to be so dangerous about him. At last, late in the evening, the innkeeper approached him cautiously. "Are you certain you actually want more ale, young sir?"

"Of course! Didn't I just order it?"

"Yes, certainly you did. But you have been drinking ale all day, eating little or nothing, and looking like a black cloud full of thunder and lightning. That's a combination which leads to trouble as often as not, and I wish no trouble in this place."

"Trouble? I've given you no trouble yet, innkeeper, and I'll give you no trouble so long as you continue to bring my ale."

The innkeeper shook his head firmly. "No more ale this night, young sir."

Haram put a hand on his sword, glowering up at the innkeeper. He was suddenly reminded of Astaran berating Orizd for getting drunk and making such trouble in the town of Ninantha on a previous visit that they did not dare to pass through it. He grimaced, then forced a smile onto his face. "And why should there be trouble between us? For certain, you'll still have ale tomorrow, and that is another day. And I shall be going to bed."

He hauled himself upright again, as the innkeeper moved back slightly, still watching him carefully. Haram discovered he was not steady on his feet, and that brought him to consider what would have happened if he had drawn his sword there. "Be lucky not to run myself through," he muttered, smiling ruefully.

For all that, he made his own way to his bed. His sleep, however, was troubled with dreams, dreams which fled at his wakening and left him only with a feeling of unease.

He understood in the morning the unwisdom of drinking so much ale the day before. With an aching head and a churning stomach, he saddled his horse. He set out northward from town, and was soon drowsing in the saddle, trusting the horse to follow the road.

It was about noon when he suddenly noticed an oak grove coming up on their right, and knew where they were. He pulled the horse to a stop. "By Tran and Viron, horse, would you lead me to my death? We are in Shondakar!"

For a brief moment, he would have turned the horse and galloped in the opposite direction, then his good sense came to the fore. If he were not mistaken, Drauha and his minions worked mostly in darkness, so the brightness of the day should hold no dangers for him. So long as he did not stay beyond nightfall, all should be well.

Haram swung himself down out of the saddle, grimacing as his legs nearly buckled under him. He shuffled around a little, recovering the use of his limbs, and wondered whether Korennis still lived there, or whether he had been replaced by another druid. He unslung a waterskin from his saddle and had just taken the first sip when his horse whinnied and was answered from inside the grove.

Haram looked up. His horse was directly between him and the grove, covering most of his body. His first impulse was to reach for his bow, but to string it would warn whoever was in the grove that he was preparing to fight. Instead, he reached into his pouch and took out his sling and one of the smooth pebbles he had collected along the way.

He continued to look across the horse's withers into the grove, but could see nothing. Bandits would certainly try not to harm the horse, since it was a precious animal; they might be tempted into a long shot at Haram's head or upper body eventually, but they would wait a while, even for that.

He saw no movement in the woods, but a man was suddenly there at the edge of the grove, a tall man clad in a brown robe. Haram stepped from behind his horse. "Korennis!" he said.

The other nodded. "And you are Haram the Venturer, a little older, with more experience behind you. What brings you here?"

Haram grimaced. "I was drowsing in the saddle, trusting my horse to know the trail north from Halan Howrdas, forgetting that the trail forks, with one branch of it leading off to Shondakar."

Korennis nodded. "Many times animals will find their way to this grove, in particular if they are hurt or distressed. So you did not seek me out?"

"By Tran and Viron, no! I have an amulet against the God of Lies, but of my own will I wouldn't trust in it so near to his own territory. At least, I assume that the lord of Shab-nazdig is continuing his work?"

"He is."

They stood in silence for a while until Haram began to feel a little uncomfortable. He extended his hand with the waterskin. "I have little to offer in the way of hospitality, but if you would care for a drink of water, I have that."

The druid smiled. "A drink of water would be welcome." He strode forward and took the waterskin. He took a short swallow, then handed it back.

"In fact, it is I that ought to be offering hospitality, this being my home. But if you would come into my grove, you would have to put aside your iron armour and your iron weapons. Does that offend you?"

Haram smiled. "Nay, not at all. As a guest in your home, ought I not to comply with the wishes of my host?"

"If you wish to unsaddle your horse, and set the saddle with your other things there by yonder tree, the horse might come into the grove, and no one will touch your equipment while you stay with me."

As he put off his armour, Haram wondered for a moment if this might be a trap, but he quickly dismissed that notion. Everything he had heard of druids said that they were straightforward persons, that any harm they did was done openly, in response to provocation, and not slyly. And he could think of nothing he had done to provoke Korennis.

He followed the druid back into the grove, noticing that it seemed to be full of wildlife. "They come here," said Korennis in response to the question Haram did not ask, "mostly out of need, and they stay for longer or shorter times, then go their ways again."

"But do they lose their fear of men by

staying here? One might think that they would thus make themselves easier prey to hunters."

Korennis laughed. "No, that is not the way of this grove. Sometimes I try to heal the worst of their hurts, as the God guides me, but for the most they do not seem to know that I am here at all."

"And what of me? Will they not take fright from me? Or will the grove cover me with its cloak as well?"

"All my experience heretofore says that they will not likely notice you, either. Do not fear, Haram, if I thought you would be a disturbance to my grove, I would never have invited you in."

A little ways inside the grove there was a rough cabin, small but weathertight. There was a well outside with a stone-built casement and a wooden bucket attached to a short rope. The cabin was built for the use of one person, a neat bedroll rolled up at one wall, a small table and two chairs, and in the fireplace a bronze kettle was staying warm by the fire. One of the walls was completely covered by a curtain of rough cloth.

"Be seated."

Haram pulled out one of the chairs and sat down. "Do You have company here from time to time, then?"

Korennis looked around. "Ah, the two chairs and all. Yes, from time to time I have visitors here. There are some of the folk of the countryside who come to me for healing and the like. Though I am not a healer by profession, I do not like to turn away those truly in need. They have learned, though, not to come for love potions or for curses on their neighbours." There was something in his voice which made Haram very glad that he had not come for a love potion or a curse.

The stew was good, with large lumps of meat in it. Haram looked at it, then at Korennis, who smiled. "Yes, it is meat. Did you think it forbidden to us? Nay, creatures of the wild eat meat, and the God is a God of nature as it is, not as some city-dweller might like it to be. And no, there is no hunting allowed in this grove, not even for myself. But there is a great expanse of land outside this grove where I can and do hunt. All that the God forbids is waste, to kill what you cannot use."

When they had finished eating, Korennis said, "Now then, tell me of yourself. What has happened to your companions?"

"Dead," said Haram shortly.

"Ah, indeed? And how did that happen?"

"Goblins ambushed us in the morning," said Haram, wishing that the druid would cease asking such questions.

But Korennis appeared not to notice Haram's brusque answer. "And you? How did you escape this ambush?"

"I was knocked on the head during the fight, and when I came to myself again, the fight was over and the goblins were dividing up the spoil. When they found me still living, they kept me as a slave. After about a year, I was rescued when they accidentally encountered another band of Venturers." He was surprised that he could keep his voice so steady speaking of these things.

Korennis nodded quietly, as though all this was merely confirmation of something he had already known. "You have been alone since?"

Haram shook his head. "Nay, I was with the band who rescued me, first as merely a companion, then as a full member."

"And why did you come here? Did you not know that the God of Lies will still be seeking you?"

"Yes, I knew that, but as I've already said, I have an amulet which is supposed to offer me protection, and I had not planned to stay long, nor to come so close to his dominions. I merely intended to visit with Terrial, the girl we had rescued. But I hear from her father that she has gone off herself to become a Venturer."

The druid nodded gravely. "Yes, she came by here on her way. She had been taught to handle a sword, but other than that, she had few skills and little knowledge. She hoped that I would be able to teach her the sorts of things she would need to know. There was little I could do for her. Most of the magic I know is the sort that takes years to learn. I gave her such advice as I could, and taught her one or two things, mostly the lore of plants. Then she was on her way. I have heard nothing of her since."

They sat in silence for a time. Finally, the druid asked, "What of you? Where do you go from here?"

Haram shrugged. "For some time now, I

have not been planning beyond the immediate day, or sometimes as much as a week. I have no plans, no goals. If I truly need money, I have money being held for me in Ifan Sor. I suppose I shall go back to Aradair and travel the roads, to see what changes and chances might come upon me."

"So. Let us go outside. The day is too fine to be wasted indoors."

They went outside, then, and sat on a bench beside the wall of the house, talking of this and that. Korennis knew much of the world outside his grove, and Haram remarked on it.

"How should I not know all these things? You remember, I told you that people come by for help and healing on occasion, and oftentimes they will talk of any number of things besides their troubles. If one listens, one learns."

There was a whinny and the sound of a horse moving up beside the cabin, and Haram thought at first it might be his horse seeking him out. But when the head came round the corner, it was only a pony. Haram glanced at it, then suddenly stared at the familiar pony face. He jumped to his feet. "Arkhwelt!" he shouted.

Chapter Twenty

The pony ambled over to Haram, who put his arms around the beast's neck and wept. He wept as he had never dared do while a captive of the goblins. Haram wept for jovial Orizd, fiery Astaran, pedantic Sagahan. "So you managed to escape?" he said finally. "You were not eaten by the goblins, then?"

Arkhwelt, being unable to answer such questions in words, nuzzled his head against Haram's chest in the fashion which meant that, whatever else might be going on in the world, he expected to be fed. "So you think you ought to be fed, do you? Shame on you, then, with a stomach so fat as yours, wanting to be fed again! Nay, it will do you no good to bump against me so, I have nothing to feed you!"

Korennis was smiling. "He came to me last year, he and a large black beast. I was sure I had recognized them, but I wished to be certain that you had not merely abandoned him somewhere. The big black was in terrible condition. Wolves had been at him, and his right hind leg was dragging. I thought that I might be able to save his life, but he would only live a life of misery after, so I gave him mercy and killed him as quickly as could be. The pony, aside from a few scrapes and scratches, and aside from being as thin as a rail, was still hale, so I have kept him here."

Haram dried his face. The sorrow for dead companions was still inside, but seemingly more manageable now. "You didn't think I had abandoned him!"

"Nay, I didn't think that of you, but you will remember that we were together for but one day and one night, and that there was much else happening as well. And I have lived so long because I learned long ago the folly of judging people too quickly, either for good or ill."

"The big black. That would have been Orizd's horse?" And his last memory of Orizd, sorely wounded and still fighting like a bear at bay, came near to bringing fresh tears to his eyes.

"Yes, as I remember it. And that was another reason for not believing that the horses had been abandoned. The Shondakranian would not have abandoned his horse, though he himself must starve. The others are dead, then?"

"The goblins came upon us in the early

morning," said Haram. "We woke fighting. In the battle, I was struck across the head with an iron-shod spear-butt. The fellow who struck me clearly thought he had killed me, or he would have run me through to make sure. Or perhaps his attention was attracted elsewhere before he could make the stroke. However, it was. I woke to find the others dead, and myself in the midst of a band of goblins. I never saw the horses, but I'm sure that at least one of them was killed by the goblins for meat."

"And once again, you are alone?"

"Yes, I am." Haram thought about that. "There was a young fellow, Merrit, a close friend of mine, who joined Orizd's band at the same time as I. But we came across Saradon's band in our travels, and he arranged a place for himself there." He went on to explain how Merrit had agreed to arm-wrestle for the place with Saradon, and how he had ensured his success. "And so my best friend left me, and cheated me in order to do so."

A thought suddenly struck him, and he looked up at the druid. "You know, I think I have even blamed Orizd and the others for deserting me as well. Foolishness, for they died in fighting, as I nearly did myself. And then I also blame Vorath's band for deserting me. In their case, they merely decided that they had sufficient money to fulfil lifelong ambitions. And since I had no particular goal in mind, I was left alone. Would you not call that foolishness?"

But Korennis only smiled. "Are you quite without plans, then?"

"As near to it as makes no difference," answered Haram. "The only plan I have in mind is to attempt to avoid the swordsmen who have been sent to kill me."

"Swordsmen? Sent by servants of the God of Lies, I suppose?"

"Exactly!" Haram was about to ask how Korennis could know who had sent the killers, but realized before he spoke it would be a foolish question. Instead he said, "Twice so far I've been attacked, and twice I've managed to survive. If I stay in one place, they will surely find me. If I continue to move, it will at least take a little longer for them to track me down."

"Beware, Haram."

"I am always careful."

"Ah, but I suggest you beware of more than swordsmen. By this time, they will be made aware that two swordsmen have failed, and they will be trying other methods. Footpads, common thieves, persons shooting from ambush, that sort of thing."

"They will be aware so soon? How would news be passed so quickly?"

"You forget, these are servants of a God. They have ways and means which are not available to ordinary folk."

Haram nodded. That made some sense, indeed. "So. I shall beware."

"And if you will stand for one further piece of advice, I would suggest you find a comrade, one who will not be daunted by being hunted by servants of the God of Lies."

"Yes," said Haram. "Bare is the back with no brother." The words of Orizd came automatically to his tongue, but they brought memories with them, and nearly started tears in his eyes again.

Korennis was looking at him. "That was something that Orizd used to say," Haram said, wiping his sleeve across his eyes. "And after so long a time without giving more than a second thought to them, I find suddenly that I weep like a babe if but remember the least thing about them."

"They were good people."

"Good people? Yes, they were good people. They had their faults, to be sure, but they did their best by me, and I tried to do my best for them."

"And if one does one's best for his companions, is there then any more he can reasonably be asked to do?"

Haram nodded. "So do I say to myself, and yet sometimes I wonder if there was more I could have done."

For a while they sat in silence, then Haram got up and drew water from the well, washed his face, and said, "Best I should be going, I think."

"Even though you do not know where?"

"Ah, I know where, now. I will go out and see if I can find Terrial. If I find her, I will try to convince her to go home and visit her father, or at least to send him word from time to time to say that she is well."

"And the pony?"

"I am of two minds there. If I seek to take him with me, will he truly come? Or would it not be better to leave him here in relative safety?"

"That is a decision with which I cannot

help you."

"Unless I mistreat him," said Haram with a smile.

"Unless you mistreat him," agreed Korennis with an answering smile.

"So. Let us first see if he wishes to come." Haram stood up and then walked out of the grove. As he walked, he called to Arkhwelt, and the pony trotted agreeably after him.

"It would seem that he still considers himself your pony," said the druid.

"It would seem so. Farewell, Korennis, and my thanks for your hospitality."

"Farewell, Haram. Perhaps we will meet again."

"Perhaps." Privately, Haram thought that there was little chance of that; pure accident had brought him so near to the domain of the God of Lies, and he doubted that any such chance would happen again.

He came to the edge of the grove, recovered his arms and armour, saddled his horse, and was on his way, Arkwelt in tow.

After a bit more than a week of uneventful riding of the dusty grey roads, Haram came to Intalis, on the northern border of Yosanair, the northernmost of the kingdoms which made up Aradair. He dismounted, and led his horse and the pony Arkhwelt down the main street, searching for the inn. As he went, he felt a bumping at his hip, where his wallet hung.

Whipping round, he drew his sword.

The fellow who stood there was several years older than Haram, wearing rough brown homespun, and leaning on a homemade crutch of inferior quality. Whatever Haram would have done was forestalled by a potter in his stall at the edge of the street, who shouted, "Ho! Thief!"

Chapter Twenty-One

Suddenly, there was a raging mob around the lame man. Out of the stalls and shops they rushed, knocking the cripple man down and jostling for the privilege of kicking him. Haram hesitated a moment; this was none of his affair, was it? But there was something about this scene reminiscent of the way goblins acted.

That thought settled the matter for him; he vaulted into his saddle and turned the horse, riding him straight into the struggling mass. "Stop this!" He shouted. "Stop! There was no theft! Get back, now!"

The horse forced some of them back, but Haram was forced to use the flat of his sword as well to discourage others. Finally, he had driven them back, though they stood glaring at the pair of them. Then the potter who had started it all, a squat fellow with a red face and a thick thatch of hair to match, stood forward.

"The half-elf bastard is a thief, sir, and ought to be dealt with!"

"Thief, is he? And what has he stolen?" asked Haram.

"Why, he was at your own coin purse, sir. Did you not notice?"

"Oh, aye, I noticed, but there was nothing taken, unless this fellow is able to take money from a purse and close it up again, without the owner of the purse being any the wiser. And if there was no theft, then what you were about was murder, no less."

"Murder? Murder, you say? Why---"

"What else would you call it, when an innocent man is killed? Now be off about your business. And let me tend to mine."

For a time it seemed as though they might defy Haram, sword or no. They stood round him, muttering and growling, waiting for someone to lead them. Finally, the potter snorted. "Let it be, then. If he will decide to save the life of a thief, so be it. And sometime soon he will regret it." He turned back to his stall, and the others drifted away as well, until at last Haram was left with his two horses and the crippled man on the ground. He dismounted.

Haram extended a hand to help the lame man to his feet, surveying the man as he rose. He was no taller than Haram when he stood erect, with a fine frame and long slender arms and hands. His hair was fair, and his lower left leg was bound in splints. "Had you asked me, I would probably have given you a coin or two. There was no need for theft."

The lame man smiled wryly. "I suppose it's the effect of this village. They don't like me here, you see, and I felt no great hope that you would be any different."

"And why don't they like you here?"

The other shrugged. "That's a long tale, too long to be told standing here in the street. But if you buy me a bit of bread and meat at the inn, I'll be happy to entertain you with my misfortunes."

Haram laughed. "You lack little for boldness, at any rate. Come along, let me feed you and hear your story."

As they made their way to the inn, he asked, "What can I call you?"

"I was called Darith-Gan by my mother and have been called many worse names since."

"Darith-Gan it is, then. And I am Haram."

"Haram, you say?"

"Yes. What of it?"

"Nothing. Only I seem to remember hearing of the name in connection with the killing of an ogre to the south of here."

"Yes. That was some time ago, when I was with Orizd's band."

By this time, they had come to the inn. "The landlord may not wish to have me inside here," said Darith-Gan.

"Ah, but perhaps I can change his mind," said Haram.

And indeed, as soon as Darith-Gan stepped through the door, the landlord was rushing over, frowning at him. "Get out, get out, you beggar! I give nothing to worthless vagrants!"

Haram stepped forward. "This man is my guest, landlord. Unless you would desire me to take my custom elsewhere?" He drew a gold coin from his wallet and held it up so that the landlord could see it. The landlord looked from the coin to Darith-Gan and back again, then looked at Haram.

"No Sir. You are welcome here indeed, sir. But do you know who it is that you call a guest?"

Haram set a hand on his sword-hilt. "Yes, I know his name is Darith-Gan, and I also know that I do not like to find myself challenged by every fat fool in town. Bring us ale and food, and do it at once!"

The landlord turned pale and quivered. "At once, sir!" He fled for his kitchen.

The food and drink were brought out shortly, and Darith-Gan went to work on it. After he had eaten and drunk a bit as well, Haram looked over at the lame man and said, "Well, you promised me a story; will you tell it now?"

Darith-Gan returned his look. "It is something of a long story, if you have the patience. And it must begin with my beginning, if you will.

"My father was an Elf of the Woods up in Trethision. He met my mother at a fair and fell in love with her. But he could not stay with her, nor could he take her with him immediately, for there was some sort of contention taking place among the Elves at the time. But he promised my mother that he would return, leaving her a ring in token of that promise.

"He never did return, and we never knew what happened, though rumours did come out of the Woods that he had died in some sort of feud. However, it was, I was born without a father.

"My mother did her best for me, and her own father stood by her, keeping the two of us as though there had actually been a marriage. When grandfather died, however, it became more difficult, for my eldest uncle had little love for Elves at all, and he claimed that my existence was a shame to the family. In the end, he drove mother out.

"We wandered after that; my mother was a skilled weaver, and could work at her trade wherever she could set up her loom. Unfortunately, she could not change my features, nor alter the fact that my father was not present. We would stay a few months or a year in a town, long enough to almost become established, then rumours would begin to spread, and eventually ill-feeling would mount to the point where we would be forced to travel on.

"To have a bastard son, that was one thing, and might well have been overcome with time. But a bastard half-Elven son, that was something else indeed, something to be mistrusted and distrusted and driven out."

He took a drink from his ale-mug, then went on.

"By the time I was eight years old, I began to understand why we were always moving, but there was nothing I could do to prevent it. When I was nine years old, I became apprenticed to one of the Hidden Folk. Do you know of them?"

Haram nodded. He had indeed heard of the Hidden Folk, master spies and assassins, with special abilities some swore were magical, while others maintained they were no more than carefully learned physical tricks.

Darith-Gan looked at him carefully. "Yes, no doubt you have heard of us, and all sorts of tales, rumours, and downright lies. However, when I left my mother, as I reasoned, that would leave her free of the stigma of my presence, free to settle down and stay in one town forever.

"I served my apprenticeship well, learned all my master's skills, and was allowed to go out on my own. I will not tell you of my exploits; better for you that you know nothing of the things I have done. In any case, after some years I finished up here, in this town.

"And you have been wondering why I admitted to you that I was one of the Hidden Folk? We do not make ourselves known, save when we are seeking to be hired, and then only to as few as possible. In this case, it would do me no good to try to hide my trade from you, for the whole village knows it, and would be sure to tell you if I did not. There is a wise woman here in the village, Old Kora by name, and on the night I took a room at this inn, she sought me out. She had never seen me before, I am sure, but before the whole company she announced, "*'You are Darith-Gan, one of the Folk who call themselves Hidden. You shall not leave this village unscathed or alone.'*"

He frowned down into his ale, which was practically gone, and Haram signalled the landlord for more. When it was brought, Darith-Gan went on with his story.

"I know not whether she was placing a curse, or merely foretelling. Whichever it was, as I was riding out of town the next day, my horse stumbled and fell. Ordinarily I would have escaped something like that with no more than a bruise or two, but this time I broke my leg.

"Worse still, my horse broke his leg as well, and had to be killed. As for myself, Old Kora set my leg and put it in splints, and I made a crutch to get around on. But I am in no condition to walk for any distance, so I stayed in town.

"However, after my money was gone, I found life a bit more difficult. The villagers would neither feed nor house me without payment, and they insisted on money. I have a spare dagger and the like, but no one would buy them. Thus, without money, I was put into a distressing situation. And as for the villagers, you see that they are getting the best out of it. They accepted my money while I had any, but now they hope I will either starve to death, or be caught in the act of stealing, which will permit them to execute me legitimately. And incidentally, all my goods would be forfeit to the town."

Haram's mouth tightened. "You know, I have a mind to stay in this town for a while, to enjoy the hospitality. Would you be so good as to be my guest in return for directing me to the local points of interest?"

The other suppressed a smile. "Though not a native, I think I can show you everything the town has to offer. Perhaps the most noteworthy part is the road out, though we may want to save that for the last."

The next day, Haram said, "I would like to talk to this woman, Old Kora."

"Well, she live at the edge of town, and her place is easy enough to find. But what do you hope to achieve?"

"A fair question, but one for which I do not have an answer. Just satisfaction of my curiosity, I suppose."

Darith-Gan shrugged, and led him to a cottage at the edge of town, a small thatch-roofed cottage with a fenced plot of vegetables and herbs out front.

Haram had no idea what to expect, and would not have been surprised if Kora had condemned him for his meddling. She was a stout lady, old, but still hale, with grey hair tied back at the base of her neck with a leather cord, and she was working in her vegetable garden when they arrived. She looked up to see them come in, but did not greet them.

"A good afternoon to you, Madam," said Haram politely.

"And a good afternoon to you as well. I see that you have found each other."

Haram looked at Darith-Gan in surprise, and found Darith-Gan looking back at him, equally surprised. When they looked at the old lady once more, she was grinning. "I see many things," she said. "Is it surprising that I should also be able to see when one of them is fulfilled?" She brushed back a wisp of hair that had escaped from the cord.

"You saw this?" demanded Darith-Gan. "Why did you not say so, rather than exposing my trade and putting a curse on me?"

"But I did say so, and I put no curse on you. You recall, I said that you would not leave the village unscathed or alone. It was a foretelling, not a curse. And now you are not unscathed, and you are not alone."

"But why should I be singled out? Why a foretelling for me rather than for anyone else?"

She beamed again. "When I am told to speak, I speak, and I do not ask the why nor wherefore. But I think I might hazard a guess. Without offending the Great Ones, I would say that this young man requires a companion."

"And I am to be his companion, whether I will it or no?" demanded Darith-Gan. Haram was thinking much the same thing.

Kora chuckled. "Oh, I imagine that you could reject this fate if you wished. But you would be going against the will of the Great Ones. This might entail suffering."

"Suffering?" Darith-Gan slapped his crutch against the splints on his leg. "Suffering? Does this not count as suffering?"

"If you think it so. But you might ask your companion about suffering."

It was Haram's turn to be mystified. "And what do you know about me, and how?"

"I know what most of Aradair knows, that you are Haram, and that the story has it that you spent some time as a slave of goblins. But that is common knowledge, and the story has been going the rounds of the cities and towns for some time of Haram of the Grim Face."

He was puzzled. "My fame had escaped me. I had hardly thought I had done anything to be famous for."

"Not even surviving a year with the goblins? People have claimed fame on fewer grounds."

Haram returned to something she had said earlier. "But you said that the Gods wanted us together. Why?"

"As to that, that is the business of the Gods themselves, and I seldom question their decisions. Would you not feel safer with a companion beside you?"

"Yes, but I would as soon choose my own. Someone who is forced to join me, willy-nilly, is not likely to be the best companion when trouble comes." He turned to Darith-Gan. "Whatever the Gods say, I do not insist that you follow me unless it is your own will to do so."

Darith-Gan looked back at him, then smiled. "Now, if I had anything better to do, I might accept that offer. But as it is, if you are willing, I will accompany you. At the very least, I owe you my life."

As they made their way back to the inn, Haram spoke. "I know little more than rumours about your people. You are the first one of the Hidden Folk I have ever met."

Darith-Gan shrugged as best he could while walking with the crutch. "And that is why we are the Hidden Folk; very few know who or what we are." He flashed a quick smile at Haram.

"They say you are assassins, killers for hire."

Again came the shrug. "Some are, some are not. We are trained in the use of the bow, sword, spear, knife, and many other weapons. Some make assassination their trade, but for the most part, we are spies. If a Lord is planning to make war on his neighbour, he might hire one of us to see what preparations that neighbour is making. Or a Lord may hire us to find out whether his neighbour is planning to make war on him. Or a merchant may hire us to look into the business of a competitor. As I say, some make their living by killing, but most do not."

After a few moments, Darith-Gan asked, "And what of you? Is it true that you were a slave of the goblins for several years?"

"Only a year, if that. It is not a time I like to think of. They came upon us in the morning, by surprise, and in the battle I took a knock on the head. When I woke, the goblins were plundering the dead. At first they were about to kill me, but then the leader gave me a choice: I might die, or I might live as a slave. I chose life."

"A wise choice. While one lives, one has a possibility of altering one's condition. Dead, one can do nothing."

Three nights later, they were seated in the inn, amid the noise and the bustle. Smoke from the fire and from torches on the walls curled up around the low wooden beams of the ceilings, and the same torches cast a flickering orange light over the scene.

The landlord and his helpers were hurrying here and there; a merchant with a mule caravan, including muleteers and caravan guards, were staying the night in town, and it seemed that each and every one of them felt he should be served first.

Haram said to Darith-Gan, "Your leg appears much improved."

"Much, thank you."

"What would you think of the notion of leaving this town tomorrow?"

"Tomorrow? We could, but I am still lame, and I might hold up your travelling."

"But you may have noticed that as well as my horse, I have a pony. The pony is trained for riding, if you would be willing to ride him."

"I have no argument with that. But we will have to find riding tack for him."

"We'll do that in the morning."

In the morning, the innyard was all confusion. As the merchant was shouting orders intended to organize the confusion and set his train on the road, Haram and Darith-Gan set off for the local leather-worker's shop.

The leather-worker was a tall spare man, his red hair now turned almost completely white. He looked at Darith-Gan with distaste as the two entered his shop. "We'd like to trade this tack, built for a large horse, for something more suitable for my pony," said Haram.

"I will not deal with *him*," declared the leather-worker.

Haram leaned forward, his left hand on the counter "You may have heard," he said, striving to keep his voice conversational, "that I was a prisoner of goblins, and for a year or more forced to endure whatever cruelties they might put to me, simply because I was a human among goblins. All this has left me less tolerant of those who decide, on some whim or other, that another person is not fit to be dealt with. It has also left me subject to ungovernable rages. Such things are fine for the Wilds, of course, but not so appropriate in towns. It would be a shame if your hands were to be broken, and all your stock slashed to bits. Of course, I might be caught and hung for it, which would certainly help yourself and your family to endure the difficult times until your hands were healed again. Look at my face, fool, and tell me I'm jesting!" The last words were spoken in a sudden, sharp tone.

The leather-worker was suddenly less sure of himself. He began to show his stock, and eventually Darith-Gan had equipment for Arkhwelt.

Haram held out a silver pony. The leather-worker looked at it, then at Haram.

"Bad-tempered I may be, and hardly fit for the company of humans, but a thief I am not. New work for old is scarcely a fair trade. Take this as well."

The dusty road they followed was marked by the traces and tracks of the merchant-train which had preceded them some hours earlier.

As they travelled casually eastward, toward the town of Lisan Wer, they heard the sound of pounding hooves ahead. Over the hill and down toward them came a horse, wild-eyed, bleeding from several wounds. It evaded all their attempts to capture it, and as it rushed by, Haram saw an arrow protruding from its shoulder.

"Goblins!" he shouted.

"You're certain?"

He smiled bitterly. "If any man of Aradair could distinguish a goblin-arrow at a glance, I think I would be that man."

"What do we do, then?"

"I will not speak for you, but up ahead there are people under attack by goblins. I go to give what aid I can!"

He strung his bow and set out, noting as he did so that Darith-Gan had strung a small black bow as well. It was not over the next hill, but over the next hill after that, that they came upon the scene of the fight.

Chapter Twenty-Two

Down below, the trail wound past a willow-covered hillside. The goblins had lain in wait on the hillside and had loosed their arrows as the pack-train passed by. They had loosed more arrows into the confusion that had followed, then had rushed to the attack. Most of the guards, who had been targets of the first arrows, were down, and the attacking goblins numbered about thirty. The caravan-master, who had himself taken an arrow in the shoulder, was trying to organize the remaining guards and muleteers into some sort of defence.

Haram loosed his first arrow and was pleased to see it take a goblin through the neck. He loosed his second arrow, but it went wide, as did his third. By that time he noticed that Darith-Gan was shooting as well, short black arrows which struck with amazing accuracy.

Snorting with disgust, Haram dropped his bow, drew his sword, and urged his horse down the hill. He galloped into the midst of the goblins, striking with his sword, and felt the blow go home, but the horse carried him past before he could tell what damage he had done. He turned the horse and saw a goblin spear thrusting up at him.

He slipped that with his shield, then struck a return blow. He missed, but again the horse carried him past before he could strike again. It occurred to him that fighting on horseback was a little more difficult than he had imagined. Kicking free of the stirrups, he dropped to the ground.

A swarthy goblin came snarling at him, slashing with a sword. Haram caught the sword on his shield and stepped in with a return thrust to take the goblin in the stomach. As he pulled the sword free, he saw the others closing in around him, and suddenly a red haze descended over his eyes. As if from far away, he heard his own voice shouting in the goblin language.

Suddenly his vision cleared, and he was standing blinking in the sun, gasping for breath. Across from him, a group of men were staring at him, fear plain on their faces. His wits came back, and he remembered someone-- yes, Vorath, that was it-- warning him about the battle madness and how men might feel about it.

He looked around him; there were no live goblins in sight. Stooping, he wiped his sword on a goblin-kilt, then sheathed it.

Haram walked over to where the merchant stood with his people. They all shrank back from him, save for the merchant himself, who, making an obvious effort to master his own fear, held his ground. "May I know your name, sir," the merchant asked, "that I might better show my appreciation?"

"My name is Haram."

"Haram of the--- Yes, of course. I am Agarad, a merchant of Nori Lantam. On behalf of myself and my men, I thank you, Haram. And best we should see to your wounds immediately."

Haram looked down at himself and grimaced. "No, despite the gory mess you see, little of this blood is mine. I have only a few nicks and scratches. But yourself, Agarad, you ought to have that shoulder bound up."

"Is there nothing we can do for you, then?"

"Yes, perhaps there is. If you could get me a skin of water and a bowl, and perhaps a rag of cloth, I would appreciate it very much."

Agarad turned and walked away, calling out as he went, "Amalad! Come here, boy!"

Haram sank down slowly where he stood, sitting cross-legged on the ground.

Darith-Gan was suddenly beside him. "You left your bow behind," he said.

"I left my wits behind."

Darith-Gan was grinning at him. "Oh, indeed. There is no doubt of that. I have caught up your horse, unstrung your bow, and stowed it with the rest of your gear."

"I thank you," answered Haram.

"Ah, so formal! After all, you had other things on your mind."

Haram snorted. "I had no mind at all. And all the folk of the merchant train fear me. What of you, Darith-Gan? Do you fear me?"

"I fear you? Ought I to fear you? Is it not your enemies that ought to fear you? No, Haram, I do not fear you. At least not yet; not until I have done something to arouse your anger."

Suddenly there was a small boy in front of Haram, a boy of about nine or ten years, carrying a waterskin, a bowl, and a towel. "Sir?" he said diffidently.

"Ah," said Haram, "the water. Good. What is your name, boy?"

"Amalad, sir."

"Thank you, Amalad. Now Darith-Gan, if you would be so good as to pour about half of that waterskin over my right side, I would be grateful."

Darith-Gan complied, and then Haram, still shivering from the water, began to work his way out of his chain armour. The rings chimed softly as he dropped the chain-shirt to the grass in front of him. He looked at it. "That will have to be dried and oiled soon, ere the rust begin to work on it. Amalad, would you go to your master and ask him if he will allow you to help me for a while, then if he agrees, find some oil and come back and deal with my armour?"

"No need to ask, sir. He will let me, I am sure."

"And so am I, but out of politeness, he ought to be asked first. Go on, now."

As Amalad hurried off, Haram washed himself. "It only comes on me when I fight goblins, you know."

"What is that?"

"The battle-madness. I've fought in other times and other places, but it is only when I fight goblins that the battle-madness comes. And not always then, either."

"However that might be, it has served you well. Only some five or so of the goblins escaped. At first they thought you easy prey, then when they discovered their mistake and began to try to escape you, it was too late."

Haram shivered, and it was only due in part to the cold water. "I killed very many, then?"

"Yes, you did. Sufficient to be sure that all the men of the caravan will walk carefully around you."

"I hardly needed that. Respect is one thing, fear quite another."

Amalad was back then, with assurances that his master had given him permission to do whatever Haram might require of him. As he watched the boy go to work, Haram asked, "What did you do when the goblins attacked, Amalad?"

The boy reddened. "Dived under a bush," he muttered.

"Now that is good sense for you," said Haram. Then, seeing the look on the boy's face, he said, "No, I mean that. Some boys of your age might think it necessary that they stand up to goblins with their bare hands, and die for it. A good part of the trade of a fighter is in knowing when not to fight. Am I not correct, Darith-Gan?"

"You are quite correct." But then Darith-Gan leaned down and whispered, "One who rides full-tilt into three dozen goblins by himself ought not perhaps to preach caution to others."

Haram laughed.

While Haram was washing, Darith-Gan collected the spoil from the goblins. He brought back three gold crowns, twenty silver ponies, another six silver coins of other sorts, and a number of copper ones. There were also three gems which appeared to be valuable. "I thought it not worth the bother to collect goblin-weapons or armour," he said on his return.

"No, not unless there was some particularly decorative weapon that we might sell to some townsman as the sword of a goblin-chief."

"Is that not a trifle dishonest?"

"Well, if I were to begin by saying that this was truly the sword of a goblin-chief, it might be. But if I say the truth, 'very few goblins own a weapon such as this,' and let the prospective buyer draw his own conclusions, then I have cheated no one. As it is, it is hardly worth the bother of taking such a weapon along."

A little later, the master of the caravan approached Haram once more. "What reward do you ask for your assistance?"

Haram shrugged. "No reward is necessary, Master. Perhaps you would let us travel with you so far as Sandaris, if you are going that way."

"Sandaris? Yes, we go that far, but surely you will want more than our company?"

"Master Agarad, we took enough from the goblins to maintain ourselves for several weeks. But if you would do more, you might seek for news of a Venturer, a swordswoman named Terrial. If you hear of her, send word to me through an inn at Ifan Sor owned by a man named Vorath."

"A swordswoman named Terrial? Yes, I can seek news of her. If I should meet her personally, is there a message?"

"Only that Haram sends his regards, and if she wishes to send a message to me, she may send it to the same place, Vorath's inn at Ifan Sor."

At the end of several uneventful days, they were resting in Sandaris. Darith-Gan asked Haram, "Where are we bound from here?"

"I am bound southward to Rathahan, then back west once more to Yath Hawr. You needn't accompany me all the way."

"Ah," said Darith-Gan with a grin, "but you recall what Old Kora said? If I desert you now, what might happen to me? And you did save my life."

"And I may not be safe to travel with. The god Drauha has a grudge against me."

"Indeed?"

"Indeed. Twice I have fought men bearing his symbol, who sought me out to kill me. I have been warned as well, by one who ought to know, that there may be hired killers out for my blood, men who also serve the God of Lies, but who will not approach me openly. And if you are too near, you may suffer as well."

"Ah, but if hired killers are seeking you, would it not be a help to you to have one by your side who knows many of the tricks of the trade?"

"I had thought that you denied being an assassin."

"No, I didn't deny it. Though truth to say, I have killed no one for hire as yet, only using my weapons in self-defence, which is not assassination. And I am trained in all the tricks, as I have said."

"Well, if you wish to come, I will be glad of the company." And as he said that, Haram realized he was indeed very glad for the company.

So they rode south to Rathahan, then turned west. Without incident, they rode through Ninantha, then the long distance to the great wood, and the town of Lisan Hawr, down to Sandan Hawr, then northward again to Yath Hawr. As they went, Darith-Gan aided Haram in the evenings to practice his sword-work, and taught him as well a few tricks regarding the use of the dagger and staff.

On the evening before they finally arrived at Yath Hawr, Darith-Gan asked, "Do you hope that by always moving, you will evade those who seek you?"

Haram frowned, then said, "I hadn't thought of it in that light, but belike it will serve to do that as well. No, I continue to travel for the reason that I have yet to find a place where I would like to stay."

"So. If I were a killer seeking the life of one who was constantly travelling, I would probably not follow him from hither to yon, unless I knew that I was a day or less behind him. Rather, I would wait in a city, for such a traveller would almost certainly come to a city, eventually."

"Do you suggest that I should avoid the cities, then?"

"No, not entirely. But I would suggest that you walk more warily in the cities than elsewhere."

Their first night in Yath Hawr was uneventful. They found an inn, one frequented by Venturers, and engaged rooms. That done, they approached the Venturers in the common room, drinking ale with them, and seeking any news. There was a good deal of news, of people who had gotten rich by fighting goblins, ogres, trolls, dragons, gryphons, and the like, of people who had been killed in fighting goblins, ogres, trolls, dragons, gryphons, and the like, of people who had gone seeking treasure and fallen afoul of the Elves, and much more.

One of the of the crew, a pop-eyed little fellow, more than a little drunk, said that he'd "heard of this Haram Grim-face, who's being hunted by killers sent by Draumaha, the God of Lies, out of Shondakar, but this Haram dispatches any that find him with one or two blows of his sword."

A dark-faced Rahasin nudged Haram. "Your name's Haram, is it not? Are you the one he's talking about?"

Haram laughed. "Do I look so fearsome, then?"

There was no word of a swordswoman named Terrial.

The second night was much the same; some of the company of the previous night were still there, while others had left, and new ones had taken their places. There was talk of Zilva's band. "I hear they come back out of Trethision, in quite a big rush," said one broad-chested red-faced swordsman. "but I hear they brought back some treasure. Four sacks, it was, big as my head, each of them, stuffed with silver and gold and jewels!"

"Oh, they brought back gold and silver all right." Responded a bandy-legged Shondakranian, "But that was the least of it. Besides the rest, they brought back some of this magical works the Elves are so famous for. They've got a wand that can blast an enemy to a cinder in the wink of an eye."

"I heard it was a bow that never misses its mark," declared a sender man from the Northeast Coast, showing evidence of some Rahasin ancestry in his curly dark hair.

"Nonsense!" declared a blunt-spoken southerner, his fair hair flashing in the torchlight. "They got a flute that, if you play it right, can make people or animals fall asleep, or even enchant them to do your will."

Discussion raged hot and heavy over this topic, and slipped into the topic of what might be the use of a magic wand that blasted people to cinders. If it also destroyed anything valuable they might be carrying?

Haram contented himself with listening to the discussion, and eventually he and Darith-Gan retired to their chamber for the night.

That night, Haram was suddenly awakened to the sounds of movement in the room. He was reaching for his sword when he heard a blow on flesh, then something clattered to the floor. A moment later Darith-Gan's voice said, "Haram? Would you make a light?"

Chapter Twenty-Three

Haram lighted a candle and looked around. On the floor was the body of a slightly built man, clad in black from head to foot. Near his hand was a short dagger. Darith-Gan was kneeling over him, a bloody dagger in his own hand. He wiped his dagger on the man's jacket, then looked up at Haram.

"So, now you have saved my life, Darith-Gan. I warned you it that would be dangerous travelling with me."

His companion rose from the floor and sat on his bed. "I fear that I am in danger, whether I travel with you or alone. I suppose the time has come to tell the full truth.

"Some time back, the _harnasp_ of Shab-nazdig put two gold coins in my hand, with the promise of more if I should bring back your head. He asked me if I would swear allegiance to Drauha, but I declined, and went my way. I swear to you that when I approached you first, all I saw was a young man with a full wallet. When I *did* find out who you were, it was too late. I have been riding with you for some weeks, and you are still alive. If that word has not yet reached Shab-nazdig, it is only a matter of a week or two. After that, there will be a price on my head as well."

Haram frowned. "This fellow," he indicated the dead man, "is he one of the Hidden Folk?"

"I believe so. You needn't worry; the brotherhood of the Hidden Folk is not so tight-knit as all that. It could not be, do you see? If one man is hired to protect the secrets of a lord, and another is hired to uncover those secrets, someone is likely to die. Oh, members of the brotherhood who are not under hire at any time might possibly give aid to another brother in need, if they make some private agreement between themselves.

"No, I've made myself your friend, and that will follow me whether I continue to travel with you or not."

"Then I suppose that we'd best continue to ride together, that each might watch the other's back."

Darith-Gan grinned. "I suppose that's the only answer. I hope you are not angry with me for keeping all this from you."

"How should I be angry? Didn't you save my life just now?" Then, to change the subject, he asked, "And what of this fellow? What shall we do with him?"

"He came in at the window. If we dump him back out the window, and deny all knowledge of him, that should serve."

"So. Will you take his head or his feet?"

While they were disposing of the body, Haram noticed a small grappling-hook lodged in the window-sill. It was attached to a thin rod, which dangled down toward the street. "Look at this!"

"Ah, so this is how he came in. A very useful tool." Darith-Gan drew the rod in, giving a careful twist at certain places to break it down into several sections, each no longer than his arm. "You see, one may toss a hook up to a window-sill, but if someone within that room is awake, or even merely a light sleeper, they may be alerted by the noise it makes. This way one places the hook carefully, and can pull oneself up the rod much as one would use a rope. Very useful. And this tool by itself would mark the fellow as one of the Hidden Folk; it is the sort of thing we use."

They left early the next day, riding out the north gate. They made no effort to hide their going. "After all," said Darith-Gan, "if anyone wishes to track us, it won't be difficult to find people to say which way we have gone."

However, once they had gotten out of sight of the city, they left the road and travelled east, straight into the Vorath Howr, the Great Forest. They carefully chose a place to leave the road, going over hard ground, so that the tracks of the horses might be less easily seen.

"It depends," said Haram, "on who it is that follows us. A skilled tracker would still be able to find our trail, even here. We must not depend on such tricks as this to throw them off the scent."

"Will we go into the Vorath Howr, then?"

"Yes, we will strike the road on the far side of the forest."

"I hope it will be safe. There are strange things said of that wood."

"Strange things? What manner of strange things?"

"It is said, for instance, that the deeper parts of the wood are Elven territory, places where the world of the Elves marches closely with the world of men, and that it may not be safe to trespass there casually."

"Ah." Haram considered this for a little, then said, "We shall try to move across without giving offence to any. We can also hope that the tales of the Forest will convince our pursuers that we would not go that way either."

Darith-Gan frowned. "I don't like it."

"There is some risk, no doubt. But it ought to throw our pursuers off the track, which would be to our benefit."

It seemed at first a forest like any other. There were trees, large old trees which lifted mighty branches toward the sky; there was underbrush, willows, thorns, and the like, and here and there a trail made by animals of some sort. It was these trails which made it possible for the travellers to go through, for the brush was otherwise too thick to allow passage.

During the first day, nothing untoward happened. In the evening, however, after they had lit their fire and eaten supper, they heard a faint and far-off chiming of bells.

Darith-Gan heard it first, and said, "Hush! Do you hear that?"

"What?"

"There are bells ringing far away. Do you hear them?"

Haram listened carefully. "Yes, I can hear them now. What are they?"

Darith-Gan shrugged, but his expression belied his casual manner. "I don't know. They seem far away, in any case."

From time to time that evening, they continued to hear the bells, but the sound never drew nearer. When they had eaten, they spent a while practising with their swords, then prepared for bed. Suddenly Haram noticed something.

"Look!" He pointed at a tree. Perched up in the branches was a manlike figure. He was squatting down, and his knobby knees were higher than his head. His long skinny arms were stretched out to the sides, as though for balance, and the hands rested lightly on the tough bark of the old bough. He was naked, save for some sort of wrapping round his loins, and he did not seem to be armed. He had thick dark hair growing in a bunch on his head, and his eyes shone in the light of the dying fire. His long, pointed ears twitched back and forth rapidly. He said nothing.

Haram stood up. "Hail!" he called. "A good evening to you!"

The ears twitched again, and the long arms moved, and suddenly he was gone. Haram moved toward the tree; Darith-Gan stepped up and took his arm. "Wait!"

"Where did it go?"

"Up higher into the tree and away, I believe. And there may be more of his sort waiting out in the darkness for us."

"You are right. And I believe that it would be wise for us to take turns keeping watch tonight."

Despite the watch they kept taking turns sleeping, they did not see the strange being again that night.

But the next day. About noon, as they were riding along a narrow animal trail through the deep woods, Haram looked up suddenly to see the spindly creature, again seated in a tree and watching them ride by. He pointed it out to Darith-Gan, and they watched it warily as they rode. Its face seemed utterly without expression, though it seemed to be more than a mere animal. Suddenly, just as it had done the previous night, it vanished.

From time to time it would reappear along their track as they went, always squatting somewhere. It seemed to favour the boughs of trees, though it also showed itself occasionally under a bush, and once atop an old moss-covered rock.

It never said a word, only watched them with pale yellow eyes as they rode by.

It was noon of the day after that they met the Elves. As they were riding along a game-trail, two men stepped out in front of them. The men were tall and slender, fair-skinned, with yellow braided hair hanging down their backs. They had bows and arrows slung behind them; they wore well-kept chain-mail and helmets, with long swords at their belts. Over all they wore grey cloaks, and in their hands they held sturdy spears, which they presented toward the travellers.

The one on the right spoke first, in a language which Haram did not understand. He looked at Darith-Gan, who said "They are Elves, and they are asking what we do here."

"You understand their language?"

"A little."

"Then speak to them and explain our intentions."

Darith-Gan spoke, a little stumblingly, in the same language as the Elves, who did not seem to relax a whit at hearing their tongue spoken.

The Elf-spokesman listened to Darith-Gan's speech, then answered in the language of Aradair, though strangely accented. "You have chosen an ill time to be wandering in these lands. There is trouble abroad, and I myself cannot give you permission to pass through. That is the province of my commander."

"Can you take us to him, then?"

"No, I cannot leave my post here. But I can send a pair of my warriors to guide you." He put two fingers in his mouth and whistled, and a dozen or so Elves, armed and armoured much as he and his companion, stepped out of the brush along the trail.

The leader of the band spoke briefly in his own language, and two of the band stood forth. "They will take you to the commander. And be careful that you do not stray from the trail as they guide you, for as I said, these are perilous times. If they think you are trying to escape, they will slay you."

"Escape? No, we wish only to pass through the woods in peace. If it must be that we must seek permission, then permission we will seek."

So off they went, with one of the Elves going on ahead, and one bringing up the rear. The Elf who led them stepped so lightly and quietly that Haram could neither hear the sound of his footsteps, nor see any place where his footsteps had disturbed the ground.

He tried conversing with the fellow leading them, but the Elf only turned and spoke brusquely to him in Elvish. "He says that he does not speak your language," said Darith-Gan, "and from his tone, I think he does not wish to speak to you at all."

So they continued to ride on in silence. A little while later they saw again the gangly creature which had showed itself beside their path previously. The Elf at the rear saw it as well, and brought it to the attention of the one in the lead. The leader also glanced at it, and said something in return. Haram looked at Darith-Gan, who shrugged.

"A word I don't know. Probably a name, by the sound of it. And I think it best not to ask too many questions."

The leader turned and spoke briefly and brusquely again. Darith-Gan translated, "He

259

says that this is no country for idle chatter, and he will thank us to keep our mouths shut." Haram nodded.

So they travelled on in silence for a ways further, coming at last into a large clearing. In the center of the clearing there was a large tent, done in red and gold. Its front flap was open, and in front of that flap was a simple wooden table. At that table, with his back to the tent, sat an Elf, working over what seemed to be lists and maps.

The Elf in front led them forward toward the tent, and suddenly other Elves appeared before and around them. The Elf ahead of them spoke briefly, and Haram noticed that he was as brusque with his own kind as he had been with the travellers under his escort.

Thus they came to the tent, the two Elves, Haram, Darith-Gan, and several curious Elves at a little more distance. The Elf at the table looked up, and the leader of their escort spoke to him.

"This must be the commander;" thought Haram, "this fellow is being polite to him."

And so it seemed, for the Elf at the table dismissed the two escorts with a few words, then looked up at the two travellers. Haram swung down from his horse, and saw that Darith-Gan had done the same thing. He looked at the commander. This was an older Elf, and his dress was somewhat more elaborate than that of the others. His chain-armour had small golden flowers decorating the shoulders and the chest, and his sword had a slightly more ornate hilt. He wore no cloak, but he had hose of a dark brown, such that if he were to put on one of the grey cloaks, he would easily be able to disappear in the forest. His head was bare, and it was clear that he was an elder, for his brow was weathered and wrinkled.

"I am Kyth-Woldan, and I command here. Who are you, and what are you doing in these parts?" he demanded.

"My name is Haram, and my companion is Darith-Gan. We are passing through the wood, and mean no harm to anyone."

"Passing through?" There was scepticism in the eyes of the old Elf. "Why do you pass through? Do not men usually avoid passing through this part of the wood?"

"Yes, so they do, and that is a part of the reason why we wish to pass through. We are being pursued, and hope thus to discourage the pursuit."

"You are fugitives, then? You do not come to claim some patrimony for your comrade?"

"No, not at all!"

A hint of laughter showed in the eyes of the old Elf. "No, I suppose not. And you did not even think that your companion would be recognized for what he is, and thus perhaps give you free passage through our land?"

Darith-Gan could hold his peace no longer. "No, not at all! My father stayed long enough with my mother to get a child on her, then left," he said bitterly. "The tale was that he could not take her with him immediately as there was some sort of contention in Elf country. But then we all know that many women have been deluded by such stories through the ages, and many will be in ages to come. I have no feeling that anything is owed to me by any Elf, whoever he might be."

"And what might your father's name be?"

"Lyssar-Gan was the name he gave to my mother."

"Lyssar-Gan?" mused the commander. "Yes, there is a tale behind that. But we have little time to converse here; as you may have noticed, we are at war. The question now is what to do with the pair of you. We cannot allow you to wander freely."

"We are prisoners, then?" asked Haram.

The commander shook his head. "That is one choice. I would prefer not to make you prisoners, though. Would you consent to be guests, staying in a comfortable tent I shall provide for you, as well-fed as can be managed in these times, with your weapons and equipment with you? This would last for a day, or two days at the most, after which time you will be free to go your way. The alternative to that is that we take your weapons away and put you in bonds until it is safe to decide what ought to be done with you."

Haram glanced at Darith-Gan, then looked back at Kyth-Woldan. "I will not presume to speak for the both of us, but for myself I will accept the status of guest, so long as it does not last for an unconscionable length of time."

"I will agree to that as well," said Darith-Gan.

Kyth-Woldan nodded. "Very well, then. I expect matters to be settled in a day's time, three at the most. At that time I will give all the explanations I can give."

By nightfall, Haram was almost sorry he had given his word so easily. To be sure, they were still granted their arms and armour, the food was adequate, and the tent was comfortable enough. But they were not permitted to go more than a spear-shaft length from its front entrance, and even to go outside at all was frowned on. The guards were under orders to converse with them as little as possible; they answered not at all when Haram spoke to them, and they answered tersely when Darith-Gan spoke in Elvish. They were not prisoners, but for all Haram could see, they might as well be.

He was wakened in the middle of the night by shouting and clashing of arms.

Chapter Twenty-Four

The tent was not completely dark. There was sufficient moonlight coming in through the open front flap that Haram could see that Darith-Gan was also awake. Darith-Gan went to the opening and spoke to the guard, who responded brusquely. Darith-Gan turned to Haram and said, "I asked what was happening. He said that the camp is being attacked, and that I should get back inside."

Haram nodded. "Whoever is attacking," he said, "will they be able to tell that we're only guests here? I think it would be best if we were to dress and arm ourselves."

The sound of battle rapidly grew closer, and there was much shouting in Elvish as the defenders rallied themselves. Several times while the two were dressing, arrows tore through the walls of the tent.

When they were ready, Haram went to the front of the tent and peered out carefully. The battle had come to within three or four spear-lengths of the tent. The Elves had formed a line which stretched, in a wavy fashion, across the clearing. A little in front of the tent, Kyth-Wolden and his guard held the center of the line, under the standard of the blue swan on a white field. On the far side of the line were the enemy, leaping and hammering against that line...

"Goblins!" said Haram.

But these were not the goblins who wandered throughout Aradair in ragged makeshift bands, armed and armoured with whatever they could find. These were larger, and grouped according to the armour they wore. There was a small group that wore plate armour, then another contingent, perhaps a quarter of the total number, who wore chain-mail. On the flanks of these were contingents in scale armour, studded leather, leather, or merely padded cloth jackets.

"The Elves are hard-pressed. Perhaps we should join them."

"Kyth-Wolden may not thank us."

"On the other hand, if they are beaten, as they might well be, we are dead. Best we lend our aid while it will yet do some good." It was only afterward that Haram realized he had never even thought of running away.

"If you go, then so will I."

Haram leaped out, past the guard, whose attention was all on the battle, and rushed forward. Even as he moved, he saw the Elves' standard fall. In the shouting, shrieking, hammering din, it was not possible to say truly that the goblin-noise redoubled at that sight, but it seemed that they flung themselves more wildly at the center of the line.

Then Haram was there, confronted by a goblin-chief near as tall as a man, wearing plate-armour and swinging a large mace in both hands. The mace swung right to left; Haram swayed back out of range, and as the weight carried the goblin's upper body nigh halfway round, Haram struck.

The goblin went down; others were coming up to take his place, though, and Haram took a hard blow on his shield, and returned it. Then a red haze descended over his eyes, and he heard himself shouting in the goblin-tongue.

Then the sun was rising and Haram was leaning against a tree, his sword hanging down at his right side. He was panting, and around him he could see some eight or ten dead goblins. There was a throbbing pain in his chest, and he looked down. There was a large rent in his armour, and blood was pouring forth.

'So,' he thought, 'one is not immune to wounds while battle-mad.' Then a feeling of weakness came over him. Suddenly Darith-Gan was beside him, saying something.

'So this is how it is to die,' thought Haram. Consciousness left him.

Haram woke again, lying in a soft bed, looking toward the flap of a tent, through which sunlight poured. He seemed to recall half-waking a time or two before, once as his wound was being dressed, then again late at night, to see the worried face of Darith-Gan leaning over him. He looked around. It was a large tent, and there were several other beds besides his, each one with a wounded Elf in it.

There was another Elf, a Healer, checking the bandages on each of the patients. Haram was aware of a great hunger, and he opened his mouth to call to the Healer, to ask for something to eat.

He must have fallen asleep, for suddenly it was twilight, and the Healer was gone, and he was still hungry. He did not go to sleep immediately this time, but lay there wide awake for a while.

There was a movement at the door of the tent, and he looked. Darith-Gan walked in, looked around, and came to Haram's bed. "So you are back with us, then?" He was smiling as he spoke, but he did not feel so light of heart as his words made out.

Haram tried to speak, but his mouth and throat were so dry that all he could manage was a weak croaking sound. Darith-Gan immediately took up a cup from beside the bed, filled it from a water-bucket beside the door of the tent, and brought it back. After Haram had drunk a little, he was able to speak at last. "The battle was won, then?"

"Oh, yes, the battle was won. Just about the time you hurled yourself against the goblins, more forces of Elves were coming out of the trees. How do you feel?"

"Very well, save for what seems to be a hole in my chest. I thought I was about to die."

"They said that you were very near to it. Some of the Elven Healers used some powerful spells on you, I understand."

"I suppose. I am hungry, Darith-Gan. Do you think you could steal a crust of bread for me?"

"I'll do what I can. I'll be right back."

He went out the door of the tent and was gone for some time. When he finally returned, he was carrying a bowl in his hands. "Broth," he said, a little apologetically. "The Healers have said that you should not try to eat anything solid just yet. You've been unconscious off and on for three days, and they are concerned as to whether or not your stomach is able to stand it." "Well, broth will have to do, then." And he found indeed that he was weaker than he thought, for he could not pull himself into a sitting position. Darith-Gan put a hand under his head and lifted it sufficiently for him to drink down the broth. Despite his hunger, there was a moment when he thought perhaps he might not be able to keep it down, but in the end, his stomach settled itself.

"Kyth-Wolden wishes to speak to you when you are well enough. I'll tell him to come in the morning."

"Fine. I doubt that I will be going anywhere soon."

After a few moments, Haram closed his eyes. When he opened them again, it was morning and Darith-Gan was still there.

"You have been here all night?" he asked.

"Me? No, not at all! I went and slept, then came back this morning!" But his eyes said that he had not slept well. "Are you feeling better this morning?"

"Yes, I am," said Haram, and as he said it he realized with surprise how much better he was feeling than he had the previous day.

Darith-Gan nodded. "The Healers said that they had used powerful spells on you, because of the nature of your wound. They said that without the spells, you might well have died, and that the spells would continue to work on you for some days yet. And now, if you wish, I will go find some food for you."

"Yes, if you would." Then Darith-Gan was gone, and Haram lay there waiting. He wondered if he ought to get out of bed, and as he was wondering about that, the Healer came in. The Healer was an old Elf with a long face, and he moved from bed to bed in the tent, looking at bandages, feeling wounds with his palm, and inspecting them all closely. Occasionally he would say a word or two, but at the first he was too far away for Haram to hear. When he came closer, Haram realized the words were in Elvish, so he would not be able to understand them in any case.

When he came to Haram, the Elf peered at him closely, then put a palm on his chest at the site of the wound. Haram felt a tickling which seemed to begin deep in his chest and work its way out, then the old Healer removed his hand and looked at his patient. He muttered something in Elvish, and was about to leave when Haram said, "Sir, do you think it would be well for me to get out of bed yet?"

"Eh? What? Oh, you do not understand our language, then?" The Elf himself spoke the language of Aradair without fault, save for a slight musical cadence. "Ah, yes. Probably you will be well enough to get up later today. But when you *do* get up, see that you do not work too hard. You have been grievously wounded, and your body has been working hard to repair its hurts."

"Thank you, I shall remember."

The Elf continued to stand there for a moment, his face melancholy, then he turned and walked out of the tent. As he went, he was muttering under his breath, in Elvish. Darith-Gan, coming in, glanced at him in startlement.

Coming over to Haram's bed, he said, "You are fortunate. As well as the broth, they are allowing you a small piece of bread this morning. Did he say aught to you?" He jerked a thumb in the direction of the tent door where the healer had just left.

Between sips of the broth, Haram recounted what had passed between himself and the Healer. As he finished, he could see that Darith-Gan was near to laughter. "What is it, then? What is so amusing?"

"It is just what the Healer was saying when he left. *'Warriors!'* he said, *'So they all promise, and yet none of them do.'*"

Haram himself laughed at that, but at that moment, another figure appeared in the tent doorway. It was Kyth-Wolden himself, and he looked up and down the rows of wounded, then walked over to where Haram lay.

"So you could not keep to your bargain," he said. But he was smiling as he said it.

Haram attempted to shrug, but found that it was difficult to do while lying down. "You were hard-pressed," he said, "and as I told my comrade at the time, better we should lend our aid while it was still of some use."

"You credit me with so little skill as a commander, then? We were the bait for an ambush, you see. I had already given the signal, and at the time you were rushing into the thick of the goblins, screaming in their own language, the trap was closing."

"And we were to guess at all this? You told us nothing, Commander, and we had to deal with matters as we saw them."

Kyth-Wolden's expression turned grave. "And yet we could hardly trust you, could we? You are strangers wandering in our land, and your companion has a grudge against at least one Elf; how far does that grudge extend to other Elves? We could not know. We could only try to keep you out of our way.

"And I will admit that the enemy came at us a little by surprise; there are more ways of travelling in this land than by road or trail. And thus it was that the fighting took place near enough to your tent for you even to see it, let alone take part in it.

"And also, you came at the moment when our standard was falling, and that might have turned the battle, or at least made our ambush less effective; for that I owe you something."

Haram shook his head. "I feel no debt, Commander. I have my own reasons for disliking goblins."

The Elf nodded. "So I would guess. There must be a tale behind that, and the way you speak the goblin language. By the way, in a battle between goblins and Elves, it may not be a wise notion to be heard shouting in the goblin language; there are some who might misunderstand."

Haram smiled. "Even when I am fighting goblins myself?"

"Even then. But the Healer made me promise that I would not weary you with my presence. He also said that you probably would be up and about this afternoon. If that is the case, I would appreciate it if you would come to my tent then to talk further."

"I will be happy to."

Chapter Twenty-Five

That afternoon the Healer came in again, inspected Haram, and said, "There is no more need for you to lie in bed here. Go carefully for the next day or so. Do not tire yourself too much. And you will find that you are very hungry; eat as much as you can. The spells are helping to heal you, but they will require food to rebuild your body."

Haram was in the midst of thanking him for his care when the Healer turned and walked away to the next patient in line. Haram looked up at Darith-Gan, who smiled. "You're well and no longer need his care, so he wastes no more time on you, but goes to see to those who still need him."

That afternoon, the two of them went to the tent of Kyth-Wolden. The Commander had set out a pair of chairs for them, and invited them to sit. He poured a cup of wine for each, waited until they had all had a sip, then spoke. "We have many things to speak of," he said, "but I think that I would like to begin by telling what I know of the tale of Lyssar-Gan.

"When he was called back to his home, it was indeed due to a contention over inheritance. He considered bringing your mother, but felt that it would be unwise to take her into such a situation. I will not trouble you with the whole story of what happened. Since you know none of those involved, it would mean little to you.

"But your father strove with all that was in him to find an amicable settlement to the contention, and when none was to be found, he joined the others in arms. In one of the many skirmishes between the parties, he was slain."

Kyth-Wolden paused for a time then, thinking. "Even so, you were not abandoned altogether. Your father's close companions watched over you as you grew. They could not take you into Elf-country, of course, since your arrival would be seen as a renewal of the struggle over the inheritance, and they knew that they had not the strength for such a contest. They did what they could, though, to see that you were safe and cared for. Did you never notice as a child that most times when your mother did any work for Elves, she received higher pay than usual?

"Oh, there were things that could not be prevented, neighbours causing trouble and so on, but be sure that if there had ever come a time when your lives were in danger, you would have had help.

"There was some consternation when you left home and began your apprenticeship; how far did the protection extend which was offered in your father's name? It was eventually decided that upon your leaving home the protection would lapse, save for whatever courtesy might be extended to you by your father's kin whenever you should chance to meet. Your mother, however, is still protected.

"You may think of travelling into the Elven Lands to claim your father's inheritance. I would advise against it; the folk who watched over you during the years since might feel bound to join you, but the outcome of the struggle would still be the same, and however right your cause, you could look for little help in Elfland. Most would wish only to be left in peace and would be loth to have old quarrels dragged up again."

Again he paused, and Darith-Gan only nodded, saying nothing. Kyth-Wolden spoke again. "I tell you all this because I think it fair that you should know, that you should not harbour secret animosity toward your father. And also because I wish to reward you, and the reward I would give requires you to realize your status. I know you do not think your deeds worthy of reward, but you risked yourself to give help when you thought it was needed, and I would give you a reward which fits the thought and the deed."

He leaned down and picked something up from behind the table, and set it on the table's top. It was an arm-ring wrought in copper, a succession of small leaping dolphins attached nose to tail. "It is made of copper, the less to attract the attention of thieves and so on, but it is still valuable for all that. This is a sign which will make you free of all the Elven Lands, should you choose to travel there. Come visit us sometime, use the arm-ring and my name if you are ever challenged, and learn something of your father's people."

He took the arm-ring and fastened it on Darith-Gan's upper arm, then returned to his seat. He turned his eyes to Haram. From beside his chair, he picked up a small silver horn, which he set on the table. "It is silver, but it is small enough that you ought to be able to keep it out of sight. If you sound it in need, the Elven Folk who are near will come to your aid."

"A worthy sentiment," answered Haram, "but I'm not likely to travel into the Elven Lands."

"Ah, is that what you think, that I would give you a gift of so little use? No, you do not know how and where the Elven Folk travel! I tell you, even should you sound the horn in the midst of Ifan Sor itself, you would find Elves coming to your aid!"

"Truly? Then this is a reward beyond all proportion to the deed, Kyth-Wolden! For the sake of one battle in which I gave aid where none was desired or needed, you would give me this?"

"For the fact that you were willing to give aid in a battle which was none of yours, and which you yourself said looked lost, I honour you. Will you take it?"

"Yes, I'll take it, though I hope I never find cause to use it. I thank you, Kyth-Wolden."

"No, no," protested the Elf, smiling. "It is I who give you this gift in thanks!"

After Haram had taken the horn, Kyth-Wolden refilled their cups, then settled back. "Now, a matter of my own curiosity. Tell me how it is that you speak the goblin language."

So Haram told the tale, finding that the passage of time had made it easier to speak of. He still felt his throat constrict when he spoke of the death of Orizd's band, and that he merely glossed over his own captivity among the goblins in two sentences, but he got through it well enough. When it was done, Kyth-Wolden was looking at him in admiration.

"Now this is a tale, indeed! You lived with goblins for a year, and survived! And I suppose it is no wonder that you hate goblins so."

"However that may be, I have found that the battle-madness comes on me only when I am fighting goblins, and indeed not every time."

"I hope not. You almost died of it this time. And I have another thing to ask; in all this, you have not explained who it is that you are fleeing from, that you would trespass in these woods."

So Haram found himself telling the story of the rescue of Terrial and the pursuit by the God of Lies, up to the present time. Again the Elf-lord was amazed. "So much adventure in so short a life! Beware, Haram! You may tempt fate too much."

"I do not seek these adventures, Kyth-Wolden. And what can I do now? I live as quiet a life as I can, but still these folk pursue me. What can I do about that?"

Kyth-Wolden nodded. "I would not presume to give you advice, but it seems to me that at some time you are going to have to face the one who pursues you."

"It is not one, but many who pursue me."

"No, no, I mean not the folk paid to seek you out, but Drauha himself."

"I should seek a conclusion with Drauha? A man fight against a god? He would squash me like an ant."

Kyth-Wolden shrugged. "As to that, I cannot say. The relations of men to their gods are not a thing that Elves concern themselves with to any degree. All I can say is that I have a feeling that sooner or later, this must be done."

They stayed in the camp of the Elves for another night, and in the morning, they were on their way. It was a long journey to the city called Nori Lantam, though it would have been longer had they travelled by way of the road. Instead, they cut across from Rathahan to Dan, then followed the road southeastward through Masol to the city.

At Nori Lantam, on the advice of Darith-Gan, they did not stay at an inn frequented by Venturers. "Those who pursued us from Yath Hawr may have been put off the scent by our trip through the woods, but there will be others who may have stayed in this city in case we come this way. And if they're here, they'll likely be watching just those sorts of inns."

It was even with some misgivings that he went with Haram in the evenings to seek out Venturers to discover what news might be had. "If they're watching the inns, they'll very likely see you whether you come in only for an evening, or whether you stay the night."

"How many are they likely to be?"

"In one city? Perhaps a dozen, perhaps twenty."

"And in those numbers, how will they watch every inn? Even if they do see us, will they attack immediately, or will they go to find their companions? After all, we have not proven easy to kill so far, have we?"

"Yes, I suppose you're right." But it was clear from his tone that Darith-Gan did not like the situation at all.

"Look, I have a task to do, and it will be impossible to do that task if I'm going to spend all my time hiding from assassins. If you will help me and watch my back, I'll be as careful as I can, but I won't let the minions of the God of Lies prevent me from doing my work."

So Darith-Gan followed Haram, with some misgivings, to seek out what news was to be had regarding Terrial.

At the start, they discovered nothing. No one had even heard of Terrial. In the second inn they visited, however, there was a man who claimed to know her. He was a grizzled old fellow, with a double-bladed axe close by his right side and a scar running down his face across the right eye. "Yes," he said, "I know

Terrial. With a small band she was, though I don't know the leader. They've gone across to Rahasin, some town named Shilka in the province of Lammasitu. They've got a contract to fight Grizalak in the hinterland. I was asked to come along as well, but I've fought Grizalak before, and I want no more of them. Look like rock-lizards grown huge, they do, and they fight like fiends."

"How long ago did the band leave?"

"How long? Six weeks, I think."

And in response to questions about Zilva's band, he said, "Yes, I've heard of them. They went up to Elven country seeking treasure, and only one of them came back. A fellow named Merrit, I hear, and he brought back a magic sword with him."

"No!" objected another. "It was a magic ring to increase his strength!"

Another spoke up. "No, neither of those! It was a pair of magic gauntlets!"

"But Merritt did return, for certain?"

"Oh, for certain," said the man who had spoken of magic gauntlets. "He's been seen here and there, though I'd suggest he is more bandit than Venturer these days."

"Is there any word as to what happened to the rest of his band?"

"I'd wager that Merritt knows more of that than he wants to admit. If I were to go on a Venture with him, Tran and Viron portend, I'd be sure to sleep lightly and walk carefully, particularly if we found any wealth more than a couple of bent coppers."

Haram would have liked to protest that his boyhood friend could not have sunk so low, but he remembered too well when Merritt had gone off to join Saradon, and further, Saradon's reticence about Merritt's reasons for leaving *his* band.

As they strolled off to another inn, Darith-Gan asked, "Do we go to Rahasin to seek her?"

This brought Haram's mind back to the real reason for his present wanderings, Terrial.

"I suppose we must, unless we hear some more recent word of her whereabouts."

"And what shall we do for money?" asked Darith-Gan. Haram's purse had been full when he had started out from Ifan Sor so long ago, and even at Yath Hawr, he had been well supplied. By now, however, much of his money was spent.

Haram shrugged. "At the very worst, we could go back to Ifan Sor and refill my purse. But perhaps we could work our way across; there may well be merchants in harbour willing to hire guards for a voyage. We'll manage it somehow."

As the last stop of the evening, they chose the Sleeping Dwarf inn. This one was much favoured by Venturers, and would most likely be under close watch by the servants of the God of Lies. But Haram promised they would go in and come out quickly, so Darith-Gan agreed.

They stepped into the common room and looked around. Over in a corner, with a half-dozen young and rough-looking fellows, sat Merrit!

Chapter Twenty-Six

Haram paused a moment. He had been asking for news of Merrit mostly out of curiosity, and he had no idea what, if anything, he had to say to the companion with whom he had departed Ifan Sor back then. *'Tran and Viron! Was it only a bare handful of years ago? And everything and everyone is altered out of all recognition!'*

Darith-Gan was beside him asking anxiously, "What is it, Haram? Is there someone here you know?"

But before Haram could reply, there was a stir behind him and a voice called, "Ho, there! Make way for the Watch!"

The two moved quickly out of the way as a party of a dozen soldiers of the City Watch marched in. They all wore chain armour, and all save the leader were armed with six-foot spears, and swords as well. The leader had only a sword at his side, but he had a small red plume on his helmet to mark him as the commander.

As Haram watched, the party marched over to the table where Merrit and his companions sat. Merrit still sat there, watching their approach with a look of faint disdain on his face. His hands lay flat on the table, and he had put on a pair of gauntlets; Haram remembered the story of what Merrit was rumoured to have brought back from his trip to the north.

The detachment of the Watch came to a halt in front of Merrit's table, and the soldiers spread out a little. The commander spoke. "You are Merrit the Venturer?"

"And if I am?" asked Merrit insolently.

"Merrit the Venturer, I arrest you for various crimes against the people and land of Aradair. Put aside your sword and come with us."

Merrit stood calmly, still disdainful, his hands on the table. "Ah, but I do not think I care to be arrested," he said. His hands shifted on the table and gripped it by the edge. He gave a heave, then the table, solid wood and near as heavy as a man, was up and flying through the air. It struck the commander and the nearest two of the Watch, edge first, flinging them back and down.

Merrit stepped forward. The soldiers of the Watch, though taken by surprise, were not easily dismayed. They presented their spears and advanced on Merrit. He had still not drawn his sword, but when the first man thrust at him, he batted the spear aside with his left hand and stepped forward quickly. His right fist came up and struck like a hammer to the side of the man's neck, and he dropped. The fellow beside him had turned to thrust his own spear, but Merrit's right hand dropped and caught the shaft; he gave it a jerk, and the soldier was pulled off balance, falling toward Merrit, who struck him in the chest with a fist. The soldier staggered away two steps, then fell.

Now Merrit drew his sword. The fellows with him had also drawn swords by this time, and they began to fight. Merrit took the brunt of it, and it was clear his sword-strokes also derived benefit from the strength given him by the gloves. Spear-shafts splintered before even glancing blows, and chain armour tore like cloth. In a few moments, the last of the detachment of the Watch lay dead or wounded on the floor.

"Come on, lads!" called Merrit, "Let us be gone from here!" He and his six made for the door quickly.

There was a general movement to the door by all present; there would be more of the city Watch coming along soon, and it would not be healthy to be found in the same place as a dozen of their dead and wounded comrades. Indeed, there were many present who would not care to come to the attention of the Watch at any time.

Darith-Gan was tugging on Haram's sleeve. "Come, Haram, best we not hang about here!"

But Haram stood still beside the doorway, watching Merrit approach. Merrit, for his part, did not notice Haram until he was in front of him. "Hah! It is you, is it?"

"It is I, Merrit. I'd heard you were seeking for me. Well, you'll have to continue to seek, for I must leave here, and I have no wish to tarry here sparring with you until the rest of the Watch arrives." He stepped past. "Good luck in your search!" he called, mockingly, as he went out the door.

Haram stood there wondering at Merrit's words. What had he meant? It sounded as though he were expecting Haram to be hunting him down with vengeance in mind. *'Vengeance? For a cheating trick played on him some years ago? What could make him think that?*

But now Darith-Gan was pulling vigorously at his arm. "Come on, Haram! Will you stand here all night, waiting for disaster?"

Shaking off his thoughtful mood, Haram turned and followed Darith-Gan out the door.

A week and a half later, they were coming into the harbour at Shilka, on the Island of Rahasin. Shilka was a small city, not so large as the cities of Aradair, but larger than any of the towns. It was circled by a stone wall, with towers at regular points along the wall. The city itself was built of bricks, plastered with lime. The houses were all squarish, blocky things, some of which showed over the top of the wall.

Captain Lichtan, of the ship *Lichtan's Venture,* was a squat little man, who looked as though he might have some Dwarvish blood in him. He had a thick chest and heavily muscled arms, and his crew all walked carefully around him. He was going a little bald on the crown, too, and was sensitive to that fact, for he frowned whenever it seemed someone was looking at his head.

He had charged them a rate for their passage, which was a little lower than some, but still it had taken a good deal of their money to get there.

"Shilka," he said in a tone of satisfaction. "She's none of your huge cities of Aradair, but she'll do for me."

"Tell me, Captain, would you be able to suggest to us where we might find work for a while?"

"Work? Ah, yes, you're the fighting men, aren't you?"

"Yes, we're Venturers. We might serve as caravan guards or the like."

"Work for fighters?" he murmured to himself. There was something in his tone which suggested that men who made their living as fighters were not quite fit company for honest seafaring folk. "Well, I could not say for sure, you see, but I have been led to understand that there is always room for more people willing to fight against the Grizalak. You know of the Grizalak?"

"We've heard of the Grizalak, but I wouldn't say we know much of them. Great lizards, I have been told."

Lichtan exploded into laughter. "Great lizards, you say? Great lizards! No, you do not know them. They are a sort of people who greatly resemble lizards, and they live mostly in marshy territory. They are large and strong, mostly larger than a full-grown man, and fierce to fight.

"Of late, they have been encroaching on our territory, and our people have had to fight them. In previous times, fighting them was no terrible task, for they used as weapons mostly spears and clubs. Recently, though, they appear to have taken up the art of metalworking, and they have produced for themselves swords of iron, and various other weapons as well. If you go to fighting them, do not expect to have an easy time of it!"

The city was small but busy, with small swarthy people bustling about on their many errands. A good many of them spoke the language of Aradair to some degree, well enough that Haram and Darith-Gan could make themselves understood. When they told the people that they sought someone to hire them, perhaps to fight against the Grizalak, they were directed to a large building in the centre of the town, and told to ask for the Lord Omar-hendath.

The building was under the guard of several soldiers, armed with spear and sword, wearing metal helmets and scale armour. They were lolling about the courtyard, working at mending their kit, or gambling with dice. But when Haram and Darith-Gan approached, they stood and took their weapons.

Their commander spoke. After a bit of talking back and forth, the two Venturers convinced him they did not understand his language, and that they were from Aradair. He turned and bawled a name, and a somewhat pale young man came hurrying over. He proved to speak their language adequately enough to be able to translate for them.

There was a good deal more talking back and forth, and eventually they made clear what their purpose was; they wished to take employment fighting against the Grizalak. Once that was done, they were taken to a man who seemed to be a clerk, albeit one with considerable power and influence. Like all the others of that part of the country, he was short, heavy-set, and swarthy. Haram was reminded of Afal-kayyon, but the mage had been taller and less broad than these folk. The clerk also had his hair and beard carefully curled and oiled, a fashion which appeared to be restricted to the lords and powerful people of the land.

He spoke the tongue of Aradair with some accent, though not so much as to render his speech difficult to understand. He greeted them with a smile and said, "I understand you wish to fight the Grizalak?"

Haram returned the smile and answered, "No, Lord, we wish only to earn some money. And since the only trade at which we have any degree of skill is the trade of arms, then it is such work that we must seek."

The official's eyes widened. "Now there is an interesting answer, to be sure! Most of the warriors who come to fight for us hasten to assure me how much they hate the Grizalak, and how dreadfully well they will fight. But you speak openly of the fact that you are fighting for pay. This being the case, then, how well will you fight? What assurance can you give that you will not merely take the money that is given you and flee?"

"I had assumed that your folk would have seen to that already. I doubt that you would give us our whole pay until the end of the term of the contract, for instance."

The clerk nodded. "Quite true. There is an allowance given for the purchase of food, but the bulk of the pay is not issued until the end of the contract. And we also send inspectors out with the bands who go to fight the Grizalak, to ensure that they do not merely sit in camp for several weeks, then come back for their pay."

"So, then. Will you hire us?"

The clerk considered the matter for a short while, then nodded. "You will understand that we cannot send out an inspector to accompany two men. Our standard is one inspector with ten to twenty warriors. But you need not worry; there are always more warriors coming in, and there are groups who come back to the city to renew their contracts and may require reinforcements. I would expect to send you out within two days."

Black Hargi was tall, standing head and shoulders above Haram, with black hair and beard, unusual in a man of Aradair, which gave him his name. He looked at the pair before him, and did not appear to like what he saw. "My usual rule, he said, "is to take no man into my band who I do not know, or who cannot be vouched for by one I know. But I need men. I had six, and Gerrid had six, so we joined forces, agreeing to take the leadership day by day. But Gerrid died our third week out, and we lost three others as well. So now we have come in again, and Lord Omar-hendath will not send us out unless we bring ourselves up to strength.

"So, what are your names?"

"I am Haram, and my companion is Darith-Gan."

"Haram? Not Haram of the Grim Face?"

"I understand that some call me that, yes."

"And you spent years in captivity with the goblins, escaped, joined a band of Venturers and went hunting goblins for revenge? And you were with Vorath's band when they slew the Great Dragon?" The tone of his voice said that he did not believe all this.

"I spent about a year in captivity with the goblins, and was rescued by Vorath's band. And I was with Vorath's band when we fought a dragon, but it was a small young dragon we fought."

"I had heard that all Vorath's band got rich from that deed. If that is so, and you were with them, why are you here hiring yourself out to fight the Grizalak?"

Haram shrugged. "Much of my money is in trust in Ifan Sor. We have come out here seeking someone, and when we arrived, we found we are low on funds, so we hire ourselves out in order to refill our purses before we continue on our quest."

Black Hargi grunted. "You will not become rich here, you know."

"I do not need to be rich, only to be able to supply myself and my companion while we look for the person we are seeking."

"And who is this person you seek? I'll have no one with me who is seeking some private vengeance on someone else; such persons tend not to be reliable, particularly if they come upon the person they are seeking."

"I assure you, it is not a matter of vengeance. I seek a Venturer, a young woman named Terrial, and I have a private message to take to her."

"Terrial? I have heard the name, but I do not know the person. Have you asked the clerk? He will likely be able to tell you if she is here, and if so, where she is."

"No, I had not thought of that. In any case, we will still need money to live on, no matter where she is."

"Well, I will allow you to come with me, then. But I warn you, there is little to be had in the way of loot from the Grizalak. In all the time I have been out there, I believe I have seen one gold coin and about twenty silver. I have heard that pickings are a little better in the villages, but we have yet to find a village."

Haram shrugged. "Be that as it may, so long as they pay us, we will come with you."

"Oh, yes, they pay us. And they make sure that we earn our pay."

Two weeks later, Haram could testify to that. They were sitting in a rough shelter on a woody hillside, trying to stay dry in the constant rain. "This is the kind of weather the Grizalak like," said Black Hargi. "It fills up their lakes and ponds. They prefer marshy country, you see."

"If they prefer marshy country, why are we hired to drive them out? Surely most marshy country is not being used for anything else."

Black Hargi laughed. "I had thought about that myself, a time or two. But you see, what they do is come down to a stream and block it up, forming a fair-sized lake on which to build their habitations. In the course of this, they often destroy farmlands and even on occasion flood villages. Much of our work is finding such lakes, driving the Grizalak away from them, and unblocking the streams. They seem to be contemptuous of men, regarding us as worth little or nothing."

"What do we do, then? Patrol every stream and lake within our territory?"

"Yes, that we do. But mostly we go to the places where they have built before. They seem to return to the same place time and again, no matter how often they are driven from it. Of course, from time to time they choose new places as well, which we have to find and destroy as well."

"How large are their bands?"

"They usually send out ten to fifteen males to do the initial work of making the dam. If we do not find them quickly enough, those are soon reinforced by another fifteen or so males, with a number of females and children as well. And when that time comes, a band the size of ours may well not be able to attack such a village outright."

"In such a case, what do you do?"

"Then we hang about near the village, picking them off in ones and twos and small groups until they are few enough that we can attack them with some chance of success. And make no mistake, they are no mean fighters, for all that their weaponry and armour are so backward."

Two days later they went out patrolling, the rain having slacked off. When they came to the nearest of the places where the Grizalak had been attempting to make their dams, they found a small group of armed men were there already.

Black Hargi cursed. "Farmers!" he snorted, and strode toward them, drawing his sword.

Chapter Twenty-Seven

They were indeed all farmers of Lammasitu, and they understood nothing of Black Hargi's shouting. Even when he calmed himself and attempted to speak to them in the language of Lammasitu, they appeared not to understand, merely stared at him with truculent expressions on their faces.

There were twelve of them, and though they had no armour, their weapons looked serviceable and well-used. Most of them bore spears, and two had short hatchets tucked into their belts as well. One of them, a little smaller and more lithely built than the others, bore a short bow.

Black Hargi threw up his hands and turned to the inspector, a squat man with a wide face, who kept much to himself in the field. "Tibo-kila-hazzan, ask them what they are up to."

The inspector nodded, then spoke quickly to the farmers. One of the spearmen appeared to be the leader, and he answered. Tibo-kila-hazzan turned back to Black Hargi. "The Grizalak have stolen a girl-child from the village, and these villagers have been tracking the culprits."

"The Grizalak have stolen a child? How do they know it was the Grizalak?"

Tibo-kila-hazzan translated the question for the farmer, and as the spokesman was answering, the bowman broke in, a little angrily. The leader looked at him, then shrugged.

Tibo-kila-hazzan translated, without expression, "He says that some of them can read tracks as well or better than any red-poll foreigner."

Haram watched Black Hargi smile at the broad categorization of people from Aradair as *'red-polls.'* "I suppose that may be true," he said mildly. "But what do they hope to accomplish, a dozen of them against fifty or more Grizalak?"

The inspector spoke to the spokesman of the farmers again, then turned back to Black Hargi. "They had thought that the Grizalak were building here again, as they have before. But the tracks lead on from here, and they suspect that the Grizalak have gone back to one of their main villages. They wonder if you would wish to accompany them?"

"Accompany them?" roared Black Hargi, his temper getting the better of him. Then he paused and continued more quietly. "They have nerve, you know. A band of farmers, setting out after the Grizalak, and then to ask Venturers to accompany them." He paused again and thought for a moment.

"Tell them this," he said. "Tell them that we will accompany them on the condition that I am in charge when it comes to fighting, and that if we find and attack the Grizalak, they will take my orders."

Tibo-kila-hazzan spoke with the farmer for a few moments, discussing the proposal put by Black Hargi. Then he turned back. "He agrees, on behalf of his people. And he trusts that if it comes to a fight, you will treat his people as though they were your own."

It was a broad hint that Hargi should not arrange for the farmers to take all the brunt of the fighting, while the Venturers cleared up afterward, and collected the loot.

For all his temper, Hargi merely frowned at that. "Done. Let us go then."

The Grizalak were somewhat slowed by the child they were taking with them, but even so, they stayed ahead of the pursuers for a day and a half. The Venturers had joined the pursuit at about midday, and by the end of the next day, they were close enough to their quarry to see them arrive at their home place.

It was a large pond, vaguely kidney-shaped, with six angular buildings set about it. The buildings were clearly meant for more than a single family each, for there were some thirty Grizalak in sight.

The male Grizalak were each slightly taller than a man and resembled large lizards. They walked on their back limbs and had a tail with which they balanced themselves. Their arms were long and sender, ending in sharp-clawed hands. Their faces consisted of a lizard's snout, with small eyes above it. Haram wondered if they could speak any human language, with such strangely shaped mouths.

The party which had brought in the girl were all armed with round wooden metal-studded shields and long swords. They were greeted as they came to the village by other males, and by females and children as well. The kidnapped child was taken into a walled enclosure, inside which the tops of two more buildings could be seen.

The Venturers and the farmers kept themselves well back out of sight, and discussed possible plans. The leader of the farmers wanted to rush right in immediately, trusting in surprise to allow them to rescue the child and escape.

"Against fifty or sixty of them, in broad daylight?" demanded Hargi. "You may wish to throw your lives away, but we do not!"

"You are afraid?" Tibo-kila-hazzan looked a little concerned as he translated that for the huge foreigner. But Black Hargi only looked at the farmer calmly, "By Tran and Viron," he said, "I had thought the point here was to rescue the child. I had not thought we were supposed to kill ourselves instead. Had I known that, I would have chosen poison, or some such thing, rather than being hacked by swords. Tell him that if he wishes the child rescued, we are willing to help, but if he merely wishes to trade insults, then we have better things to do."

The leader of the farmers muttered some sort of apology, then they began to suggest and discard various plans. After the discussion had gone on for some time, Darith-Gan finally spoke up.

"If you wish, I could go in and bring the child out by myself."

As Tibo-kila-hazzan translated that for the farmers, Black Hargi turned to Darith-Gan. "We are making plans here, lad. We have no time for braggarts."

Darith-Gan merely smiled. "I do not speak idly," he said. "I am able to do it, if you wish me to try. And Haram will be able to tell you something of my abilities, if you wish."

Black Hargi flashed a glance at Haram. "My companion is not given to boasting," he said, "and from what I know of his abilities, I'd say he is able to perform what he promises."

Black Hargi frowned. "So? Well, rather than having to fight all the Grizalak at once, I'd be inclined to allow you to show what you can do. Let me talk to these others once more."

Tibo-kila-hazzan had been translating the conversations all the while for the farmers, so they already knew the proposal. It took a little more time to convince them it was worthwhile to give Darith-Gan a chance to show what he could do.

So it was that after dark that night, the band crept close to the village of the Grizalak. Darith-Gan was dressed in a black shirt and trousers. His sword was slung over his back to keep it out of the way as he climbed. He put a few items into pockets of his dark suit and took up a coil of light rope with a grappling hook on the end of it.

Then, as the band watched from the cover of the brush, Darith-Gan set out for the enclosure. For a few minutes they watched him, then suddenly he was no longer visible.

"Has he some sort of invisibility spell?" asked Black Hargi.

"No, I think not," answered Haram. "I think rather that he is skilled at his craft."

Black Hargi muttered something, and they continued to watch. For a long time, there was no sign of Darith-Gan. The Grizalak had guards who walked around the village from time to time. As one such party of guards had passed by and was out of sight of the enclosure, there was a sudden movement by the wall.

From this distance the cord was not visible, so it seemed as though Darith-Gan climbed the wall unaided. He was up and over in a moment, and again they waited.

For a time, there was no sound nor movement. The farmers, being totally unused to this sort of thing, were sure that something had gone wrong. They wished to charge in immediately to retrieve the situation.

Black Hargi, arguing in violent whispers, held them back by the force of his personality as much as anything.

"Delays are to be expected, aren't they? The man has not been gone very long, has he? And might it not be possible that he would have to search for the girl?"

Finally, those who were not convinced realized that they were too few to do anything if they made an attack, so they broke off. But their expressions made it clear they were not pleased with the situation.

The moments stretched out, and even some of the Venturers were becoming restless. Most of these were sufficiently experienced that the restlessness did not come out in the audible shifting and movement of the farmers, but rather in the deep breathing and shifting of the eyes.

Suddenly there was a movement along the top of the wall, and a black figure slid over and climbed down. The figure seemed oddly hump-backed, and Haram breathed, "He has her!"

The leader of the farmers muttered something under his breath, and they continued to watch.

Perhaps it was the fact that he was carrying the child on his back, but Darith-Gan did not seem to blend into the underbrush so well on the return trip. From time to time, he would pause, then move again. When his circuit of the village brought the sentry of the Grizalak into view, Darith-Gan halted and waited. Many times, one can go unnoticed simply by standing still, particularly at night. This time, however, the Grizalak stopped suddenly, as though he had heard something, and surveyed the area carefully.

"The boy is seen!" muttered Black Hargi.

The Grizalak was still staring out in the general direction of Darith-Gan's hiding place. Then he gave a loud bellow and began loping toward the Venturer. Darith-Gan did not move. The leader of the farmers was muttering out loud to Black Hargi, and Haram needed no translation to know that he was demanding to know what Darith-Gan was doing. The leader of the Venturers did not answer, and was probably wondering something very like that himself.

Then, just as the Grizalak reached him, Darith-Gan was up on his feet. Like a moving shadow, he closed with the Grizalak, then moved away, leaving the foe to crumple to the ground. Then Darith-Gan began moving rapidly towards the place where his companions were hiding.

He was carrying the girl slung over his shoulders, her wrists tied to her ankles with a piece of cloth. She was sleeping, though not soundly.

"What happened?" demanded Black Hargi.

"I had given her a small draught to make her sleep; it was necessary," he added quickly, as the inspector translated for the farmers. "She was terrified, and she was about to start screaming. If that had happened, neither of us would have escaped. But she wasn't sleeping soundly enough, and as we were waiting there, she made a little moan, just enough for him to hear us. And when he'd heard us, it was not difficult at all for him to see us."

The leader of the farmers said something, and Tibo-kila-hazzan translated, "The shout the monster gave will waken the others. We ought to leave, and leave quickly."

Black Hargi shook his head. "I thought so at first, but now I'm not so sure; if we flee, they will pursue us, and we will be slowed by the child. Eventually we would have to fight them, so why not fight them now, when we can take them by surprise, and possibly discourage them from coming after us?" He looked around at the faces surrounding him. "Look, we have a very good place for an ambush, and it is night. Let us stay only long enough to make them wary of us."

The farmers eventually saw the wisdom of this, though it was clear some still were not happy with it. Black Hargi positioned them all throughout the bush, with the farmers all in supporting positions to the better-armed Venturers. The one with the bow he placed where he could have a fair view of the oncoming enemy, but where he would not be sending stray arrows into his fellows down the trail.

It was soon clear that they had been well-advised to wait in ambush, for about thirty of the Grizalak came loping out of the village. They paused for a moment by the body of the sentry and some of them cried out, though whether the cries were grief or anger, none of the men could tell.

Then the Grizalak were on their way towards the brush where the men waited.

The trail was so narrow that the lizard-men could go only two abreast along it. They clearly had no thought of ambush, for they ran down the trail, pursuing the fugitives as though they were sure the men were fleeing ahead of them. Haram, stationed somewhere near the centre of the ambush, got his first clear look at a Grizalak warrior close up.

They did indeed look like great lizards, and the large snouts had sharp carnivorous teeth in them. The skin looked like green leather, and they breathed heavily as they ran. Each clutched some sort of weapon, most of them having long swords and round shields, a few making do with clubs which seemed to be no more than limbs wrenched off trees and trimmed of twigs.

Then Black Hargi shouted, and the ambush began. The farmers and the Venturers leaped out of the brush, weapons up.

Chapter Twenty-Eight

The Grizalak were taken completely unawares. Several, including the leaders, went down in the first assault before they could even raise a weapon. There was turmoil and confusion among them as the half-light of the moon filtered through the trees. The Grizalak knew only that they were being attacked, not by who or how many.

Surprised and leaderless, the Grizalak pulled back, but the rest of the column was engaged in a struggle all along its length, so that an orderly escape was difficult. As each running Grizalak infected others with his panic, it rapidly became an each-for-himself rout.

The Grizalak burst back out of the brush, fleeing for their village, with the ambushers in pursuit. Black Hargi called them back, and the Venturers eventually held their ground. The farmers, however, kept on going. Their blood was up, the Grizalak were fleeing before them, and they were not to be held back. Even commands in their own language from Hargi and Tibo-kila-hazzan had no effect.

Black Hargi looked at his Venturers and shrugged. "Once the greenskins collect themselves a bit, they'll see who's chasing them and turn around and fight. Then woe betide the farmers. What do you say, lads? Do we leave the farmers to their lot, or do we go see to it that the Grizalak have no time to collect themselves?"

The Venturers had got their blood up as well, and there were shouts of "Down the greenskins!" and the like.

"So be it!" cried Black Hargi. "After them!"

So off they went, across the open area to the village. It was a near thing too, for some of the Grizalak were already beginning to rally, and it would be only a few moments before the Lizard-men realized they were fighting against men with poor armour and arms, and men with little fighting-skill either. The armoured Venturers came charging in among the Grizalak and broke them up before they could rally, seeming by their very ferocity to be several times their true number.

For a time they battled fiercely by torchlight and moonlight there amidst the buildings of the Grizalak town, smiting and struggling and striving. It was a scattered battle, and after the first few moments, there was no front line and no rear, only warriors fighting all about.

Several of the Grizalak rallied to fight, but only in twos and threes, and never in groups large enough to make a difference. The females and children began to flee, and the males fled as well, covering the retreat of their families.

Then, almost suddenly, the Venturers and their companions were left in possession of a Grizalak town, empty save for the bodies of the dead.

Black Hargi called his people together, and they found their losses were amazingly light. Three of the farmers were dead, as well as one of the Venturers. All the others had wounds, ranging from one of the farmers with a severe slash across the chest to Black Hargi himself, with a nick on the arm.

"Well," said Black Hargi, "we have possession of the village; let's see if there is anything here worth the taking. We shall have to work quickly, for they may recover their courage sooner than we could wish."

They went about in pairs, searching all the buildings for anything that might be of value. Darith-Gan and Haram went together to the walled enclosure. Within it was a small building and a larger one. Darith-Gan nodded to the smaller one. "There's nothing in there. It's only a building used to house captives."

"But I thought the Grizalak did not take captives."

Darith-Gan shrugged. "So we had been told, but still that building was used to house captives."

"You speak as though there were more than one."

"There were spaces for more than one, and signs that there had been several there, but there was only the child present."

"And we have found no captives elsewhere in the town. Where are they all, then?"

Darith-Gan shrugged again. By this time, they had come to the door of the larger building. Haram tried it and found it locked. "Let me try," suggested Darith-Gan.

He took out a small knife and inserted it in the keyhole. He manipulated it for a few moments, then there was a click, and the door swung open. They stepped inside.

They were inside a large porch screened off from the rest of the building by a long curtain. To their right was a rough wooden chest. It was not locked, so when they opened it, they expected to find little or nothing. Indeed, most of what it contained was pottery, dishes, jugs, flasks and the like. Some of the flasks had small amounts of liquid in them. Darith-Gan said, "They may be potions, perfumes, or wines, but we have no time to test them to find out which. And such things as this will not be easily transported either; leave them."

There were four small leather bags as well. One contained seven gold coins, of varying weights, while the rest contained mixes of copper and silver, a rough count giving twenty-nine copper and nineteen silver. They were about to close the chest when Haram spotted a gleam of copper at the back. He looked closer and found a thin rectangular sheet of copper, incised with runes.

"Hah! Look at this, my friend! This will pay us enough and more than enough for what we will need!"

"What is it?"

"It's a page from the books of Drum-na-Drum." Darith-Gan looked puzzled, so Haram explained. "I was told that, back in a Former Age of the World, the wizard Drum-na-Drum inscribed his books on sheets of copper, so that they would not be lost. But war and troubles and the changing of the ages destroyed the wizard, and scattered his books, so that only bits of them remain. Wizards, and collectors of wizardly lore, will pay well for any inscribed sheet of copper, and especially if they can read it sufficiently to tell that it is part of the books of Drum-na-Drum."

A grim heaviness fell on him, then, as he recalled Orizd's band and his last memories of them, Orizd fighting like a wounded bear over a dying Astaran, with Sagahan defending himself with fire and lightning.

Abruptly, he was aware of his companion speaking and looking at him anxiously. Haram shook his head to clear his thoughts.

"What is it, Haram?"

"Nothing but poor thoughts and bad memories. Let's finish up our search."

They went through the curtain into the main part of the building. This part of the building was lit, albeit dimly, by large candles along the walls. At the end of it was a large, dark object. As they drew near, this was revealed to be a large sandstone, roughly carved into an approximation of a Grizalak. In front of it was a shallow dark pit, and as they came closer still, they saw the pit was full of ashes and charcoal.

Haram stepped to the edge of the pit, and suddenly he could see that some of what appeared to be partially burned sticks were actually charred bones. A closer examination of one of the lumps of charcoal revealed it to be a small human skull. It was only when Darith-Gan said "What is it?" that Haram realized he had spoken aloud.

"Look!" he said. "This is why there was so much space in the other building! They were offering the children as sacrifices!"

Darith-Gan exclaimed in horror, then looked at Haram. "How long has this been going on, I wonder? How many of the local villages have found themselves missing a child or two from time to time, a child who they could never find? Achh! Let us be gone from this place, Haram!"

But as they went out, Darith-Gan seized one of the candles from the wall. After they had passed through the curtain, he held the candle to the curtain until it was well and truly on fire, then tossed the candle over against the chest in the porch.

"Perhaps it will burn, perhaps it will not. I hope we might see it destroyed."

Chapter Twenty-Nine

Several other members of the band, including Black Hargi himself, had heard of the Books of Drum-na-Drum, but none had ever seen one, or any part of one.

"I will admit," said Haram, "that my experience in the matter is limited to the sight of one scrap of copper which the magician with Sagahan's band declared to be a part of a page of one of the books of Drum-na-Drum. But I will say that this bears a great resemblance to the one that I saw."

At this assurance, some of the band wanted to go back immediately to town to sell it, and then return to Aradair. Black Hargi refused.

"I do not know how the rest of you feel, but for myself, my word has been given with this contract, and I will carry out what has been promised."

There was some muttering, but in the end, no one objected too seriously. Over the remainder of the contract, they saw only a few minor skirmishes with the Grizalak. Then they marched back to Shilka.

After they had been to visit Lord Omar-hendath to pick up their pay, they went to see what price they could get for the piece of copper. However, the town of Shilka was a small one, and few of the wizards, sorcerer, or soothsayers had heard of Drum-na-Drum, and fewer still could be convinced of the value of one small sheet of inscribed copper.

They settled at last for a sum which, while high enough to make most of the band happy, still seemed low to Haram. He suggested they take it across the strait to Aradair, because they could get more for it in a larger city, but most of the band were willing to settle for real money in their pouches that instant.

Black Hargi and the others took their money and sought passage on a ship bound for Aradair. Haram and Darith-Gan stayed in Shilka.

"Well," said Darith-Gan when they were once more on their own, "Will you go out now to seek Terrial?"

Haram shook his head. "No, I think not. She and her group will be coming in to have their contract renewed; let's wait here for them."

Careful inquiries revealed the band would come back to the city within three weeks. For the first week, the pair roamed the city. There was always something new to look at and talk about. In the second week there was little left to see or do, so they spent a good deal of time in practising their weapon-skills. The middle of the third week found them frankly bored.

They took to spending much of their time waiting at the gate of the city, watching for parties arriving from inland. Haram wondered if he would recognize Terrial when he saw her; they had not been that long in each other's company. It had been some time since then, and she was now a Venturer. He doubted that the small half-frightened girl he remembered could survive long as a Venturer and not be changed.

There was no mistaking Venturers from Aradair; they were taller in general and usually had red or reddish hair. Twice such parties came through the gates, but the first party had no women at all and the second party had one woman, tall and strongly built, with yellow hair. Darith-Gan looked at her, then looked at Haram with a question in his eyes.

"No, she might have grown somewhat, but not so much. And I doubt she would have changed the colour of her hair."

They continued to wait. It suddenly occurred to Haram that Terrial might have died in battle and been buried out in the hinterland somewhere. He considered that unwelcome thought, then dismissed it. If she did not come in by the end of the day, then he would go to the office of the Lord Omar-hendath next day to see what he could find out.

Eventually Darith-Gan went off to find some food for them. Haram waited at the gate in case she should come in the meantime.

Finally, a little after lunch, a band of Venturers, fifteen strong, came in the gate. Among them was Terrial.

She had grown a little since he had seen her last, and she was clearly more muscular. She wore a jacket of leather, strengthened with iron studs, and she had a round shield slung at her back. On her head was a helmet, also of studded leather, and she had a small case of darts slung over her right shoulder. A sword and dagger at her waist completed her equipment.

She had a small scar on her right cheek, apparently a sword-scar, and her right arm had the usual tiny scars of a sword fighter's arm. She was paying little attention to the crowds around the gates, and did not see Haram. He did not attempt to draw her attention.

Darith-Gan came over to Haram. "That was not her either?"

"Oh, that was her," replied Haram.

"Yet you said nothing to her?" asked Darith-Gan.

Haram smiled. "Imagine yourself coming in from up-country, tired and dirty and probably at least a little hungry. How would you feel about some fool leaping out and greeting you, talking about old times and keeping you from your pay? We know she is in the city, we know who she is with, and we should be able to find her when we want, later on."

Darith-Gan smiled and nodded. "Wisdom indeed! And what shall we do in the meantime?"

Haram shrugged. "I would suggest that we return to our inn and rest."

As they walked back to their inn, Darith-Gan spoke softly. "There are some people following us; at least two of them, but there may be more."

"What sort of people?" asked Haram.

"Folk of Aradair, from the hair. I doubt they are of the Hidden Folk; they're too large and visible for that. But they're following us for certain," answered Darith-Gan.

"So then. Let us be careful. I suppose it was too much to hope that we might have thrown them all off the trail," said Haram with a scowl.

"We threw them off, but they picked up the scent again. I wonder how many they are altogether?"

Darith-Gan was soon able to tell that there were only the two of them. "They're seeking a likely place in which to attack us."

"Shall we oblige them?" asked Haram.

"Perhaps you're right; better to have them attack us when we're ready than to wait and perhaps have them attack us when we're no longer expecting it," replied Darith-Gan.

They walked down the winding streets of Shilka then, and finally came to one of the poorer quarters of the city. While folk might report to the City Watch a fight that took place in the Main Market, people in the poorer quarters generally avoided attracting the attention of the Watch.

As it happened, it was not even necessary for Haram and Darith-Gan to pick a quarrel with their pursuers. As they turned into one particularly deserted street, Darith-Gan hissed, "Here they come!"

And indeed they did. There was a rush of feet and the two were rounding the corner, swords up and ready. As he reached for his own sword, Haram remembered something.

"Trrik trrak Drauha vrrak!" he said.

For just a bare instant, the two attackers paused, then they were coming again. The pause was time enough for Haram and Darith-Gan to draw their own swords. Haram would have preferred to be able to use his shield as well, but the sword would have to do.

The attackers had the advantage of having shields ready as well, but Haram was quick and well in practice, having spent much of the past week drilling with Darith-Gan. As well, the two had noticed the effect of the small charm which Haram had used, and it concerned them. As well as fighting with Haram and Darith-Gan, they were also alert for other charms and magic spells.

For his part, Haram concerned himself with trying to get past the guard of his opponent. At one point in the fight, he noticed that Darith-Gan had reached into a pocket and drawn out a length of light chain with a weight at each end. He wondered what its purpose was, but he had no time to watch what was happening.

The course of his own fight put him with his back to Darith-Gan for a moment, and he heard the sound of a sword striking flesh. He could not take his attention from the man in front of him, even if Darith-Gan had been wounded or killed; all he could do was wonder.

Then his opponent was attacking him ferociously, and his first thought was that Darith-Gan had gone down and he was about to be attacked from behind. He suddenly noticed the desperation in the man's eyes, and realized that it was Darith-Gan who had conquered, and the other was trying to kill Haram and escape.

In the midst of the fierce attack, Haram found an opportunity; he beat the sword aside and lunged, driving the point of his own blade past the shield and into the man's throat. Darith-Gan was stepping up beside him as his opponent fell.

"So. You managed, did you?" asked Haram.

"Oh, yes, with the aid of a few tricks that fellow was never taught." With one hand, Darith-Gan coiled up the chain and stowed it in his pocket again. "And you managed as well?"

"Yes, once the fellow saw that the odds were against him, he became reckless," answered Haram.

Haram knelt by the man's side and opened his coin purse. From it, he took what he expected to find: the symbol of the God of Lies. He held it up. "They found our trail, by whatever means."

"The questions to be asked, then, are whether it was just this pair that found our trail, and how many others are likely to be following *them*?" asked Darith-Gan.

"Well, since we're unlikely to be long in Shilka, we need not worry too much," replied Haram.

Chapter Thirty

They found the inn where Terrial and her group were staying by the expedient process of looking in at the inns nearest to the office of the clerk in charge of payments. At the third inn, they saw Terrial and several others sitting at a table in the common room.

When he first saw her, Haram had a moment of doubt that this was really Terrial. He still held in his mind the small, soft-featured, withdrawn young woman he had escorted out of Shab-nazdig. Her size had not changed, and she was drinking a mug of ale with her band, and her expression said that she simply had nowhere better to go. But she was no longer soft. She was tanned, and looked to be slim and lithe as a javelin, and perhaps even as deadly. Her red hair had been cut short to accommodate her helmet, which was lying by her right foot as she drank her ale in short sips.

Haram walked over to her, with Darith-Gan following him.

As they drew near, Terrial looked up. Her expression changed from puzzlement to recognition to stubborn anger. "A good evening to you, Terrial," said Haram.

"A good evening to you, Haram. Did my father hire you to seek me out and bring me home?" Her hand dropped to her dagger.

"No, no!" protested Haram, as the other members of her company turned hostile faces toward him and Darith-Gan. "I came to seek you on my own, for my own reasons, though your father <u>did</u> send a message, if I should ever find you."

She had changed, to be sure. Haram reflected that a merchant's daughter, after a year or so as a Venturer, might well find herself changed as much as Haram had after a year or so enslaved by the goblins.

She relaxed a little at his reassurance. "You have not come to take me back, then? You swear it?"

"No, by Tran and Viron, I swear I have not come to take you anywhere against your will, nor even to try to persuade you to go anywhere or do anything, save perhaps to speak to me."

"Why?" There was dark suspicion in her voice.

Haram shrugged. "Because once many years ago we faced a danger together, and because I have become sufficiently well-off that I need not worry every moment about what I will eat tomorrow. Thus, I had the time to seek you out, and when I sought you, I found that you had left home to become a Venturer. So I set out to find you. Along the way, I encountered my companion, Darith-Gan. May we speak with you?"

The eyes of Terrial's companions were a little less hostile than they had been, but Haram knew that all that would be required would be for Terrial to seem to be distressed by him, or for her to utter the word, and they would be up and fighting him on her behalf. Though she did not seem happy to be with the group, still she was a member of the band, and they would defend her if need be.

"Yes," she said presently. "Shall we find a table of our own?"

There were some of her compatriots who did not seem to like this notion; she ought not to have secrets from them. She sensed this and turned to them. "Have no fear, Yuga. When we are done, I will come and tell you everything."

Then she rose and, carrying her mug, went in search of another table.

When they had taken their seats, she looked up at Haram. "What of your comrades, the ones who were with you when you rescued me? Are they no longer with you?"

"They are dead. A little after we left you, we were attacked by goblins. The others were killed, and I was taken prisoner."

"Haram? Then you are Haram Grim-face, who was a prisoner of goblins, and escaped, and now hunts goblins to be revenged on them?"

"So I am led to believe. But I don't hunt goblins, any more than any other Venturer. And I didn't escape. I was rescued by Vorath's band, though I will admit that the rescue was unintentional."

"Yes, it was Vorath's band, I recall. And then you fought a drake west of here and slew it, and all became very rich."

Haram grinned again. "All partially true. But it was a young dragon, and somewhat inexperienced. And when all was said and done, we were not so rich as some might have believed. The hoard of a dragon is usually cursed, imbued with the evil of the monster himself. The wizard who was with us picked out from the hoard what things were the least affected by the curse, and that was enough to make even the least of us well off. And I was the least of them.

"So it was that Vorath's band broke up, each going off to do the various things each had wished to do if he had the money. I had no goals of my own, so I went off by myself, with the vague idea in my head of seeing how it was with you. When I got to Halan Howrdas, I talked to your father and found that you had left long ago. He asked me to take a message, if I ever found you, to come by and visit him sometime. He seemed very lonely."

She nodded. "Yes, I suppose he would be." She was silent for a time, looking down at the table top. When she looked up, her eyes were flashing.

"Do you know why I left? No, I think not, since I told no one, ever. When you brought me back, and after he had an amulet made for me, my father began treating me as though I were some precious porcelain figurine, as though I might break if treated too roughly, or as though I might be stolen away by a thief in the night.

"Can you understand how difficult it could be to protest against such treatment when you know that it is being done out of love for you? I convinced him to allow me to learn how to handle a sword, arguing that if I could handle a weapon, it would be less easy for kidnappers to take me again. At the time, I had no thought of running off to become a Venturer. It was merely a way for me to be allowed to have some say in my life, even though my father disapproved.

"But that was not the worst of it. No one truly knew what had happened when I was kidnapped, and there were a good number of stories told about it. I heard many of those stories, some told out of spite by people who wished to hurt me, and some I heard in coming upon conversations unawares.

"Before my kidnapping there had been talk, nothing like a contract, nor even so firm as an understanding, that when I came of age, I would marry the eldest son of one of the other rich merchants of the town. After I was brought back, there was no further such talk, though I did not at first understand why.

"The end of it was when I was on a stairwell one day and heard one of my father's business associates talking to him, offering one of his younger sons in marriage so that 'my shame might be covered.' And for this, he sought a major share in my father's business!

"I did not wait to hear what answer my father might give. I packed up some clothing, some food, and my sword, and rode away. I left a message to tell my father what I had done, but I did not say which direction I was taking. I have heard since that he had been seeking me, but I sent him no messages in return. I have no idea whether he feels as his associate does, that it was a shame on me to have been kidnapped and held prisoner, nor do I wish to know."

"Had you any trouble becoming a Venturer? I know there are a number of women Venturers, but you are still young, and you were smaller then."

Her expression grew stern. "You recall I had taken lessons with the sword before I left? The leader of the first group laughed at me when I sought to join him, so I offered to fight anyone in his group to demonstrate my ability. When I won, he denied that there had been any sort of agreement that I would be allowed to join them. But the story had gotten around, and the next person I approached had heard of me, and had a place in his band, so I joined.

"Since that time we have lost old members and taken on new ones, so that there is no longer anyone left of the old band, not even the leader."

"What places have you been?"

"We did much as you did, I expect, wandering about Aradair seeking for anything or anyone to fight. In the mountains north of Intalis, we came upon a band of three ogres, which we fought. We came away from that with a fair bit of treasure, but we lost four of our members, including one mage.

"After recruiting more members, we hired on as caravan guards for a merchant who was planning on taking the trip to Rahasin. His trading did not go as well as he had hoped, so he paid us off at Shimshara, from which we worked our way to here."

Haram nodded. "Have you ever thought of going home?"

The half-smile was gone from her face as though it had never been. She began to rise from the table. "So you have come to take me back! You---"

"No, no!" interrupted Haram. "I swore to you that I had no intention of bringing you back, only to deliver your father's message."

She settled back, grudgingly, keeping her eyes on him. Yes, time had changed her as much as it had changed him. Still glaring at him, she spoke. "Then you have passed your message, and you can leave me now!"

"I apologize, Terrial. I had no intention of upsetting you! Let me explain. You see, when I was rescued from the goblins, it took some time before I was truly fit for human company again. I have passed through Ifan Sor a time or two since, and in fact I stayed there for a few weeks the last time, but I have not gone to visit my own father. And when I left home, it was with his knowledge and permission. I have thought at times that I ought to go back and greet him, but there are other difficulties involved.

"My friend, Merrit, left home against his parent's wishes, and was not happy to be with such an ordinary band. An opportunity came to win a place in another band of more renown, and he cheated to win that opportunity. I understand that he has left that band under shady circumstances, and is now as near an outlaw as makes no difference.

"So if I go home, my father will ask about Merrit, and will want me to take news of Merrit to his father as well, and what can I say? Particularly now. For once, I had only stories that he was in bad company. Now I know that he has gained a bad reputation in his own right." For a little while he was silent, then he spoke again. "Perhaps I ought to go, despite all. If I must talk to Merrit's father, then I must, but I ought to speak to my own."

He looked at Terrial. Her face had softened again. "Perhaps you may go home again, but I cannot. At least not yet. But if you are going back to see my father, you can take him a message for me. Tell him that my leaving did not mean that I do not love him, but that... I could not stay... No, tell him only that, that I love him, even though I left him, and that one day I will come home to visit him."

The common room had become very crowded by now, and the gathering was so loud and boisterous that it was almost necessary to shout in order to be heard. Terrial looked at Haram. "Let us go upstairs to our chambers, where we can talk without having to talk to all of Shilka."

After she took a moment to inform Yuga, they went upstairs. There they talked of many things, of the sights they had seen, of places they had been, of things they had done, and of how the land of Aradair compared with the rainy country of Rahasin.

After they had talked for some time, Terrial was smiling. They sat in silence for a time, merely enjoying being together. At last Terrial looked up at Haram. "Ah, Haram, I could wish we had met in better circumstances."

He looked at her, puzzled.

"When I began my life as a Venturer, I decided that if I were ever to go to bed with a man, it would be by mutual consent, not because he was stronger. And I have fought a time or two to enforce that decision." She fingered the scar on her cheek absently. "Even for us to be alone here will mean that some will start the whole business over again. If I will go to bed with one, why will I not go to bed with all and any?"

"What if I were to join you? If we were together, no one would fight the two of us."

She considered that for a moment, then shook her head. "Yuga would not have it. Our band is already six people, and he thinks that too many. There were three bands totalling sixteen who went out fighting the Grizalak, and the six of us are all that are left. Out of respect and companionship, Yuga consented to let the remnants of the other bands join with us, but he will have no more, not until we lose a few more."

Haram would have spoken again, but he felt he heard something beyond the words Terrial was speaking, that she was not quite willing to get so close to any man, not just yet. He smiled and said, "Well, I will take your message to your father, and perhaps come back again to see how you fare. Would you mind?"

Tears showed suddenly in her eyes as she said, "No, I wouldn't mind. But we might be gone from here; how would you find us?"

"The same way I found you this time; Ask people until I hear news of you, and travel in the direction of the rumours until I come to you."

She stood, and Haram stood as well. "Perhaps we had better be going back downstairs; I will have trouble enough for being here for so long, and the longer I stay, the worse the trouble. Come here, Haram."

He stepped closer to her, and she put a hand on each side of his face and pulled him close for a kiss.

There was a sudden flash of brilliant light, and the two sprang apart, reaching for their swords. There was a pillar of light in the centre of the floor, a pillar which reached from the floor to the ceiling. Amid the pillar was a figure of light, something in the shape of a lizard standing upright. Its eyes were flashing red within the sockets as it stepped out of the pillar.

It seized Terrial in massive hands, pinning her arms at her sides. It glanced at Haram, then stepped back to the pillar. Just as he was leaping forward with his sword drawn, the pillar disappeared. The room was dark, lit only by the small candle on the table, and Terrial was gone.

Chapter Thirty-One

Yuga was not pleased. He was a man of action, not careful forethought, and his sword was two inches out of the scabbard by the time Haram was half-finished with his somewhat jumbled explanation.

Haram himself felt a sense of desperation and grudged every moment it took to make explanations. He was himself very close to drawing his own blade and taking his chances about being able to kill every man of Yuga's band, then going off on his own. Only the knowledge in his mind that it would not stop with Yuga allowed him to maintain some measure of calm. If he could deal with Yuga and his men, not necessarily a certainty, he would have to answer to the local magistrate, which would mean more delay and troubles that a bare blade would not solve.

"Listen," he said urgently, "What kind of tomfool would I be to bring such a story to you if it were not true?"

Yuga was not easily mollified. "And a shrewd man might come with just such a tale, trusting in its very improbability to convince others. I've heard tales of you, and I would not trust a man who's spent time with goblins."

This was a new attitude towards his time with the goblins, one Haram had not considered before, but this was neither the time nor the place to argue the merits of the notion.

"Listen, you have a wizard with you, I see. I'm certain he knows some sort of spell to tell the truth from falsehood. Let him test me and see if I'm lying!"

"Why bother the man? Why do we not simply begin taking you apart until you tell us a truth that a man can believe?"

Haram drew a deep breath, and by strength of will alone, kept his hand away from his sword hilt. One more try, then. "Yuga, you have heard stories of Haram Grim-face, probably all painted larger than life and in great colour. But has anyone ever suggested that Haram Grim-face could not or would not fight, if a fight was necessary? If a fight starts here and now, there will be dead men on the floor before it is done, and how many besides me are you willing to see die?

"Why not let your wizard do what he can before you begin something where the outcome might be in doubt?"

He was careful not to make any statement regarding the fact that Yuga was directly in front of him, and would be the first target of any attack he might make. That could be construed as a challenge to Yuga's courage, one to which the most likely response would be an immediate attack.

The wizard, a tall and slender man of a breed Haram had never seen before, with dark hair and an aquiline nose, stepped forward. "There's some sense to what he says, Yuga. I could tell if he's lying, and even if he's got some kind of spell to counter my truth-detection, I could tell that too. Let me have a try, and you can always cut each other to pieces afterward."

Yuga, his eyes still on Haram, released his sword and let it slide back into the scabbard. "So, then, Optikkaz, do your spelling."

Yuga's expression said all Haram needed to know about what might happen if the spell said he was lying. Optikkaz muttered some words quietly, and Haram felt a tingling all over. The hair on the back of his neck stood up, and his eyes began to feel dry.

"What city are we in?" asked the wizard.

"Shilka," answered Haram. The wizard put up a hand to forestall Haram's question in return.

"Please bear with me. This is a necessary part of the spell. Now, what is your name?" asked Optikkaz.

"Haram," answered Haram.

"Have you hunted the Grizalak?" asked Optikkaz.

"Yes," answered Haram.

"Ah, fine, fine! Now, tell us once more the story about how Terrial was taken," urged Optikkaz.

So Haram went through the tale again, rather more calmly than the first time, though inwardly he was still impatient at every moment's delay.

When he had done, Optikkaz mattered a few words again, then turned to Yuga. "He tells the truth, Yuga. It happened as he told it."

"Hmph!" grunted Yuga. "And what do you plan now, Haram of the Grim face?"

"I think first of all I need to find a seer, and ask what this means. From what little I know of seers, I think I will need something that belonged to Terrial for hm to seek her by."

"We'll bring her kit. Her helmet, here, she wore it enough that it ought to serve. We'll have to wait until morning, though."

Haram was nigh ready to scream with frustration, but he knew Yuga was right. If they woke a seer up at this time of the night, he would not likely be in a good frame of mind to be helpful, and Haram was beginning to suspect that they would need all the help they could get.

He finally took a seat with his back against the wall, certain that he would not sleep at all, but some of the other patrons of the inn swore that they'd tie him down if he did not cease pacing. Then suddenly it was dawn, and he lifted a groggy head from his chest, and remembered what had happened.

Haram looked across the table at Gwylior, the seer. He was of Rahasin, one of the segment of that people who seemed to have some Dwarfish ancestry, for he was short and stock, broad-faced, with a dark and heavy beard covering his chin.

The walls of his shop were covered with charts, some carefully done with coloured inks on parchment, others seeming to be little more than rough sketches on bits of wood, leather, or tree-bark. Haram wondered briefly if all or any of these had any function at all, save to impress the seer's customers.

Rather than telling the whole story and asking for an interpretation, Haram passed the helmet across the table and asked, "The one who wore this, what can you tell me of her?"

As the interpreter translated, the seer was turning the helmet in his hands, holding it lightly but firmly between his palms, and looking, not at it, but at Haram.

Then he stiffened, and his eyes rolled up into his head. Haram automatically reached for him, but the seer's assistant, a very young boy, laid a hand on Haram's arm and spoke.

The interpreter translated. "He says not to worry. The seer is in his trance, and he sees what he will see. Only wait."

Then the boy busied himself with mixing herbs into a pot and heating water in a small copper vessel.

For some time nothing happened, only the buzz of the town life outside the dim shop. Haram, despite the assurances of the seer's attendant, was on the point of attempting to get the seer's attention when suddenly the man stirred.

Gwylior spoke in a dry and gravelly voice, very quickly, so that the interpreter was hard pressed to keep up.

"Gwylior says that this is a matter of the Gods, and that mortals had best not interfere. He says that there was a bargain between the God of Lies and Vssthak, the God of the Grizalak, for the God of Lies was prevented from touching his prey, while Vssthak was angry with you, and wished to cause you as much pain as possible. He says that the woman was the prey of the God of Lies, and that he has her once more, and will not let her go."

"How could he have her? She had an amulet to protect herself from him!" protested Haram.

There was a pause while the interpreter put this to Gwylior, who then responded.

"Sometimes the Gods meet and make bargains. The amulet protected her against the God of Lies, but was not so effective against Vssthak. And given time, the God of Lies will be able to overwhelm the strength of the amulet." Translated the interpreter.

"Is there any way I can find her? Anything at all I can do?" asked Haran

The seer was quiet for a while again, staring through the walls into some far distance. Then Gwylior spoke.

"Hard, hard, the task to be done! No mortal can do it alone, and will any God interfere? There is a grove of oak trees, and a druid, and that is all," said the translator.

"That is all? What message is that?" asked Haram in frustration.

"That is all the message. If you do not know what is meant, I fear I cannot help you." answered Gwylior through the translator.

Haram stood. "I understand a little, but I am not sure that it makes any sense. The grove of oaks and the druid, I think I know, but what the druid might be able to do, I cannot say."

The boy brought a cup of infused herbs to the Dwarven seer, who began to drink in careful sips.

Haram paid the fees of Gwylior and the interpreter, then they all went out.

Yuga shook his head. "I've fought any number of things, but this is a business of the gods. Terrial was a companion, but how does one fight against the gods themselves?"

Haram was too full of thoughts and conjectures on the seer's words to spend even a moment's inward sneering at Yuga's protestations of comradeship out in the street. He turned to Darith-Gan. "I plan to do what I can for Terrial. I'll not blame you if you prefer not to come."

"The seer's words mean something to you. What is it?" asked Darith-Gan.

"You recall what I told you about the God of Lies, about our first brush with him? When we took Terrial away, he found us outside the grove of trees where the druid Korennis lives. If there is a druid or grove of oaks to be connected with this story, that would be it. What it means exactly, I can't say, but I think I'd better go there without delay. Korennis may be able to tell us more." answered Haram.

"We go to Shondakar, then?" asked Darith-Gan.

"I go to Shondakar. I'd not expect you to fight against gods on my account," replied Haram.

The half-elf smiled, "if I let you leave me behind, what might happen to me? I broke a leg so as to be ready and waiting for you in that little village. If I let you go on without me, could I expect some broken ribs as well?"

Haram smiled. "I'm ashamed to admit that I'm glad you feel that way. I dislike the thought of this, gods and all, but I'd dislike it even more without a friend at my back. Shall we go to the harbour to see about a passage across to Aradair?"

There were several ships in the harbour, all of them intending, eventually, to sail to Aradair. The soonest departure was two days, however, and for most of the other, the time stretched to a week or even two.

Haram, striving to conceal the desperation he felt, began bargaining with the Captain of the *Lady Windchaser* to leave immediately.

Captain Arrag-hiphon, a squat and swarthy native of Rahasin, shook his head. "Couldn't leave today If I were to want to," he declared in the tongue of Aradair, heavily accented. "Crew's scattered Wave-god knows where, over half the inns and whorehouses of the town. Day after tomorrow's the best I can do."

'And I have to be in Ifan Sor as soon as possible, and can't wait that long. Captain, I'm sure a man such as yourself would never let himself be caught so short as to be unable to leave when he wanted to. And I'd be willing to pay for the ability to leave tomorrow morning."

"You think so, do you? Now who's been telling you I work miracles? And just from curiosity, what were you thinking of paying me to work this wonder?"

"Twenty silver ponies." *'And may the spirit of Astaran help me.'*

"I wouldn't sail across the harbour for twenty silver ponies, boy. Suppose we say six gold?"

"Suppose we assume that no one has written 'rich fool' across my forehead? Twenty-two ponies."

With various protestations of poverty and accusations of unconscionable greed, the bargain was eventually made that they would be transported to Ifan Sor and provided with meals during the trip, all for a price that Haram knew to be somewhat high. He knew, however, that speed was important, and the captain had some sense of that himself, so the seaman was able to press for a higher tariff than he might otherwise have done.

"You've spent practically everything we have!" expostulated Darith-Gan as they returned to the Inn for their gear. "What will we live on after we reach Ifan Sor?"

"Vorath has been holding my money for me. I expect we'll be able to get at least enough from him to take us to Shondakar."

"And what then? We're fighting against gods, but your only plan is to get to the druid's grove?"

"You're right, it is a slender reed on which to lean a plan, but it is the only hint we have. But I do know this, I will not simply let this matter drop. If there is something to be done, I shall find it and do it. May Tran and Viron help me!"

A beam of sunlight suddenly flashed through the clouds and shone on Haram. For a moment his armour gleamed like silver, then the sunbeam was gone. Haram stood blinking for a moment, wondering. Was it an omen? Had Tran and Viron heard him?

The trip to Ifan Sor was a long one, long enough that Haram had to continually force himself not to think about what might happen to Terrial in the meantime. He succeeded at this by putting himself into the same state he had been in when he had been a prisoner of the goblins. At that time, he had kept his mind only on his sword, waiting for the chance to take it and make his escape. Now he concentrated on the oak-grove and Korennis, to the exclusion of well-nigh everything else.

He barely noticed that the sailors had begun to walk carefully around him, and that none of them spoke to him any longer. If he were in the way, someone would speak quietly to Darith-Gan, asking him to request his companion to move, but they did not speak to Haram directly.

After they had left the ship at Ifan Sor, Darith-Gan said to Haram, "Well, this will be another addition to the story of Haram of the Grim Visage, for sure."

"Truly?" asked Haram absently. "How so?"

"How so? No, I suppose you have no idea of how you have been the past few days. Believe me, if anyone had thought they had seen you with a grim face before, they had not yet seen the genuine item."

They went first to Vorath's inn, a fine, large building with a colourful sign above the door proclaiming it to be The Dragon's Hoard. Haram smiled slightly. "So the Dragon is remembered even after his death."

Vorath was busy overseeing the inn, watching the servants in their tasks and keeping an eye out for trouble from the customers. The inn had apparently already become a favourite for Venturers, and with such custom quarrels, brawls, and outright battles were not unknown. Vorath had been a Venturer himself, and could usually predict when a quarrel was about to become more serious, and would step in then to prevent trouble.

When Haram came in, Vorath was calming a dispute between an axe-wielding Dwarf and a rather inebriated Shondakranian half-breed.

The Shondakranian was speaking in a slurred voice, but very audibly for all that. "Dwarves? Best use for any Dwarf I've ever met is in a circus!"

The Dwarf, with the touchy pride of all that race, said nothing but reached for his axe, stepping forward into a suddenly widening ring.

Clearly, Vorath had been watching this situation well before it had begun to develop.

He placed himself in the Dwarf's path and began to speak in conciliatory tones. "Now, Master Dwarf, you know we don't allow trouble in here. And think on it, if everyone was to be challenged for words spoken in their cups, the world would be sadly short of people."

The Dwarf was not easily calmed, though. "If some grinning apes were to be held to account for words spoken in their cups, the world would be a much more polite place. Look at him, smirking behind your shoulder! He spoke as he did, knowing you would protect him from me, but I am determined I will have my satisfaction! Step aside, Vorath!"

Vorath took a glance over his shoulder, where the Shondakranian was indeed grinning drunkenly at the scene he had caused. The Innkeeper turned back to the Dwarf again, clasping his hands in front of himself, the very image of the servile innkeeper.

"Ah, but Master Dwarf, why should we let such a fool as this spoil our pleasures? Listen---"

And suddenly, with no warning whatsoever, Vorath spun and drove a fist into the Shondakranian's belly. As the man bent over, his face encountered Vorath's knee coming up swiftly and decisively. The Shondakranian collapsed on the floor. Vorath, scarcely breathing hard, turned his attention back to the Dwarf.

"Now, Master Dwarf, it would be unsporting of you to carve the fool to bits while he is unconscious. Mind you, I am not putting a price on your pride, but I'd be willing to buy you a nice mug of ale if you'd like to go back to your table."

It was clear the Dwarf was not altogether mollified, but he also recognized that dismembering an unconscious drunk would do serious damage to his own reputation, so he allowed himself to be led back to the table, where one of Vorath's inn-servants was already pouring the ale.

Vorath went back to his counter. As he was going, he saw Haram.

"Haram! By Tran and Viron, it is Haram for certain! Welcome back!"

"And a good evening to you as well, Vorath. Vorath, this is my companion, Darith-Gan. Darith-Gan, this is Vorath, in whose band I once travelled."

"As a companion of Haram, you are welcome to my inn, Darith-Gan. How long do you plan to stay, Haram?"

"Just for the night, Vorath. We're in something of a rush."

"Indeed? You will have time to sit and talk for a moment, won't you?"

"Yes, for a little while. But we must leave early in the morning, and will have to be early to bed."

"So then. Just a moment." He turned toward his assistant, who was off in a corner. "Graf! Graf! Watch things for a bit, will you? I have an old friend to talk to."

When the three of them were finally seated with a mug of ale each, Vorath turned to Haram and said, "Well, then? What is this task that brings you in and out of the city like a rushing wind, so quickly that you cannot even stop to visit old friends and companions?"

Haram hesitated a moment before speaking, then said, "It is something of a long story, Vorath, and it goes back to the days before we met."

"You recall me telling you that when I was with Orizd's band, we rescued a girl named Terrial from the God of Lies? Drauha has never forgiven nor forgotten that. I think he may have even had something to do with the goblins finding us that morning. After I left you here, I eventually made my way to Halan Howrdas, and found that Terrial had left, some time ago, to become a Venturer herself. So I decided to seek her out and pass on a message from her father."

He continued with the rest of the tale, the burning of the Grizalak temple, the happenings in Shilka, and the hints given by the seer.

"So you see," he finished, "I am on my way to the druid's grove, and I stopped here to replenish my wallet for the trip."

Vorath looked around uneasily. "I could leave Graf in charge of things while I come with you. You seriously think that the druid will be able to help you against Drauha?"

"No, no," Haram protested, "I didn't come to you seeking your company on this journey! I am on a quest, the outcome of which is very far from certain. The seer gave no foretelling, merely hints of what I should seek, and the danger into which I go is not one to which I would drag any other person, no matter how willing! By Tran and Viron, I have no wish to have your death on my conscience, Vorath!"

"What can I do for you, then? To be sure, you can stay the night if you wish, but there must be some way I can aid you."

"There is. I told you that we came away from Shilka in something of a hurry, and we spent a good deal in order to come quickly. I left much of my money with you here, and I need to fill my purse before I leave."

"Money? For certain, there is money available. I could let you have twenty silver ponies now, if you wish. If you wait until morning, I could give you twice that, or more."

"We will have to wait for morning in any case, since we will need to buy provisions for the trip. And I may wish to talk with Afal-kayyon as well. Now, all business having been dealt with, how goes it with you, Vorath?"

Vorath then recounted his various adventures in the process of setting up an inn, all the things that had never occurred to him before he began, but were in fact vitally important. He told the tales of how one or two merchants tried to cheat him in the matter of supplies, but when he and Tanno had strapped on swords to go visiting the merchants, the shortages were suddenly made up and the overcharges suddenly disappeared. After that, they had found it very useful to mention in their dealings with merchants the fact that they had been Venturers, and that they had on occasion been hired to hunt down and kill bandits and thieves.

In the morning, Haram and Darith-Gan went out to purchase supplies. They visited Afal-kayyon's establishment, which was becoming dusty and dingy, filled with odd-looking jars and bottles, with herbs, spices, and reagents hanging from the rafters and stuck on shelves in a seemingly erratic fashion.

Afal-kayyon greeted Haram warmly, but when Haram explained where he was bound and why, the mage's face turned grave. "A nasty business, fighting against gods," he said.

"I know that, but what else can I do? If there is any chance at all to rescue her, I must take it," said Haram.

"Yes, I suppose you must. Is there aught I can do for you?" asked Afal-kayyon.

"Other than ensuring that my amulet is strong enough, I think not," answered Haram.

"What of your companion? Will you buy an amulet for him?" asked Afal-kayyon.

"No, this task is for me. There is little hope of coming out of it alive, and I will not drag someone else into such danger," replied Haram.

"No! I will accompany you, Haram!" protested Darith-Gan.

Haram turned to Darith-Gan, "You will not! This is my task, and I will bring no one else to suffer my fate with me!"

"Don't be a fool, Haram! You recall what Kora said? I am meant to be with you, and I will come with you. How do you propose to stop me? If you forbid me to accompany you, I will follow you at a little distance, and join you at your destination. You're not the only one who knows the roads of Aradair, you know." Darith-Gan stood his ground.

Haram stood quietly for a moment, then said, "Well, if you must come, then come. But it will be more dangerous than anything we have done hitherto."

"And what sort of companion would I be if I only accompanied you when there was no danger?" grinned the half-elf.

Afal-kayyon was smiling. "So, then, another amulet for your companion, then?"

When he had finished the amulet, the mage gave it to Darith-Gan with the warning, "This will help protect you against the God of Lies, but do not rely on it altogether. The full strength of a God is considerable, and if he should exert himself, the amulet might well fail. But in general, it will do what it is meant to do."

He turned to Haram. "Haram, this sounds very much like a trap, set to catch you. Terrial is the bait to bring you into the territory of Drauha, and when you arrive, he will be waiting."

"If that is the case, why did not the God of the Grizalak take the two of us?" asked Haram.

Afal-kayyon shrugged. "Perhaps it is all a part of the plan, that you should run free for a while, thinking to rescue Terrial, so that your despair would be the greater when you fall into his hands. And perhaps it is merely that your amulet is stronger than Terrial's, so that Vssthak could not take the two of you."

The road to Halan Howrdas was long, and since they had no idea what they might meet when they arrived at the druid's grove, they could make no real plans. As they neared the town, Darith-Gan asked, "Will you stop to speak to her father?"

"No, what could I tell him?" Haram looked over to Darith-Gan, "That his daughter is once again taken by the God of Lies, and that I have something less than half a plan for her rescue? I think it best if we simply pass through; when all is done, if we have succeeded, we may be able to come back to speak to Lavad."

Darith-Gan nodded.

They made their camp a little to the north of the town and the next day carried on to the oak-grove.

They rode to the edge of the oak-grove and dismounted. There was no sign of life. "What now?" asked Darith-Gan. "Shall we go in to seek him out?"

"Not immediately. We will camp here, and if he does not come out to us soon, then we may go into the grove. But I, for one, would not like to go uninvited into a druid's grove."

They made their campfire and had eaten. Night was falling, and still Korennis had not appeared. By this time, Haram himself was becoming restless. "Why are seers so vague in their prophecies? He spoke only of the oak-grove and the druid, but not about how to approach him if he remained hiding."

"For all that, the seer only spoke of a grove of trees and a druid. Can we be certain that it was this grove and this druid that he was speaking of?"

Haram grimaced. "Don't say such things! Reason says that since it was Korennis who was connected with our first encounter with the God of Lies, it ought to be he to whom the seer referred. Even if it is not, probably he can direct us more certainly."

They sat in silence for some time then. After an hour or so, Darith-Gan suddenly looked up and exclaimed. "Haram, look!"

When Haram looked up, Korennis was standing there, just on the edge of the firelight. "Welcome, Haram."

"And a good evening to you as well, Korennis. Though when you hear why we have come, you may withdraw your welcome."

"As to that, I already know why you have come. And don't look so surprised; do you not remember the very first time you passed this way and camped here? I knew then who was pursuing you, and I know why you are here now."

"Then will you help us?"

"Yes, with what help I am able to give. This fight will not be the same sort of fight, though."

"It will not?"

"Oh, not at all. Now, let me make the circle around your campfire, and I will come back to tell you what I know or suspect."

So Haram waited, with mounting impatience, as the druid walked three circles around the campfire. That done, he returned. "In fact, I know little more about the matter than you do, though I have guessed some things which you have not thought of. Drauha plans his revenge on you, and has recovered the girl in order to work that revenge. And he has drawn you here because he wishes me to be involved in the matter as well; you will recall that I defied him the last time as well.

"But what has clearly not occurred to you is that he may not use the same means as he did before. The circles will protect us against him and against the creatures he brings with him. But he has other servants, ordinary human beings of this world who do his will, and they will be able to cross these barriers with only a little difficulty."

"What a fool I was, then! Vorath offered to accompany me, but I rejected his help for fear that the task would be too dangerous for him. I ought to have brought him along, him and anyone else who would come," said Haram.

Korennis smiled slightly. "Do not fret just yet, Haram. Though I usually stay quietly in my grove, I am not so feeble in a fight as all that. We may---"

At that moment there was a sudden humming, and a feeling of oppressive heat. A moment later, a pinpoint of light showed in the air, a light which expanded into a large, roiling ball. Then the God of Lies was once more before them. In one huge hand he carried Terrial, still dressed as she had been when Haram last saw her. Her head was slumped forward, and she appeared to be unconscious.

"So," he said, smiling wickedly, "You are here again. But this time you are here at my request, and this time I have the means to deal with you!"

He waved one hand, tracing a fiery arc above his head. There was the sound of movement out beyond the firelight, and suddenly the circle was surrounded by armed warriors. Leading the whole group was Merrit.

Chapter Thirty-Two

Even as he looked at Merrit, Haram felt in his heart that this was no great surprise. Merrit looked at him, saluting with his sword, and smirked. "So we meet again, Haram."

"We meet again. I cannot say that I approve of the company you keep."

Merrit shrugged. "I knew you were hunting me, and I knew that sometime we must face each other. So I found allies."

"You thought I was hunting you?"

"So innocent he is! In every town in Aradair, I would hear that Haram of the Grim Face was seeking word of me! Will you deny that?"

"No, I will not deny that, but I sought word of you only as a friend seeks word of a friend from whom he is parted. I had no ill will against you, Merrit."

"So you say now. But what if you find me sometime when I am all alone? Besides which, I doubt my master would feel kindly disposed to me if I do not carry out my orders." He glanced back over his shoulder at the place where Drauha stood waiting. He looked back at Haram and raised his sword, preparing to give the command to attack.

Haram dropped his hand to his sword, and his hand bumped against the Elf-horn. If there were a time when he needed assistance from Elves, this was the time indeed! He brought the horn to his lips and blew, even as the warriors surged forward.

The horn sounded, a high, sweet, wild call, the noise as of a storm roaring through the trees, of surf crashing on a rocky beach. There were all the sounds of summer, there were wild winds of winter blowing, there was a low warlike chanting, all in the same moment that the horn sounded.

At the call of the horn, Merrit and his company stopped for a moment. Just as they had decided that the horn was no strange and deadly spell, there was an answering horn call from beyond the firelight. With that horn-call came some two-dozen armed Elves, ready for battle.

Merrit looked around, then looked back at Haram. He was smiling again, the same wicked smirk. "So Haram of the Grim Visage has allies of his own? Well, so be it! Let us try which of the two of us is the better!" He lunged forward.

Haram parried that lunge easily, then struck in return. Merrit parried and slashed, a hard blow which jarred Haram's arm when he halted it with his own blade. Merrit was wearing the Elven gauntlets that gave him extra strength, and Haram had to remember not to allow Merrit to strike his sword square on the blade, for fear it would break or be knocked from his hand. As they fenced, he also discovered that Merrit was not his equal in swordplay. Of course, using the gauntlets, he would usually overwhelm his opponent, but Haram was a little surprised that he had not mastered the sword any better than he had. He remembered Merrit's trick the night they had arm-wrestled for the right to join Saradon; perhaps Merrit had never properly learned to use the sword, always depending on tricks to win.

Haram fought with all the skill he possessed, always slipping Merrit's blows off to one side or the other. With that necessity, his own swordplay was handicapped, but as the fight went on Merrit used less and less skill, concentrating on hammer-blows intended to smash through Haram's guard. Such blows occasionally put Merrit off-balance, but he always recovered quickly enough to avoid a return-blow from Haram.

Again he struck, a slashing blow at the crown of Haram's head, and again Haram slipped it along his own blade, directing it toward the ground on his right. This time Merrit's blade actually touched the dirt, while Haram's sword moved in a stroke that had been drilled into him by his various teachers. The circular movement of the parry continued in front of his legs and up to waist height, from where he launched a backhand stroke at Merrit's right side, still exposed from his own blow.

Merrit jumped back, but the tip of Haram's sword caught him, swinging him round and dropping him to the ground. His sword fell from his hand and he did not move. Haram turned his attention to the surrounding battle.

The rest of Merrit's warriors were either dead or fleeing, and the Elves were gathering around Haram and his group. He turned to look at Drauha, in case the God of Lies might be planning some other attack. What he saw there stunned him.

Two terribly bright figures, one male and one female, were facing the God of Lies, swords in hand. A moment later, the male figure and the God of Lies had disappeared. The female figure stooped, then turned towards Haram and the others. Though he had been continually watching, he had no memory of her having sheathed her sword, but now she was carrying Terrial in her arms.

Haram dropped to his knees as she approached, looking down at the ground in front of him. A gentle voice spoke above him. "Rise, Haram, and look up."

He did so and gazed at the bright vision of the ever-young Goddess Tran. She smiled at him. "Here, take your young friend. She is sleeping, and she will wake from that sleep refreshed and well."

Haram tried to speak, but his mouth was too dry. After a moment, he managed to croak, "What of Drauha?"

"Drauha will not bother you again. From time to time he may wish to send his people to hunt you, but if we hear of it, we shall deal with him again. Have no fear of him."

"Thank you, Lady."

Again came the smile. "It was time. Drauha was beginning to interfere too much, trying to make himself too powerful. We were forced to take notice."

"You have rescued us."

"Mostly you have rescued yourselves. Farewell, Haram."

She vanished.

Haram looked around again. The Elves were standing round, watching him. "I thank you for you timely arrival, friends."

One of them smiled at him and answered. "The horn was sounded, and we were the nearest. It is our joy to have helped to repay the debt."

"If you ever have opportunity to speak to Kyth-Woldan, express my gratitude."

"We will. Do you need any other assistance?"

Haram looked around. Darith-Gan was standing, leaning on his sword, with several dead around him. He was unwounded, as was Korennis, who stood quietly with his hands in his sleeves. "No, I think not."

"Then we shall take our leave. Farewell to you, Haram of the Grim Visage."

"Farewell, all of you."

As the Elves trooped off into the night, Haram went down on one knee beside Merrit. Merrit was still breathing, but the wound was grievous, and he would not last much longer. His eyes opened. "So, Haram, you were better than I."

"So it would appear. Merrit, Merrit, you need not have done this. Truly, I had no grudge against you."

"Truly? No, I suppose you did not. But I have done many foolish things in my life, and I suppose that the last of them has killed me. Haram, I am sorry."

"For what?"

"For the things that I have done to you. Would you do one thing for me?"

"If I can."

"Go to my father. Tell him that I am dead. Tell him--- Tell him that my last thoughts were of him."

"I will."

"Thank you, Haram. You were always a good friend." Merrit closed his eyes and Haram knew he was dead. Haram continued to kneel there, and tears filled his eyes.

In the morning, Haram coaxed a fire out of the embers of the previous night, then looked around at his companions. Darith-Gan was still sleeping, but sleeping lightly. Terrial was waking, and Korennis was watching him. "My thanks to you, Korennis."

"No need to thank me. You handled the situation very well."

"Me? I blew a horn and called the Elves. I fought and killed the man who had been my best friend. There ought to have been a better way to manage things. And this is the third time that you have helped me."

Korennis laughed, then at Haram's look said, "Your pardon, but the first time I had no intention of helping you. I wished only to save my grove from whatever wrath the God of Lies might unleash against you. I had hoped to convince you to move along, but you would not. Therefore, I had to help you, and keep the God distracted from my grove."

Haram said, "For whatever reason, you have helped me. I thank you again."

"And I will take my leave of you, Haram, wishing you well in whatever you do from this time."

"Thank you."

Haram sat back and watched the other two. When they were fully awake, he must discuss plans with them. Terrial might or might not wish to visit her father, since they were very near to her home. Darith-Gan might come with him or go off by himself, since it appeared that Kora's prophecy had been fulfilled. As for himself, he must ride to Ifan Sor, to tell Merrit's father how his son had died.

Saskatoon,
12 Mar. '94

Thank you for reading this story, please consider leaving a review.

Also by JP Wagner:

The Avantir Chronicles:

The Guardian of the Sword

The Crystal Crown

Talisman Series:

Stonecaller

Talisman of the Winds

Standalone:

The Search for the Unicorns

Railroad Rising: The Black Powder Rebellion

Maid of the Westermoor

Plague Wizards

Watch for more at J P Wagner's site.
www.revjpwagner.com